A GRAVE PERIL

A GRAVE PERIL

WENDY ROBERTS

WORLDWIDE.

TORONTO • NEW YORK • LONDON
AMSTERDAM • PARIS • SYDNEY • HAMBURG
STOCKHOLM • ATHENS • TOKYO • MILAN
MADRID • WARSAW • BUDAPEST • AUCKLAND

PLEASE RECYCLE
THIS PRODUCT IS RECYCLABLE

Recycling programs
for this product may
not exist in your area.

A Grave Peril

A Worldwide Mystery/November 2019

First published in 2019 by Carina Press.
This edition published in 2019 with revised text.

Copyright © 2019 by Wendy Roberts
Copyright © 2019 by Wendy Roberts, revised text edition

ISBN-13: 978-1-335-45566-6

Printed in U.S.A.

This book is for all the wonderful women who lift me up, cheer me on and believe in me whenever I stop believing in myself. Thank you.

ONE

EVERY TIME I find a body I hope it will bring closure to those left behind. That's a lot to ask of a corpse. The dead usually bring more questions than answers. Although I've taken a hiatus from using dowsing rods to find the dead, that hasn't stopped the stiffs from piling up or the living from wanting to bring them home. Sometimes late at night I can almost hear the dead calling.

As I stared into my laptop screen and scanned my email inbox, I drummed my fingers on the table and tried to decide if this was the week I'd go back to work. It's been months. Both my FBI boyfriend and my psychiatrist agreed I should take my time. They thought the dead could wait and my sanity was more important. I understood their reasoning, but Garrett and Dr. Chen were not the ones fielding my overflowing inbox of requests from loved ones desperate to find and bury their dead.

My dog, Wookie, came over and nudged my knee with his head. A cue that I'd been staring at my laptop on the kitchen table for too long and, meanwhile, his food bowl was still empty. An angry meow from the kitchen counter meant Fluffy felt the same.

As I fed the animals and shooed Fluffy off the

counter, I looked longingly at my laptop screen from across the kitchen.

Maybe just a little case. A simple recovery that would ease me back into my Divine Reunions business of finding the departed. I had a restless feeling in my gut that had only grown stronger every day over the past few weeks. There was that one request a few months ago...

I grabbed some coffee and sat back down at the kitchen table, then scrolled back through my emails until I found it. A mother looking for her son; a missing hiker. Searches for his body had been called off until the spring thaw. I glanced out my window at the blooming cherry tree in the center of the front yard and checked the weather forecast on my phone. It had been an exceptionally warm April. I sipped from my mug then read over the message details. Before I could change my mind, I sent off a quick request to the hiker's mother for more information and attached one of my service contracts to the message.

I closed my eyes, breathed in and said a silent prayer that it wasn't too soon to return to work.

"I'm ready." I hoped the self-confidence in the words would fill the rest of my body.

My cell phone chimed, and I let it ring a few times before I picked it up. It would be nine o'clock on the dot.

"For a moment there I thought you were going to be a second late," I chided as I leaned back in my chair.

"And for a second I thought you were going to let it go to voicemail just to tick me off," Garrett replied. His voice sounded strained and tired. "How are you, baby?"

"I'm good except you've been gone almost a week and the dog and cat are starting to fight for your space in our bed."

"Do not let the animals in our bed!" Garrett exclaimed, but his voice held no enthusiasm for our usual playful argument.

"Too late. I need someone to keep my feet warm at night."

Fluffy was once again on the kitchen counter. Wookie, the Rottweiler, noticed the infraction at the exact same time and barked sharply at the cat and then looked to me for approval.

"Nobody likes a tattletale," I told the dog.

"Fluffy on the counter again?" Garrett asked.

"Maybe I should just start to ignore it. I think he actually enjoys the spray bottle. I'm thinking I should just stop rewarding his bad behavior with attention."

"You'll make a great mom," Garrett said and then I could almost visualize him cringe. "Sorry, that just slipped out."

Still, the comment lay between us and created a sense of panic in my chest. I cleared my throat and changed the subject away from that more tender one. "When are you coming home?"

"Soon."

"Soon as in tomorrow? Or soon as in before my hair turns gray?"

"This case is just…" He exhaled loudly. "Hard. It's damn hard."

"It would make me feel better if I at least knew where you were."

He didn't reply. Having an FBI agent as a boyfriend meant a lot of unanswered questions.

"Well, I've decided to take on a case," I told him. "A simple one. Missing hiker that—"

"Already?"

"It's time."

"I'm glad you feel ready. Could you wait until I get home?"

Even though his tone was gentle, it still rankled. I hadn't taken a dowsing job for months. Sure, I had my own doubts about going back to work, but I didn't want to wait for his permission.

"I've been waiting." My back was up now. "I'm doing it. It's time."

Someone was trying to talk to him in the background and he told them to wait a second.

"Could you take someone with you?" he suggested. "Maybe call Tracey?"

Tracey was particularly useless on a hike and he knew that but if I ended up taking the lost hiker case, the drive was going to be a particularly long one. It might be nice to have someone along for the ride. "I'll ask her."

"Good." He sighed with relief. "When I get home—" he began, but then I could hear muffled voices in the background and he abruptly told me he had to go.

"Okay, I love—" But the line was already dead.

I frowned at the phone briefly, then decided to get in the shower. Later, when I was drying off, I caught my reflection in the steamy bathroom mirror and startled as if seeing a stranger. In a joint hair-dying evening, Tracey had insisted I needed to lighten things up. Quite literally. And now I was a bleached blonde.

While I dressed in jeans and a T-shirt, my phone chimed notification that I had a reply to my email. The mother of the missing hiker was thrilled I would help find her boy. She'd answered all my remaining questions, signed my service contract and thanked me profusely. Only a minute later my phone pinged again, stating she'd already paid my deposit. It was a go. I felt simultaneously exhilarated and sickened.

I wanted to go back to work and I was proud of my Divine Reunions website. I'd designed the site to help give loved ones a way to contact me about using my dowsing rods to find the bodies of their lost loved ones. I'd never expected to be so overwhelmed by requests from all over the world so, when things went to hell several months ago, I'd stopped answering inquiries. It was too hard to deal with death and dying. I was struggling just to live. My mind had been too fragile then. Was I strong enough now?

I sat on the edge of the bed and tried to do one of the many quick meditations I'd learned from my psychiatrist. When I tried to clear my thoughts, immediately one unwelcome idea popped into my head.

Wine would be oh so lovely right now. A massive glass of ice cold pinot grigio. Remember what it's like to take that first swallow? The feel of that sweet tang hitting the back of the throat?

The words flew into my head before I could stop

them. The urge to drink happened more often than I liked. I'd been sober for many months now but I still craved alcohol like a lover's touch. I pushed boozy ideas away and did one of the mindfulness exercises to help calm my pinging nerves and, when I was done, I stretched and headed to the kitchen.

"He-e-ey, Mom." As I walked by, I tenderly touched the jar containing my mother's ashes that rested in a corner of the counter.

I made myself some toast and refereed another battle between Wookie and Fluffy while I ate. Then, true to my word, I called up my friend Tracey and asked if she felt like tagging along for a ride to Hog Lake.

"Are you looking for a dead person? Oh my God, you are, aren't you? Of course, I want to come! Will I be home in time for my shift at six o'clock?"

"Hog Lake is near Spokane," I told her. "We're talking ten or eleven hours round trip driving and however long it takes me to do the hike. You'll be lucky to make it home by midnight."

"Damn."

"Don't worry about it. You can come along another time." I felt a wave of disappointment and realized I'd actually been counting on the company.

"But this is your first time since…you know."

Of course I knew, and I didn't want to talk about it. "I might not even find the body my first time out. There might still be too much snow on the trail to even give it a good look."

"Let me just see if I can switch my shift. I'll call you back."

She ended the call and I went to the spare bedroom and opened the closet. My hands shook a little as I reached far into the back, behind some unpacked boxes, for my backpack. I began to pack it with everything I needed to find the dead. Granola bars, a baseball cap, sunglasses, a scarf, and water bottles. My dowsing rods lay where I last placed them, at the bottom of the pack.

"Hello there." I took out the copper rods and stroked the length of them. A small sigh escaped my lips. "I know it's been a while."

The rods felt warm and responsive to the touch. As if they were welcoming me.

I gingerly tucked them back into my pack and let Wookie out for a pee while I went in search of my hiking boots. As I walked through the kitchen, my toe caught on a tear in the linoleum that had lifted and curled. I cursed and stomped on the offending old flooring to punish it for hurting my foot. It must've been the hundredth time I'd tripped on the exact same location.

Even though we'd lived in this house a few months already, the three-bedroom fixer-upper ranch still didn't quite feel like home. When Garrett and I decided to move in together, we looked at dozens of houses before deciding to buy this one. It was in an area of Washington not too far from the city of Everett. Close enough for Garrett to commute into Seattle, and far enough from the city that I didn't have to walk Wookie through streets lined with concrete towers. The to-do list on this house seemed overwhelming and the other houses too close. But Garrett had insisted that having neighbors was safer and that the work needed in the house was all cosmetic. He'd said we could take our time to make the place ours. At the time, I'd been weary and just hanging on to myself by a thread. When Garrett had continued to extol the virtues of a house needing work, my final answer had been a shrug of agreement. I just wanted a place that felt safe.

The biggest drawback for me wasn't the endless amount of work the house needed; it was the proximity of neighbors. Every time I let Wookie outside and whenever I walked out the door to my car it seemed that either Hairy Neighbor on one side, or Bald Neighbor on the other, were out to greet me and wanting to make small talk. They liked to hang around Bald Neighbor's fancy Alfa Romeo Spider and stare lovingly at its shiny red paint.

Garrett felt having people close by was a form of protection. He had far more faith in people than I did. When I let Wookie back inside the house, Bald Neighbor was out watering his flowers in the backyard and he stopped to give me an enthusiastic wave. Although I returned the wave, I hastily closed the patio doors and then the drapes covering them.

I found my hiking boots tucked far under our bed. They'd seen a lot of wear before we moved, and they hugged my feet nicely as I slipped them on.

"Behave, you two," I told the cat and dog as I slipped the backpack onto my back.

Fluffy was engaged in an elaborate bathing ritual and didn't even glance over. Wookie offered me a sulky look because he wanted to come along.

I walked out to my Jeep and felt the cool, misty spring air that would burn off as the April sun rose in the sky. Just as I backed my Jeep out of the driveway, Tracey called. She'd traded shifts with someone and was free for our adventure.

"This is going to be awesome!" She sounded entirely too enthusiastic about a field trip to find a dead person. Then again, Tracey wouldn't be hiking. She was more likely to be taking advantage of my heated seats and scrolling through social media on her phone.

When Garrett and I moved in together, Tracey had found a new place to rent and a new job only a few miles away. She claimed she could work at a grocery store anywhere and liked having a friend nearby. She'd packed up and moved just for me. It was the type of commitment to friendship I'd never experienced before.

When I pulled up to Tracey's apartment building a few minutes later, she struck a seductive pose, her pale pink hair draped over one eye as she thrust out her thumb as if hitching a ride. I smiled despite myself. Tracey and I were the same age, but we were darkness and light. She wore her late twenties like a glittery fairy full of the spark of life while the same years were heavy on me like a weighted blanket of trauma and drink.

"I'm so excited!" Tracey gushed as she flung open the passenger door and carefully climbed inside. A knee brace made it more difficult.

"I'm impressed you're dressed for hiking." I eyed the brand-new hiking boots on her feet, lightweight jacket over her arm, and a small pack she put on the floor at her feet.

"I know you like to hike so I bought some gear months ago when there was a sale." She slid me a sidelong sheepish look. "I may be only visually hiking because of my damn body but I want to at least look the part."

Tracey had a connective tissue disorder that made her joints unstable. She had braces that switched onto various joints depending on the day.

"What happened to your hair?" she asked.

"I had a trim." I touched my hand to my head.

"But you cut off all the pink." There was a slight hurt in her voice. When Tracey dyed her entire head pink and mine blonde she'd convinced me to pinken the tips of my hair. At the time it had felt childlike, lighthearted and fun. The very next day I'd taken scissors and cut those pink ends off.

"It's great on you." I offered her an apologetic flicker of a smile as I steered out of her parking lot. "But I don't think it's my style."

When she opened her mouth to protest, I shut her down by giving her something to do.

"Take my phone from the console and look up the notes I made about today's search, okay?"

She dug out my phone, opened the emails and read out loud.

"Douglas Prost, age thirty-one, told people he was going to hike Hog Lake in October of last year. When he didn't return home that day, his mother reported him missing. Local rescue crews went out the next day, but they stopped looking when a blizzard made the search too dangerous. His mother tried to hire some private search crews but they all turned her down because of the heavy snows this winter. Because of our extra warm spring, some crews have already ventured out, but they have yet to locate the body." Tracey turned to me. "You made a note here that says 'easy 5.'"

"It's an easy five-mile hike," I explained. "I looked it up."

While I took the exit onto I-90, Tracey fiddled with the radio until she found a station playing angsty rap songs where she knew all the words. I usually preferred to listen to audio self-help books on my drives, or guided meditations. The music grated on my nerves all the way through Snoqualmie Pass and well past the town of Ellensburg. When Tracey slumped in her seat and nodded off I shut down the radio and she promptly woke.

"Just need a while to think," I explained.

"Could we make a stop?" Tracey asked. "Need a coffee and to pee and not necessarily in that order."

We made a stop at a gas station in the next town. I decided to use the washroom too and when I came out Tracey was paying for a pile of candy bars and telling the woman at the counter all about our plans to find Douglas Prost.

"I heard about you finding dead people," the woman said, nodding sagely. "I used to live up in Blaine many years ago I knew your grandparents back in the day too and—"

"I'll see you in the car," I told Tracey.

She returned carrying two coffees and a sack of

candy all balanced precariously in one hand while she opened the door and climbed inside.

"This one's for you," she said, handing me one of the coffees.

"Thanks." I put the coffee into the cupholder, then turned to her. "Don't do that."

"What? Buy you coffee?" She blinked innocently.

"You know what I mean," I grumped. "Don't tell people where we're going and what we're doing. It's nobody's business."

"Oka-a-ay." She buckled up her seatbelt. "For the record, I never knew the woman would know about your stupid family or anything. Guess Washington State is a lot smaller than you'd think."

Not when you were trying to find a lost hiker. Then it could be pretty big.

Tracey scrolled through her phone and we sat in silence for the remaining hour of our drive. We pulled into the parking lot at Hog Lake and I put the Jeep into park.

"Do you think you'll find this Douglas Prost guy?" Tracey asked through a yawn. "Five miles is a lot of area to search."

"I don't know," I admitted. "Obviously he's not on the main trail or someone would've found him by now."

"So, you're just going to trust in your dowsing rods and hope for the best?"

"Same as always."

"Says there's a pretty waterfall." She pointed to her phone. "Wish I could see it for myself." She rapped her knuckles against her knee brace. "Take some pictures for me, okay?"

"Sure."

I climbed out of the Jeep and started to get ready for my hike. As I pulled my Mariners ball cap onto my head, Tracey climbed out of the passenger side and looked around. The gravel lot was surrounded by brush and tall trees. A crow eyed us suspiciously and cawed his displeasure from a few feet away.

"It might take me a couple hours or even more." I tossed her my keys. "If you get bored, drive into Spokane and I'll text you when it's time to come get me."

"I'm not going to leave. What if you need me?"

I glanced down at her knee brace and frowned. "If I need you, I'll text or call and then you can contact someone else to help, how's that?"

Tracey threw back her head and laughed in a way that always made me ache for that kind of light-hearted joy. "Get out of here." She made shooing motions. "You're interfering with my time to take selfies and post them on Instagram."

With a chuckle I took out my dowsing rods, then hoisted my backpack onto my shoulders and started out on the trail. Douglas Prost's mother said he wasn't a very experienced hiker and he'd chosen this hike because it was both easy and beautiful. He was scouting locations to bring his girlfriend to propose. I was guessing that the best location for that kind of thing would be near the waterfall, so I followed the trail in that direction.

The April breeze was heavy with the scent of pine and moss. Early buttercups were scattered along the rocky trail, and birds of all types sang their hearts out. All my senses relaxed at the feeling of the trail beneath my feet. It had been a long time since I'd gone on a hike and I wondered why I'd waited so long. My hands held the dowsing rods out in front as I walked but the wires held still and never wavered.

One foot went in front of the other and I paused only briefly to take a sip from my water bottle and to take a couple of pictures of birds for Tracey to post on social media.

The area surrounding the falls was private property, so you could only go so far without breaking the law. I thought about whether Douglas Prost would've risked trespassing for a better view for his proposal and I took the chance. Unfortunately, my rods never wavered even once. After nearly two hours of walking, I headed back. Doug Prost's mother was going to be very disappointed in me. I returned to the Jeep to find Tracey snoozing in the passenger seat. She jumped when I opened my door.

"Did you find him?"

"No." I opened my pack, pulled out a water bottle and finished it. "It was a beautiful hike but no sign of Douglas Prost."

"Thanks for sending me pictures of the falls and the birds. They already got a ton of likes."

I rolled my eyes.

"What now?" Tracey asked. "Besides finding a washroom because I really have to go."

"Find a bush." I nodded toward the tree line. "I haven't seen even an outhouse nearby."

"I'll wait." She crossed her legs. "I can't go outside."

I sighed because I still wanted to search the surrounding area. "I'm going to drive around and see if he might've come in from another direction." I placed the dowsing rods in my lap. "If we see an outhouse along the way, I'll stop."

As the Jeep bumped and jumped along the rutted road, Tracey began to squirm in her seat. I tried to ignore her but all this talk of having to use the toilet made me have to go too. Unlike her, though, I had no problem just stepping off into a ditch somewhere. We reached a fork in the road where construction signs blocked off access, but down a bit I could clearly make out a dilapidated outhouse. I pulled to the shoulder and nodded my head in that direction.

"C'mon."

I hopped out of the Jeep and Tracey followed.

"You're going to think I'm being silly, but I really don't like outhouses," she said, trying to keep up with my long stride.

"That's not silly." I slowed down so she wouldn't have to struggle to keep up. "Nobody likes them."

"When I was a kid we went camping and when I went to use the outhouse, a wasp stung me on my ass."

I looked at her to see if she was joking. Her face was dead serious, and I burst out laughing. Once I started I couldn't stop even when Tracey began to look more and more annoyed and my need to use the toilet intensified. When we got to the outhouse I turned to her.

"I-I'm sorry," I gasped trying to get hold of myself. "Tell you what, I'll go first and if there are any bees or wasps I'll let you know, okay?"

"There's a sign saying it's closed." She nodded toward the wooden structure and I shrugged.

"They aren't maintaining it because the road is closed. It's a hole. It won't really be closed." I handed her my dowsing rods. "Hang on to these."

"Can I play around with them and see if I've got the knack?"

"Sure."

Once I got to the outhouse, I took a deep breath before entering and peed as quickly as I could. Less than a minute later I bounded out of the building.

"Not a stinging insect in sight," I assured her.

She handed me back my dowsing rods. "No jiggling rods showing me a body either."

I smiled as she tentatively opened the door and headed on inside to do her business. After she was done, we sauntered back toward the Jeep while Tracey talked about the childhood joy of camping with her family. I listened politely. An envious ache for that normal childhood always reared when she talked about growing up. My childhood had been all about surviving brutal abuse. My adult life was still focused on moving beyond that.

We were nearing the Jeep when the dowsing rods that dangled casually from my fingers suddenly twisted to the left. Tracey was two steps ahead and still talking when she realized I'd stopped. I took the copper rods and firmly held them out in front of me to check, and they definitely swung left, so I turned and followed.

There was a steep, rocky ditch and, at the bottom, a cement culvert directed water to flow under the road. As I skidded down the rocky embankment I could just make out two hiking boots and the remnants of blue-jean-clad legs protruding from the culvert entrance.

It was the body of Douglas Prost.

TWO

IT HAD BEEN a while since I'd dowsed for the dead, and I steeled myself for an overwhelming sense of panic that didn't come. My heart pounded, and my breathing was hard, but I calmed both with a moment of meditation.

It's okay. You're going to be fine.

Deep breath in through the nose and slow exhale through the mouth.

The painful thudding of my heart wasn't fear. Instead, I realized that it was nervous exhilaration. It felt eerily good to be back using my dowsing rods. I'd been worried for months that I wouldn't be able to return to dowsing without falling victim to the full-blown panic attacks that had paralyzed me for months after the death of my mother. However, the overwhelming sense of terror and the near black-out paralysis didn't materialize. I pinched my eyes shut and sighed with relief.

I wasn't aware that Tracey had moved so that she could also see part of the body until I heard her scream like her ass was on fire. After I scrambled up the steep embankment, I hugged her tight and walked her back to the Jeep. Once she was buckled up inside and had stopped shaking, I closed the door and stood outside to make the necessary phone calls. Then I settled in to wait until the authorities arrived.

I sent Garrett a text.

I found the body of the hiker.

He called immediately.

"Are you okay?"

"Yes." I smiled because it was true. "Yeah, I'm really good actually."

"Are you sure? Do you need me to come?"

I smiled. He'd drop everything he was doing and run to me if I needed him.

"Go do your FBI things. I'm great. I've got Tracey here…" I glanced over my shoulder at my friend, who still looked pale with shock. "Yeah, so she's such a big help. Huge."

That last bit of sarcasm was wasted on Garrett because I could hear someone talking to him in the background. He was obviously distracted.

"I know it must be hard for you to get back to work." His voice was low and soothing over the line. "I'm in the middle of something, but we'll talk more later, okay? I love you."

"I love you too."

We ended the call and then I took a deep breath. A Steller's jay screeched his harsh call in a tree nearby. Dark clouds had rolled in, and the balmy April day chilled as a light rain began to fall.

Climbing into the driver's seat, I started the motor and tuned the radio to a station Tracey would like.

"We're going to have to wait a bit until the authorities come," I told her. "Are you good?"

She nodded but her eyes were still too large in her ashen face. The first time I'd found a dead body I was a child. Sometimes I forgot that not everyone had my macabre upbringing and an intimate connection to the dead.

I grabbed Tracey a water bottle from my bag and a granola bar. She ate and drank quietly. I wanted to call Douglas Prost's mother and let her know I'd found her son, but things weren't that simple. I needed to be careful what information I provided her since the police hadn't confirmed his identity.

I punched the woman's number into my phone and turned to look out the driver's side window away from Tracey. A breathlessly excited voice answered on the first ring.

"I've found a body," I told her, not even bothering to introduce myself. "I'm waiting for the police to arrive. They will need to confirm whether or not the remains are those of your son."

A strangled sob broke across the line. The rain beat harder against the window as I waited for Mrs. Prost to regain some control. It took a full two minutes before she could get the words out.

"But it's him, right? You know it's my boy?"

Yes. In my heart, I know it's him. "It's very likely. I'm so very sorry for your loss, Mrs. Prost."

Another jagged sob cut across the line. "Thank you." She sniffed. "I'm so grateful. God bless you for finding my boy."

I would take the blessing because I hadn't had

many in my life. After I told her she should be hearing from the police later, I again expressed my sympathies and hung up.

Everyone reacted differently to hearing that the remains of their loved ones were finally found. I'd had people scream out in denial and anger because they'd still been holding out hope that their loved one was alive. Once there was a body, that optimism spiraled down quickly. Some wanted to shoot the messenger. Others, like Mrs. Prost, were just grateful.

Once the phone was tucked back in my pocket, the rain ramped up in earnest. I turned on the defogger to clear the windows that were steamed from our breath.

"How do you do it?" Tracey looked at me with solemn eyes.

"Well, I'm not sure how it works." I used a tissue to clear some of the fog from the windshield. "I think the dowsing rods just— "

"I don't mean that." She tugged at a strand of her pink hair and wrapped it nervously around a finger. "I mean, how do you look at a dead body and not totally freak out?"

How did I tell her that my heart beat darker? Not all of us were raised believing that we were made from sugar and spice and all things nice. My body held the scars of abuse to prove that I'd long ago learned to control my emotions or else I'd be forced to deal with the wrath of others.

Gawd, I wanted a drink. Just a small glass. Or a shot of something hard. I could have just one. Nobody even needed to know.

I cleared my throat loudly and gave my head a quick shake.

"I know it's kind of a shock." I reached over and patted her leg. "Let's talk about something else." I searched my head for a different topic. "You told me that you had cats growing up, right? Maybe you can give me some advice on how to keep Fluffy off the kitchen counter and how to stop him from being such a dick to Wookie."

She began, slowly at first and then with gaining enthusiasm, to describe every cat her family had owned and their various silly behaviors. I nodded and smiled encouragement. The rain pummeled the car and we were nicely cocooned in the dry vehicle. However, as Tracey spoke excitedly about cats, my mind drifted to Douglas Prost lying in the culvert through rain and snow for all these months and I shuddered.

The rain came to an abrupt stop and I turned off the vehicle and lowered the windows a bit to catch some fresh air.

"So now what?" Tracey asked. "After the authorities come? What do we do?"

"Nothing. We wait for police to come and give our statements and then that's it."

She nodded. "How do you think he ended up there?"

"I don't know."

"But I bet you could take a guess because this is kind of what you do, right?"

"I find dead people, I don't make assumptions about how they got where they are because that's the

police's job but…" I glanced in the general direction
of the victim. "If I had to guess, I'd say he did what
we did. He had to use the washroom and he saw
this outhouse. Then he lost his footing. It could've
been icy at that time of year so if he slipped and fell
down that embankment, he could've been hurt badly.
I imagine it was something unfortunate like that."

"You think they'll do an autopsy?"

"Probably."

"I wouldn't want that… to be cut up and…" Her
voice had been calm but she was quickly getting
emotional again.

"Let's talk about something else." I suggested
"Ask me something. Anything that doesn't have to
do with dead people."

"Okay." She tapped a finger to her lips. "Is Garrett still away on business?"

"Yes."

"He's been traveling a lot lately. Are you okay
with that?"

"I miss him, but it's part of his job. He calls me
every morning at nine to say good morning and he
calls every evening to say goodnight."

"Are you going to have hot jungle sex the minute
he comes home?"

I burst out laughing. "I'll probably let him unpack
first before I jump him." I pointed to the brace on
her leg. "How's your knee?"

"I'll be having surgery next month."

"Oh." I frowned. "I'm sorry. You never told me."
She shrugged. "Just found out."

"Is it because of your Ehlers-Danlos thingamajig?"

"Yes. Spit not glue."

"Excuse me?"

"The doctors say I'm held together with more spit than glue." She tilted her head at me. "Hey, why did you change your mind about being called Delma Arsenault instead of Julie Hall?"

Just last year I'd been certain about changing my name. I was born Delma Arsenault but, after being abandoned by my mother at my grandparents' farm, I took on my middle name, Julie, and their last name, Hall. After my mom's death last year, I considered becoming Delma Arsenault again as a kind of tribute to the name my mother originally gave me.

"I tried being Delma for a while, but it didn't take. I guess I've been Julie Hall much longer than I was ever Delma Arsenault, so it felt like I was wearing someone else's shoes that were a couple sizes too tight."

"Plus, one day you're gonna marry Garrett and then your last name will be Pierce, so that'll be another change."

"Not going to happen." I shook my head. "I don't need a piece of paper to be committed to Garrett. Also, he did that once before, remember?"

"I guess you're living together so it's kind of the same thing. But don't you want a ring on your finger? An outward sign that shows the world you're in lo-o-ve?"

"I might like a ring one day but jewelry has nothing to do with commitment."

She wanted to talk about it more but just then the police pulled up and saved me from having that discussion. Tracey wanted to wait in the car, but I told her he'd need her statement too. We introduced ourselves to the officer and then walked him toward the location of Douglas Prost. The rain had left large puddles in the ruts in the gravel road, and we carefully dodged them as we walked. The officer and I were side-by-side and Tracey kept her distance behind us. When asked, I explained how I'd come across the body. I explained about his mother reaching out to me for help and expected a raised eyebrow or a snide remark about my using my dowsing rods, but he was obviously one of the law enforcement officers who'd heard of my skill. I'd built a bit of a reputation in Washington.

When we stopped I pointed to the culvert below.

"Careful," I told him. "It's going to be slick now because of the rain."

The officer only went down the embankment as far as was necessary to confirm the body was exactly where we said, and then he scrambled back up. Twice on his way he lost his footing and nearly tumbled on top of Douglas Prost. Tracey let out a high-pitched nervous squeal each time. Once he was safely back on the road, we walked back to our cars just as two other official vehicles arrived on scene. They no longer needed us so, after giving our contact information, we left the police to do their jobs.

It was a long drive back, but we broke it up by stopping at a diner halfway. We ate grilled cheese sandwiches and shared a plate of fries and talked about our favorite shows as if today was like any other day. Once we were back on the road, Tracey slept until I nudged her awake when I pulled up to her apartment building.

"Thanks for helping me today," I told her.

"I wasn't much of a help." She cringed. "I was just a big baby."

"Are you kidding? If you hadn't had to pee, we never would've found him."

She smiled broadly at that. "That's true. My bladder is kind of the unsung hero here."

We parted company with a possible coffee date arranged for the next day and I headed home.

When I pulled up to my own driveway, I was surprised to see Garrett's sedan in the side drive under the carport. He hadn't mentioned he'd be back tonight. I was excited to have him back, but when I walked in the door I could immediately tell something was wrong. He was in the living room with the TV blaring, feet up on the ottoman, a half empty box of pizza on one side and Wookie curled up on the other. There were deep creases of exhaustion around his mouth.

"Hey," I said dropping my pack and walking over. "Nice to have you home."

"It's nice to be home," he replied wearily.

I shooed Wookie onto the floor so I could sit down next to Garrett. I kissed him on the cheek and rested my head on his shoulder. "You okay?"

"I am now." He put his arm around my shoulder and gave me a light squeeze.

His voice sounded heavy with worry. I decided I'd wait it out and see if he was ready to talk. If it was work-related, there was a good chance he wouldn't share what was weighing on him, but he was back and that alone made me glad.

"Congratulations on finding that lost hiker," he said as I snuggled against his shoulder. "You feel okay about it? No…" He struggled to find the words. "You didn't feel too overwhelmed?"

"It was good. I was ready."

"That's great. I'm proud of you."

He kissed the top of my head and we watched television together. It got late, and I dozed on and off against his shoulder. At one point I remember him leading me off to bed. In the morning, I reached for him, but the sheets were cool. I blinked at the clock. It was nearly nine, so he was most likely already on his way to the Seattle office. Then I smelled coffee brewing and bacon frying and hurriedly swung my legs out of bed.

In the kitchen I found Garrett wearing only his boxers and standing at the stove. Wookie was at his feet gazing adoringly at the maker of bacon. Fluffy was seated on the kitchen chair, one leg in the air while he bathed himself. I came up behind Garrett, wrapped my arms around his waist and placed a kiss between his shoulder blades.

"Good morning. I take it you're having a work-from-home day?"

"Yes." He turned and kissed me on the tip of my nose. "How do you want your eggs this morning?"

"Drowned in coffee," I said stifling a yawn.

"Over easy it is."

I poured us each a cup of coffee and set the table. I'd grown up fending for myself and breakfast was never an option. Once on my own, a handful of dry cereal wasn't unusual since I rarely had fresh milk. I tended to drop weight when I was stressed and over the past months I'd felt my clothes get loose and the notch on my belt had changed more than once. Since we'd moved in together, Garrett rarely missed an opportunity to fatten me up when he wasn't traveling for work.

While we ate, Garrett asked me questions about finding the body of Douglas Prost. "How did you feel when you found him?"

Garrett's questions were mostly about me and not about the actual find. He'd seen me do it, and the procedure wasn't in question. My sanity was.

"I felt good." Mostly. "It was kind of exciting to be back at it." I gave him a smile of reassurance as I nibbled a piece of bacon. "It made me feel…" *Good. Bad. Scared. Excited.* Like I needed a drink to celebrate or drown out the dark thoughts. "A lot of emotions but, overall, it just felt good to be doing something."

Garrett's eyes were sharp as he watched me answer. If he suspected there was more than what I was saying, he didn't press further. His mood this morning was light, and whatever had been bothering him the evening before seemed to have vanished.

When we were done eating, he gathered up our plates and took them to the sink.

"I've got some news," he said casually, as he added a squirt of soap to the dishes and turned on the water. "I'm going to be working at home for a while."

Something about how he said it caused my heart to skip a beat.

"Is that right?" I waited a breath or two. "Is that a good thing?"

He didn't answer but I could tell by the vein of tension bulging in his neck that there was more. I poured myself another cup of coffee and waited for him to find a way to say whatever he was trying to work through in his head. After he was done scrubbing the dishes he came back to the table, picked up my hand in his and looked at me solemnly.

"I've been pulled from the case I was on. And I'm not assigned to anything else. They've put me on leave."

"But why?" This was a shock. "Put on leave" sounded an awful lot like he'd been fired. Garrett was the most moral, law-abiding and hardworking person I'd ever met. There was no way he could've done anything to warrant being let go.

"It's because of Faith."

He'd never spoken his dead wife's name out loud to me before. Just the weight of it caused me to feel lightheaded.

THREE

"I DON'T UNDERSTAND." I shook my head slowly. "What does…" I couldn't bring myself to speak his dead wife's name. I didn't feel like I had the right. "What does she have to do with your case?"

His wife and son were gone. Killed by a drunk driver long before Garrett came knocking on the door of my single-wide trailer asking for my help on a case. It wasn't a topic we discussed. Ever.

"It's actually about her brother. Sid."

Oka-a-ay. I didn't even know she had a brother.

He released my hand and combed his fingers through his hair. "I can't talk about the case."

"You can't *not* talk about it either." I blew air through my lips in a raspberry and immediately regretted the childish display that probably did nothing but reminded him there were a couple decades between our ages. "Look, I know you're unable to talk about your case, but it's no longer your case, right? You just said you were put on leave."

"I still can't talk about it."

"How about this? I'm going to talk about a hypothetical situation and you can just listen." I laced my fingers together on the table. "You've been working some time in an area of the FBI that deals with drug smuggling. I know that isn't always the cases you handle but I think that's mostly your jam." His lips twitched into an almost smile. "So, if I had to make an educated guess, I'd say that your brother-in-law's name came up in connection with your investigation and you, being the standup guy that you are, right away had to tell your bosses about your connection to Sid and then, just like that, you bought yourself a vacation."

"I'm not saying you're right and I'm not saying you're wrong," Garrett spoke through a sigh. "But I am saying that you'd make a mighty fine agent if you ever decided to join the Bureau."

"Ah-ha!" I laughed. Relief washed over me because this felt like a simple thing, but it still made me wonder about his mood the night before. It felt like there was more to this than what he was saying, and I bet all the guessing games in the world wouldn't help me figure it out. "What else is there? I can feel something big in everything you're not saying."

"This investigation is the biggest thing I've ever worked on. It's become a real rat's nest and it's like every stone we overturn we find another fat rat."

I could tell it was killing him not to be seeing the case through to its conclusion. Garrett wasn't a guy who liked loose ends.

"Are you home until the case is solved or until they reassign you to something else?"

"No idea if I'm home for a day, a week or longer."

"In that case—" I pointed an accusing finger at him "—have you taken a look around here?" I waved my hands around to indicate our house. "Remember when you convinced me that buying a place that needed some work was a good thing? You said I'd have to wait until you had time to do everything that needed to be done. Yeah, well, get busy, mister. Don't be such a slacker."

He genuinely smiled then and I felt a great sense of relief as if I'd dodged something big. At least for the moment.

I took Wookie for a run up the road and had to pause more than a few times to nod good morning and say that "Yes, it was good to see the sun" or agree to those who commented that it was a beautiful day. I'd spent much of my life on a farm far from anyone else and, even in school, I'd been the awkward kid with poor social skills and thrift store clothes that smelled faintly of mildew. All this random socializing because we now lived in suburbia was mentally exhausting.

When Wookie and I returned to the house, Garrett was talking over the fence to Bald Neighbor. They both turned and smiled at me and I offered a half wave as I went inside. Garrett followed a minute later.

"What's Bald Neighbor have to say? If he's complaining about Wookie taking a dump in his yard, let him know that I picked it up and he should fix his fence."

"It wasn't about Wookie, but it was about the fence," Garrett said. "He wants to replace the fencing between our yards."

"Good. Ask him if he can make it a foot higher so I don't have to see him every time I go out."

"It's going to be a joint effort. We have to pay for half."

"What? Then we're definitely making it a foot

higher!" I went to the sink and poured myself a glass of water. "Why do we have to pay for it?"

"I doubt he'll go for making it taller just because you're antisocial." Garrett chuckled. "And sharing the cost is just what good neighbors do."

"I can see it now." I took a long drink from my glass. "It'll be a joint trip to the lumber store, then a fence-building party, and it'll be another celebration when it comes time to paint the damn thing." I stuck out my tongue.

"Actually, we agreed to just hire someone to do it."

"Thank God." I put a hand over my heart and looked up at the heavens in gratitude. "This suburbia politeness is getting to be a bit much. Do you know how many people stopped to talk to me while I was out walking Wookie? A hundred at least."

Garrett wrapped his arms around my waist and planted a kiss on my neck. "Only a hundred? I would expect much more. You're a bit of a celebrity around here."

I groaned. I'd made the papers a few times over the years and my website DivineReunions.com got a helluva lot of hits locally, no doubt from neighbors googling. But I hadn't taken my dowsing rods out to find bodies in forever and definitely not since we'd moved in. I wasn't so much a celebrity as the neighborhood freak.

"If they knew you were an agent with the Bureau I'm sure you'd be a celebrity too." Garrett only told people he worked for the government. "And Bald Neighbor and his partner only moved in a week ago and suddenly I can't leave my house without one of them yelling at me?"

"Yelling?"

"Yeah, 'good morning' or 'beautiful weather' or whatever. Plus, they're always mooning over that fancy red car of his. That Alfa Romeo Spider."

Garrett laughed. "They're horrible human beings. Also, instead of calling him Bald Neighbor, try Preston. That's his name."

"It's a dumb name. Don't they even work? They're always around."

"Phil runs some kind of bookkeeping business from home, and I think Preston said he's on vacation at the moment. You'd know this stuff if you had a friendly talk with them."

"Whatever. I'm getting in the shower," I told him.

"There are worse things than having nice neighbors." He swatted my ass as I walked away.

In the shower I leaned my forehead against the cool tile and let the water hit the map of keloid scars that covered my back. They were a visible reminder of a horrific upbringing. Only Garrett got to see those old wounds and knew the horrors that caused them. While the hot spray pounded between my shoulder blades I practiced one of the one-minute meditation exercises that my psychiatrist thought would erase the ricochet of violent thoughts that occasionally flooded my mind. If I was completely honest, the exercises did help. A little. Particularly when those dark, quicksand, traumatic thoughts from the past popped into my head and a little voice whispered to me that one glass of wine couldn't possibly hurt.

When I stepped out of the shower, I walked naked into our bedroom. Garrett came into the room just as I was snagging a T-shirt and jeans from my drawer, but I never had a chance to get dressed. His arms circled my waist and drew my body against his. We stumbled into bed, his mouth still on mine and our hands exploring each other in now familiar but tantalizing ways. Afterward, as we lay breathless in the tangled sheets, I turned to him.

"I could get used to you being home every day if this is going to be the morning routine."

Garrett kissed me and murmured an agreement against my mouth. His phone rang, and he rolled away to answer it. He talked in monosyllable responses as he got up and pulled on a pair of sweatpants, then his tone changed to anger as he walked down the hall to his den. I got dressed and went to the kitchen for another cup of coffee before feeding Wookie and Fluffy. The cat rubbed up against my legs and purred while I filled his bowl. Wookie growled low in his throat.

"Jealousy does not look good on you, big guy." I laughed and rubbed the Rottweiler's large head. "Besides, you'll always be my first love."

"Hey, I'm standing right here," Garrett said as he walked in the room. "I'd like to think that I'm your first love."

He'd replaced his sweatpants with jeans and a button-down shirt and walked over to grab his windbreaker from the closet. His words were light but his face was dark, like he was forcing himself to sound nonchalant.

"Nope. You're my second love." I watched as he

put on his runners. He wasn't exactly dressed for work, but he was sure in a hurry to go somewhere. "I thought you weren't working?"

"I'm not. Not really. Just meeting up with someone," he replied vaguely. "Something I've got to get out of the way."

"There goes my dream of home repairs," I said in mock despair.

"Once this case is done—" he walked over to me and took me in his arms "—how about we do something special." He kissed my neck, then lifted my left hand and tenderly kissed my ring finger. "Not a big wedding." He kissed my finger again. "Just a quick couple of I Dos."

"Garrett…" I pulled my hand away and put my arms around his neck. "We've talked about this…"

"I know." He kissed the tip of my nose. "Can't fault a guy for trying."

He smiled but there was an underlying worry in his eyes that made me frown as he went out the door with a quickie backward wave.

Wookie and I shared a look.

"Yeah, something's not right with our guy." I scratched the dog's ears. "Whatever it is, let's hope he figures it out."

I settled onto the couch with my laptop and my coffee. Like always, my inbox was full of unopened requests to find loved ones from here in Washington all the way to Florida and every state in between. It made me feel sad and a little guilty about taking so much time off. Yesterday hadn't been so bad. Why had I waited so long to go back to work?

Because you were only clinging to your sanity by a thread, a little angry voice in my head whispered.

The voice was right.

Douglas Prost's mother had sent me a very nice email. The police had confirmed the body found was that of her son. The coroner's initial investigation included suppositions that he'd fallen into the drainage ditch and hit his head on the culvert. She'd sent the rest of my payment and wished me well.

It felt great and I was tempted to leap into taking another case, but I also wanted to pace myself. I wasn't going to decide about my next body search today. In the months I'd been away from finding the dead, I'd spent a little time fine-tuning my skills. I'd read up on grave dowsing and a couple times I'd gone out to do some fieldwork. Small graveyards scattered around the state were excellent places to dowse because they were usually vacant from prying eyes. I'd practiced with rough dowsing rods made from branches but now that my rods and backpack were back in action, it would be fun to use those. With the weather today promising to be another sunny April day, a graveyard field trip was a good way to get outside.

Early afternoon I packed up my backpack and locked up the house, making sure to set the alarm. As luck would have it, all the neighbors seemed to be out doing yardwork so just walking to my car involved a couple of friendly waves and forced smiles. A few ladies who always walked our suburb wearing designer yoga gear called me by name as they pointed out the obvious about the nice weather. One of them made a comment about my nice backpack.

It was plain, old and worn so it was just their way of wondering what I was up to. Maybe the dowsing freak was going to find a body. Thankfully, politeness overtook their curiosity, so I didn't have to answer a direct question. Let them imagine my bag was filled with the magic rods and maps leading to bodies. That wouldn't be far off anyway.

In the Jeep, I started up one of my self-help books. As I cornered off my street the audio book narrator spoke lyrically about loving yourself being the key to letting go of the past. The author had probably been thinking more about the past of bad relationships than my brutal upbringing. Still, I found peace in the words even though they didn't ring precisely true.

My phone rang just as the narrator started the ten steps to moving forward. I answered when I saw it was Tracey.

"Hello?"

"Hi, what are you up to?" she asked.

"Driving." I slowed as I approached a red light.

"I don't suppose you're driving anywhere near Sixteenth and Baker?"

"The grocery store where you work? Why?"

"My car kinda won't start."

I frowned and signaled to turn in the opposite direction of where I'd been headed.

"You don't have to come," Tracey added quickly. "I can, you know, just walk home or something."

"You live five miles away and you've got a bad knee," I pointed out. "Stay put. I'll be there in a few minutes."

When I pulled up alongside Tracey's beater of a car she had the hood up and was staring inside.

I rolled down the window. "We both know you aren't going to fix it by looking at it."

She slammed the hood down, then walked over and climbed into the passenger seat.

"One of these days you're going to have to invest in a car that actually runs."

This wasn't my first or even fifth time rescuing her from her bad choice in automobiles.

"As soon as I get a little money saved, getting a good car is like fifth or sixth on my list," she said. "I left the keys with one of the guys I work with. He's going to arrange for his brother's garage to have it towed and looked at. Fingers crossed that the repair costs less than twenty-five dollars because that's all I have in my checking account." She glanced over at my backpack in the back seat. "Oh my God! Were you on your way to find another body?"

"Not really." I steered out of the parking lot onto the main road. "I'm going to that old cemetery in Marysville to practice."

"Oh! Can I come?"

"Sure." I glanced over at her skeptically. "Are you sure?"

"It's a nice day. Might as well spend some time outside. Even if it is in a graveyard."

I nodded in agreement.

"But first, let's do something about this." She reached over and turned off the audio book. "I don't know why you listen to those." She clucked her tongue. "You ever want advice, you should just ask me."

That made me laugh so hard my stomach hurt and while I was laughing Tracey got an insulted look on her face, which made me laugh even harder until, finally, she was joining me. We stopped, at Tracey's insistence, to get a couple of coffees for the road. When we pulled up across from the old cemetery, I turned off the Jeep and grabbed my bag.

"So, what's the plan?" Tracey asked as she walked alongside me. "Your rods are just going to be crossing all over, aren't they? I mean they cross every time there's a body, right? It doesn't seem like much of an exercise for you."

We were standing in the middle of the small cemetery now and I put down my pack. "What I'm trying to do is get a little better at reading my rods. They can cross with a different intensity depending on how long ago the body has passed so I've been going to different cemeteries just to keep in touch with my, uh, skill."

"That's good. And I know exactly how to help you and make this fun."

I wasn't quite sure if *fun* was the word that should come to mind when traipsing through a graveyard. "Most people wouldn't think this was going to be such a good time."

"Yeah, well, maybe not exactly a party but at least I can help make it more interesting. I'll pick graves that are old or new and I'll cover up the markers and you'll have to guess."

"Okay but hopefully I won't be guessing." I hoisted my pack onto one shoulder and followed her. "Try to pick a marker that's not surrounded by a dozen others close by, so I can zero in on it."

This cemetery was made up of mostly flush, lawn-level stones. I always felt it was bad form to just step right on top of graves, but Tracey didn't seem to have an issue with walking right over the dead instead of keeping to the path. Eventually she came to a stop on the outskirts of the cemetery and held up her hands so that I didn't come closer. She took off her light jacket and draped it on the ground over the marker.

"Okay, do your thing," she told me.

I took the rods out of my pack and could feel their vibration between my fingers. They wanted to point in every direction but when I centered myself in front of the grave where Tracey was standing, I gained some control. I walked forward slowly, and the rods hesitated. There was barely a quiver as I walked back and forth but eventually they crossed. This wasn't new. Since I was a little girl I'd been finding bodies when my dowsing rods crossed. The new part was getting a feeling for the strength of the almost magnetic pull and an impression of the speed of the crossing.

"Old," I murmured. "This person has been gone maybe eighty or ninety years."

"Eighty or ninety? Is that your guess?" Tracey asked.

"It's as close as I'm going to get," I told her. "This isn't an exact science."

"Ta-da!" She whipped her jacket off the ground.

The engraving on the marker was faded from the elements:

Virgil Smith.
1924–1933

"You were right!" Tracey said. "The grave is, like, eighty-six years old."

"He was just a kid," I said sadly. "Nine years old."

But Tracey didn't hear me, she was off looking for the next marker. We did a few like this with her using her coat to block the dates and making me guess. Mostly I was accurate.

"Why don't we practice your pendulum dowsing now?" Tracey suggested.

I shook my head.

"But isn't that more accurate? You hold up an object on a string and ask it questions and you get answers, right?"

"First of all, it's not quite that easy and, second, it's not my jam. It's only worked for me a couple times. I need to have a personal connection to the object I'm using and the case I'm working on."

We ran through the grave marker exercise a couple more times and, although I would've liked to spend more time on some of the older graves, it started to rain so we returned to the Jeep.

A couple blocks from Tracey's apartment my phone rang and the display in the Jeep said it was Garrett's number. I accepted the call with:

"Hi, sweetheart, just letting you know Tracey's in the car with me."

There was some rustling noise, as if fabric was rubbing against the phone, but no reply.

"Hello?" I said.

Some voices grew louder but indistinct.

"Sounds like he butt-dialed you," Tracey remarked.

I agreed and was about to end the call when Garrett's voice shouted at someone. He was furious. I'd never heard him ever raise his voice in anger and it was unnerving. Before I could think to concentrate on what was being said, I reached and ended the call.

"Wow," Tracey said. "He's really pissed. I wouldn't want to be on the receiving end of that."

"Yeah." I cleared my throat nervously as I pulled up behind her apartment building. "Any word on your car?"

"Yeah," She looked through her phone. "My work friend texted that it's some kind of doohickey that needs to be replaced. It should be ready for me to pick up tomorrow."

"Good. Hope the cost of doohickeys isn't too high these days," I mumbled distractedly.

"Are you okay?" she asked me. "Don't be worried about your guy. I mean, FBI guys gotta use their mean voices all the time, right? Sort of in his job description I bet."

"Of course. Sure." I picked up the chain I wore around my neck with my father's wedding ring on it. I fingered the band nervously and forced a smile. I didn't want to tell her that Garrett wasn't even supposed to be working now.

She thanked me for the ride and suggested maybe we could get together when it didn't involve dead people. I nodded, and she waved as she headed inside her apartment building. As soon as she went inside I redialed Garrett's number and it went straight to voicemail. Instead of leaving him a message I sent him a text: I think you called me by mistake. What time do you think you'll be home?

A few minutes later, as I was pulling into our driveway, I received a reply.

Don't wait up. I'll be late.

Don't wait up? It wasn't even six o'clock. He said he was just going to talk to someone. What was he up to?

I let Wookie out in the backyard to pee and avoided making small talk with Bald Neighbor— Preston—by pretending I was on the phone. He waited patiently on the other side of the fence, but I just offered him a polite wave and headed back inside. I made myself a bowl of popcorn for dinner and dealt with an intense craving for a bottle of cold, crisp wine to go with it by having a Coke instead. I munched my dinner through the begging stares from Wookie and Fluffy and thought about Garrett. I didn't like the feeling that something was wrong. He was not supposed to be the unstable one in our relationship. I didn't like it.

"He's been called back on the case," I told Fluffy, who'd saddled up beside me on the couch. "That'll be why he's gone out."

The cat was purring, so I reached out to stroke his back and my attempt was met with an angry swat that nicked one of my fingers.

"Ouch! You're so mean."

His reply was to leap off the sofa and try to catch a fly.

I busied myself answering a few emails and looking through requests to decide on the next body to look for, but my mind was on Garrett. Maybe I could convince him to do a weekend trip to Vancouver. I could search for the body of a lost skier during the day and we could see the sights during the evening. I went to print off the details of the case, but the wireless printer decided it wasn't going to communicate with my laptop.

The printer was kept in Garrett's office, so I wandered in and played around with it for a minute or two until it spewed out the page I wanted. I sat in Garrett's chair, surprised to find the top of his desk was pristine. There were usually file folders and notes scattered all over, I guess being taken off the case, he'd cleared off the area. No doubt tomorrow it would be covered again in cryptic notes and reminders.

I whirled around in his chair and my gaze landed on a nearby bookshelf where there was a framed picture of his son, his face now for eternity frozen into a wide smile. It made my heart ache for the pain Garrett must've gone through—was still going through—at losing his family.

I took my page from the printer only to discover the ink was so faded the words were illegible. The tiny screen on the printer told me the ink was low. I looked around for a spare ink cartridge.

I went to open the top drawer of his desk and found it locked. I frowned at it, then gave it a little wiggle in case it was just jammed. Definitely locked. Although I was curious why he'd lock it, I wasn't one of those insecure, snoopy girlfriends. He worked at a job that was wrapped in all kinds of secrets, and locking things was probably just a habit. But I'd come in this office before and retrieved a stapler from this very drawer. It had never been locked in my memory. The first time I'd been inside his apartment in Seattle, before we were even a couple and I was just a person hired to find bodies, his coffee table had been littered with files and paperwork and he'd made no attempt to hide any of it. Locking stuff up was new.

I found an ink cartridge in a lower drawer and managed to get my page printed. Still, the locked drawer felt strange. Something was off about Garrett's behavior and maybe it was time we had a little heart-to-heart about it. Even though Garrett said I shouldn't wait up, I was determined to do just that. For the rest of the evening I curled up on the sofa with Wookie's head taking up residence in my lap and Fluffy giving us a stinky look from afar. I watched an old romantic comedy and sometime after a late-night talk show host's commentary I dozed off. I woke up with a start when I heard something fall in the kitchen.

Wookie also jumped and ran, barking in the direction of the sound.

A quick look at the guilty party showed Fluffy on the counter and my house keys now on the floor. My head was still fuzzy with sleep as I reached for a spray bottle I kept nearby. I walked over and sprayed a stream of water at Fluffy to get him off the counter, but he just hissed at me.

"Stop it. Seriously."

I pushed Fluffy off the counter and rolled my

shoulders in a stretch. My neck was stiff from being slumped over on the sofa. As I blinked in the bright sunlight coming in through the drapes it occurred to me that Garrett hadn't come home. A glance in the driveway confirmed that his vehicle was still gone. I hurried back to the sofa and found my phone had slipped between the cushions. I looked through, but he hadn't called or messaged. His last text was still:

Don't wait up. I'll be late,

He said he'd be late. There was no mention that he'd be gone all night. There were many times he was on a case that required him to work through the night or even, like lately, be gone for days at a time, but he *always* told me if he wasn't coming home, and he always texted or called me to say goodnight. Always.

I called his number, but it went straight to voicemail.

"Call me back. I'm worried," I said. Then fired off a text saying the same thing.

I paced the floor and tried to keep my worry from ramping into panic. The fact that he'd called me when he'd been in the middle of a heated conversation with someone also caused me anxiety and now I wish I'd listened more intently to the call. I wish I at least knew where he was or if he was back working. If he was at work, he'd have backup and other agents around to help him if needed.

I let Wookie out to pee and watched to make sure he didn't disappear into Preston's yard. As soon as the dog was inside I headed back to Garrett's den.

I was filled with a need to know where he was, and maybe notes about what he was working on were hidden in that locked drawer.

"Don't do it," I told myself as I stared at the drawer from his chair. "You have no business going through his stuff."

Chances were good he had the key with him on his keychain anyway. But he'd have a spare and, most likely, that extra key would be around here somewhere. Even as I told myself I was being silly for worrying, I couldn't stop myself from searching the den, but I had no luck finding a spare key for the drawer. I even checked the table next to his side of the bed but nothing.

"He's going to walk in any second and he'll be all apologetic about not calling and you're going to feel like an idiot," I told myself.

Wookie and Fluffy both looked at me like they agreed. I took a seat at the kitchen table and did a deep breathing, mindfulness exercise. Afterward, I made some coffee and had a piece of toast. I was still worried, but I did feel marginally better.

A couple hours later, though, the feeling of dread and worry began to boil in my stomach. I tried Garrett's phone once more, but it still went directly to voicemail.

"So, he ended up working all night and his phone battery died." I smiled at Wookie.

Still, the curt text from him telling me not to wait up and the angry conversation he'd been having with someone, combined with the lack of further contact from him, weighed heavy on my mind. The day was already getting warm and, for the first time this spring, I wanted to change into a pair of shorts. All my summer clothes were in a box in our closet. Switching out my winter clothes for summer would be a nice distraction. I dragged the box of summer clothing from the closet, snagged an old pair of cut-offs from it and tossed them onto the bed.

My side of the walk-in closet was a jumbled mess of boxes still unpacked from our move and a hodge-podge of things I should probably just get rid of. Garrett's side held half a dozen nearly identical dark suits and dress shirts. The shelf above his dress clothes was nearly vacant except for one shoebox. Curious, I stood on tiptoe and grabbed the box. Immediately I knew by its light weight it didn't contain shoes. I snatched the lid off, convinced I'd finally found where he kept the spare key to his desk drawer. Instead I discovered a black velvet ring box. My hands trembled just a little as I lifted out the jewelry box and let the shoe container fall to the ground as I popped the lid.

Inside was a beautiful emerald ring surrounded by diamonds and, when I slipped it on my ring finger, it fit perfectly.

FOUR

I STARED AT the ring on my finger. My breath came in hard and fast until I felt so dizzy I thought I'd faint or throw up. Finally, I yanked it off as if it was a painful vise wanting to splinter the bone.

"This isn't good."

I jammed the ring back into the small box and then into the shoe box and stuffed the works back on the closet shelf.

"We've talked about this."

I didn't want to get married. Not now and maybe not ever. I'd told him that before we moved in together. I'd wanted to be completely open with him about the idea because if a marriage license was a deal breaker for him, I'd rather break up than feel I was leading him on. It had taken a lot just to get me to the point of wanting to live with Garrett. He'd said he could live without a slip of paper between us, but he still might want kids. That scared me too, but I hadn't said *never* to that; only *we'll see*.

Now, what was up with the damn ring?

I walked away from the closet and into the kitchen, where Fluffy eyed me curiously from his notorious perch on the counter only inches away from the spray bottle. Wookie stood beside the cupboard where his treats were kept.

Ignoring them both, I sat down at the kitchen table and, with my hands on my knees, I drew in deep, measured breaths until my heart stopped pounding.

"It's just a piece of jewelry. It means nothing."

Garrett had casually asked me to marry him before but, every time, I'd repeated that I didn't know if I'd ever be ready for marriage. Did he have this ring tucked away in case I suddenly changed my mind? I found myself nodding at my plausible explanation. That was it and it made me feel sad because I hated to disappoint him over and over. We'd talk about this more later because, right now, I didn't know whether to be angry or worried that I hadn't heard from him for sixteen hours.

I took Wookie for a couple miles' jog to burn off the nervous energy. The air had abruptly cooled as bulging, dark clouds knit together. So much for putting on my summer shorts. We returned home just as the first fat drops hit my head and I was kicking off my shoes when the home landline rang, and it was such a foreign thing to happen that I stared at it from across the room. When I reached the cordless phone on the counter, the call display was not a number I recognized.

"Hello?"

"Hi, sweetheart," Garrett began. "Sorry for not calling earlier. My phone got damaged so I just borrowed one."

"I'm glad you're okay." I exhaled loudly. "You called the house line instead of my cell. Is everything okay?"

"Fine. Sorry for worrying you."

"I guess you're back at work."

I heard him cover the phone and mumble something to someone nearby then to me he said, "I'll be home within the hour."

"Okay. See you soon."

We said our I-love-yous and disconnected.

"I told you he was okay," I said to Wookie who answered by leaning against my thigh and then licking my hand.

It was not at all like Garrett to lose his phone. He was the careful, methodical one. The planner. I thought about the ring in our closet and swallowed.

God, I want a drink.

"Coffee," I said aloud. "That's what I need."

After I had coffee and ate an apple, I threw a load of laundry into the washer and ran the vacuum. I got in the shower and, while I was drying off, I heard the door to the house open.

I'm going to tell him I found the ring. I need to make sure we're still on the same page here.

I slipped on an oversized T-shirt and sweatpants and went to greet him. Garrett had his back to me and was pouring a glass of water from the sink.

"You must be exhausted," I told him as I approached.

"I am." He took a drink. "Look, before I turn around, let me just say it's not as bad as it looks."

"What do you mean it's..."

But the words died in my throat as he turned to face me. The left side of his face was swollen, and he had a bloody gash over his eye. It looked as though his face had made multiple contacts with a wall, or a fist.

"Oh my God!" I rushed over, feeling my throat tighten as I slipped my arms around his waist and pressed my cheek to his chest. "What happened?"

He hesitated and, in the pause, I could feel him weighing how much he could tell me.

"An apprehension got a little out of control. That's all. It happens."

"You should see a doctor." I released my hold on him and took a step back, cringing. "That cut above your eye needs stitches."

"It's fine." He picked up his glass of water and took another long drink. "Like I said, it's not as bad as it looks."

"I guess this means you're officially back at work. That didn't take long. I guess all the house repairs will have to keep on waiting."

He put down his glass and offered me a tight smile. "Yeah. It's been a long night. I'm going to have a shower and hit the sheets."

"Okay." I stood on tiptoe and kissed the scruff of salt-and-pepper whiskers on his cheek.

"Shoo," he told Fluffy, swatting the cat off the counter as he walked by, but his words did not have their usual weight and Fluffy was back in the same location before he'd even left the room.

I half listened to the sound of the shower while I folded our laundry, then opened my laptop to, once again, look over requests and think about whether to take a case. When I heard the door to our en suite open, I walked to the bedroom just as Garrett was slipping into bed. Wookie was thrilled at the possibility of napping with one of his favorite humans, so he hopped up next to Garrett and curled up on my side of the bed.

"Just going to close my eyes for a few hours and then I've got to get to the store to replace my phone." He yawned as I tugged the comforter up to his chin.

"Okay, baby."

I reached and stroked the deep grooves on his forehead. As his eyes closed I was struck by how old he looked. Garrett was over twenty years past my twenty-eight. That had never mattered before but seeing him tired and hurt made me see his age and panic a little.

I closed our bedroom door most of the way, allowing for Wookie to leave if he wanted, and returned to my laptop. I didn't want to think about Garrett getting hurt by some druggie he was trying to take down. Possibly some crackhead or drug kingpin who could've had a knife and gutted him like a fish. My hands shook as I forced the thought from my head and glanced through my emails.

An eight-year-old girl was missing and presumed dead in a park in Seattle. It was a custody battle gone in the worst possible direction, and the mother was convinced that the father had dumped her in the park. Seattle wasn't far. I could possibly even be back before Garrett woke up. After being away from dowsing for months I knew I had to ease back in slowly. Maybe taking another job so soon after finding Douglas Prost's body wasn't the right thing.

I drummed my fingers on the table as I thought

about it. Bringing the remains of a young child home was always rewarding. Maybe I wouldn't officially take on the job. I'd just take a drive to the park the mother had mentioned and see if my dowsing rods lit on anything.

My phone chimed an incoming text from Tracey.

Can you give me a ride to get my car?

I replied that I could and gathered up my back pack, refilled my water bottles and grabbed a bag of trail mix. I left Garrett a note on the counter saying I was going out for a few hours. When I left the house I nearly slammed into Preston, who was just about to knock. I let out a squeak of surprise and quickly closed the door behind me so that Wookie didn't suspect someone was here and start barking his fool head off.

"Sorry, didn't mean to startle you." Preston took a step back.

He was in his mid-fifties, over six feet and looked like he pumped iron. His partner, Phil, was working in the front garden, pulling weeds, and he paused to wave. They were the kind of guys who wore shorts all year round. Today, in addition to a pair of colorful board shorts, Preston wore a faded yellow T-shirt with a small broken lightning bolt symbol on an upper corner.

"I was just on my way out." I shifted my pack onto my shoulder.

"I won't keep you then. Is Garrett around?" He

hooked his thumb to indicate our driveway. "I saw his car so figure he's got a day off."

"He's resting. What can I help you with?"

He hesitated, obviously wanting to talk to the man of the house about manly fence issues. I resisted the urge to roll my eyes. "Is this about the fence?"

"Yes." He smiled. "I just wanted to let you guys know they'll be taking down the old one tomorrow. Wanted to give you a heads-up because of the dog."

"Oh right. Thanks." I gave him a quick smile. "I'll be sure to pass that on to Garrett as well when I get back."

I started to walk toward my Jeep, and Preston called out to me.

"We should all get together for a barbecue."

And here we go.

"Yes. Definitely." It sounded like torture. "We'll have to set a day to do that another time, Preston. Thanks again for the heads-up about the fence."

"Call me Pres!" he called after me as I walked away.

I nodded and waved back at Phil, who gave me a garden glove salute as I climbed into my car. They were nice but the thought of making regular small talk with people living only a couple yards away made my stomach ache. But if it was important to Garrett, I'd be willing to try my best to be a good suburban neighbor.

When I pulled up to get Tracey, she had a wrist brace on to match her knee brace.

"Subluxed my wrist trying to get the knee brace on," she explained. "Just need to rest it."

This was a normal thing for her condition and I knew she didn't like to focus on it, so I didn't reply. I just drove, following the directions she gave me to the garage. After a few blocks Tracey narrowed her eyes at me.

"What's up?"

"Nothing."

"Bullshit. You're all tense like you're about to explode."

I turned on the wipers to clear a few spots from the light sprinkles that started. "Garrett had a rough night at work. Came home with his face beaten up."

"Wow." She looked genuinely surprised. "I always thought he was more the office type of FBI guy and not the kind actually, you know, out there wrestling with criminals in hand-to-hand combat. Hopefully the other guy looked worse off."

"Yeah." I turned the corner onto the main road. "Also..." I licked my lips nervously because I felt like I needed another girl's opinion on the matter but didn't want Tracey to blow it all out of proportion. "When I was looking for something in our closet I found a ring Garrett had hidden in a box in the closet."

"Really? What kind of ring?"

"Like an engagement type ring with emeralds and diamonds and stuff that fit my ring finger perfectly." I offered her a quick, crooked smile.

"Shut up!" she shouted, nearly causing me to run off the road. She punched me in the shoulder. "Do you think it's for you?"

"Of course, it's for me." I slid her an annoyed look. "Who else would it be for?"

"I thought maybe, you know, it was his dead wife's ring."

"Oh." Sheesh, I hadn't even thought about that. "Wow. Maybe you're right."

"Yeah, because he probably would've kept that, right?"

I felt like an idiot for not even considering that the ring could've belonged to her. Suddenly I felt an overwhelming sense of relief mixed with maybe a twinge of disappointment. Maybe it was *her* ring and, obviously, he couldn't just toss it in the trash.

"Why did that make you look so happy?" Tracey asked. "And sad?"

"The whole marriage thing…" I shuddered. "I think it's unnecessary. Things are good. We're happy. I don't see the point. Getting a ring would just complicate things."

"I get that and there is absolutely no need for a piece of paper," she agreed. "Unless, of course, one of you really wants it."

And that was what bothered me the most. Garrett *did* want it. I thought about his most recent proposal; kissing my finger and suggesting a simple ceremony of quick I Dos. It was clearly important to him.

"So where exactly is this garage?" I asked.

Tracey told me to turn into a driveway a few blocks up ahead. Once there, I parked out front.

"You don't have to wait," she told me. "The guy said it's ready to go."

I decided to wait anyway until I at least saw her

come back out with her keys and start the car. It was a good thing I waited as a minute later she exited the building looking ticked off and stormed over, opened the passenger door and hopped back into my Jeep.

"I thought you said it was all fixed?" I asked.

"The car's ready but it's wa-a-ay more cash than I have in my account. The estimate they gave me wasn't even in the ballpark. It was like at a different baseball field a thousand miles away." She let out a long sigh and then a shrug. "Well, no big deal. I'll just bus it until payday or maybe a few paydays." She smiled. "Sorry for wasting your time. If you drive me home, I'll make you a killer cup of coffee. That is, if you can stop at the store first so I can buy the coffee."

I turned off the Jeep and climbed out.

"What are you doing?" she called after me, but I ignored the question.

I went inside and admonished the mechanic for not being more accurate in his estimates and then put her fifteen-hundred-dollar repair bill on my credit card. I returned to the Jeep with her keys.

"Here you go." I tossed her keys onto her lap.

"That's not cool." She frowned at the car keys. "It's going to take me a long time to pay you back. Like, over a year or more because I'm going to be laid up after my knee surgery so I'm not gonna be able to work and—"

"You don't have to pay me back."

"Oh, yeah, I do. I'm not some charity case, okay?" It was the first time I'd ever heard her sound angry. She was biting her lower lip, obviously trying not to cry.

"It's not charity. It's your cut," I added quickly. "You helped me find the body of Douglas Prost. I was planning on paying you anyway, so this works out perfect."

"Really?" She slid a tentative look my way as her eyes brightened with unshed tears.

"Absolutely. His mother paid me in full. If you hadn't had to pee so bad we never would've found him," I said seriously. "You were the best assistant I've ever had."

My only assistant but whatever.

She leaned over and hugged me hard with her one good arm.

"You're the absolute best friend anyone could have." She climbed out of the Jeep then. "Want to go to the coffee shop up the road so I can at least buy you coffee?"

"Sure." I smiled. "I'll meet you there."

The eight-year-old presumed dead child in the Seattle park could wait an hour.

We sat on high stools, our hands wrapped around our coffee cups, and Tracey confided that she was on a new dating site and wanted me to look at the profiles of a couple of the guys who'd messaged her.

"I thought you were seeing someone?"

"I was. I am. But we're not, you know, exclusive."

"You need to do a criminal record check before you meet up with anyone." I glanced through the profiles of guys who said they liked hiking and fine dining but who all looked like they hadn't hiked farther than their driveways and for some reason liked to pose next to oversized pickup trucks.

"No, I don't. I check all their pics on social media and google their names and I definitely meet dates somewhere public and let others know where I'm going in advance. Isn't that good enough?"

I grunted in affirmation. "Wouldn't you rather just keep dating one guy and then find someone else if it doesn't work out?"

"We've only gone out a few times. It's a little early to narrow it down to one guy."

"Yeah, well, all of these guys look and sound the same." I handed her phone back.

"Not really. I've been chatting with the dark-haired one. He's nice."

"My dog is nice."

"That's a matter of opinion."

Tracey didn't care for dogs. She was finally at the point that she didn't nearly pass out if Wookie sniffed her crotch, but she wasn't going to be snuggling with a pup anytime soon.

"Too bad you don't like dogs, because they're great protection and they're a great way to meet guys," I told her. "You go to the dog park and there are lots of single guys there with their dogs and you can tell a lot about a man just by observing him handling his pet."

"Yeah, well, I'm just going to have to do it the normal way. Online."

"Right. Well, I've got to get to Seattle. I've got a body to find."

We got to our feet and disposed of our paper coffee cups in the recycling bin.

"Wish I could help. I don't like you going alone

but I have to work in an hour. Could you put it off so we can do it together tomorrow?"

"I'm okay on my own. I've been doing it this way for years, remember?"

Suddenly someone dropped something glass behind the counter and it made a loud sound. I jumped and put my hand to my chest as a vision popped into my head of running in a dark forest away from a crazy person trying to kill me.

"Maybe it's too soon." Tracey took me gently by the elbow. "Dead people don't need you to do it today, right? Go home and take it easy. You just started back yesterday. No law says you have to jump right in and go gangbusters right away."

"I'm fine." I shrugged out of her grip on my arm. "Besides, I'm just going to drive around and get a preliminary look." At her uncertain expression I added, "Really. I'm good."

"But if you waited for me to go with you I could help out and pay you back for the money you spent on my car."

We walked to our cars parked next to each other. The clouds were parting and the sun was suddenly bright.

"You're not paying me back. I mean it. That was your share, okay?"

When we paused next to our vehicles Tracey pulled me into a hard hug.

"You really are the best person I've ever met." She squeezed harder. "I mean, you act like a serious old person sometimes and you have horrible taste in road trip listening tunes but…" She finally let me go. "You, Julie Hall, are the bestest best friend a girl could have."

"Thanks. You too," I said in awkward reply.

I watched Tracey drive out of the parking lot and felt my throat tighten with emotion. I'd never had a best friend before except for Katie and it turned out that Katie was more of a backstabber than a friend.

Before driving to Seattle to look for the eight-year-old girl, I pulled up the email I'd received from the mother. It was a sad case. The dad had a history of abusing both the mother and his little girl. When mom left him, she got a protective order and he was denied visitation. The order hadn't stopped him from sending abusive and threatening messages. One day eight-year-old Maryanne went missing from the playground at her daycare. The dad claimed to be at work at the time and a coworker initially covered for him. By the time the alibi fell apart a couple days later, police discovered evidence that Maryanne had been killed in her father's car probably immediately after he abducted her from the daycare. Dad was taken into custody, but his daughter's body was nowhere to be found and he wasn't talking.

It had been a couple weeks and police had done a huge search of the area, including nearby Interlaken Park, but no sign of Maryanne. The mom said that the dad liked to walk the park and she felt strongly that her daughter's body would be found there. Mom and a large group of volunteers had trudged through the thick brush daily without luck. The police didn't have the resources to search the entire city or even the neighborhood daily, but they'd certainly led a number of exhaustive searches of their own.

This morning I'd sent the mom an email asking for more information, but I hadn't told her I'd take the case. If I did find Maryanne, this was going to be a freebie. I knew it the moment I read the last line in the mom's email: What kind of monster kills his own flesh and blood?

I knew *exactly* the kind of monsters who killed their own. The same demons had raised me. If it hadn't been for luck and desperation, I could've had the same fate as Maryanne, and my body was a road-map of scars that proved that point.

As I took I-5 south to Seattle, my head was a minefield of quicksand thoughts that threatened to drag me under, but I fought back. Blasting over my speakers were positive and uplifting Ted Talks followed by healing meditations that I knew by heart. I said the words out loud, pushing out dark thoughts and trying desperately to replace them with good.

Maryanne's mother had provided the address of her ex-husband and I drove to the street only to find it still clogged with lookie-loos, those curious about a murderer living in such a normal house in this afflu-ent area. From his house I drove the few blocks to the park where Mom suspected her daughter might be.

I pulled my dowsing rods from my pack and rested them on my lap as I drove into the park on East In-terlaken Boulevard. Large cedars towered over the park road, blocking out the sun, and thick vines and shrubbery encroached on the paved drive. I'd taken Wookie for a run through the park a few times when we were living in Garrett's condo, so I had a good feel for the area. Although it was in the middle of bustling Capitol Hill, it was also over fifty acres of heavily wooded trails thick with dense brush. A great oasis to take you away from the busy city. Lots of trails and paths that were great for joggers, bikers and walkers. And a good dumping ground for the body of a little girl.

Although I was driving the park now, I knew Maryanne was bound to be off the trails and obviously not in an area frequented by a lot of traffic or else she would've been found by now. I had hoped for some kind of tremor in my dowsing rods as I drove to give me an idea of where to start my search, but the copper rods remained motionless in my lap. I drove through and around the park another time waiting for a tremble or a quiver in my rods to indicate I was nearby but they remained motionless.

Finally, I parked near the Nineteenth Avenue entrance and took one of the less used trails. I encountered a dog walker who looked at me and my dowsing rods curiously but that was the only activity on the trail. Of course there was an excellent chance Maryanne's mother was wrong and her body wasn't here. Maybe Daddy drove her out of town. Even though this park was densely treed, it was still risky to drag a body through a park in the middle of town.

"C'mon, little girl, if you're here give me a sign," I murmured as I stepped off the worn path and into the dense forest.

After traipsing off trails and through scratchy bushes I gave up and returned to my car an hour later.

I turned up the air-conditioning, pointing the vents on my face to cool me off, and drank some water. I decided I'd done enough walking at this end. Before heading home I'd drive around to a different side of the park and maybe do some off-the-path walking from there. With my rods once more on my lap I circled the park but, again, there was no movement to indicate Maryanne was close.

I circled onto East Boston Terrace and became blocked in traffic only a little way down the road. The park was on one side and stately houses were on the other. One of the houses was undergoing construction, and the road was narrowed to one lane of alternating traffic because of heavy machinery blocking part of the street. A flag person held up a stop sign ahead, so I put the Jeep in park and sat patiently.

Drumming my fingers on the steering wheel, I thought about Maryanne's short life and how my own could've ended at the same age. Only my body wouldn't have been dumped in a forested park. I would've been buried somewhere on the farm.

I was breathing deeply and rhythmically to clear my head when the guy in the car behind me leaned on his horn and broke my spiritual concentration. The flag lady had changed her sign from Stop to Slow and was waving it at me.

"Okay, don't get your panties in a bunch, everyone. I'm going."

I put the Jeep in Drive and eased forward. I'd driven only a few yards past the flag person when the dowsing rods in my lap trembled. I glanced down and, just as I reached the driveway of the house undergoing renovations, the rods swung to the left, away from Interlaken Park.

I slammed on my brakes and received another horn blast from the vehicle behind me. Resisting the urge to show him my middle finger, I pulled over to the side of the road and parked directly in front of the driveway. The car behind me accelerated past at a high speed just to show me his displeasure, but I didn't care. I was already climbing out of my Jeep with my rods held out in front of me.

The copper divining rods pulled me unswervingly onto the driveway of the house under construction and directed me right up to a massive, overflowing construction dumpster.

"Damn, Maryanne. Your daddy tossed you out like trash." I reached and placed a hand against the rusted metal. "I'm so sorry, little one. You didn't deserve this."

FIVE

WHEN THE POLICE ARRIVED, one of the officers shimmied up the side of the dumpster and over the side to confirm what I already knew. Buried deep in the large container filled with renovation rubble was a black canvas bag containing the bloodied and broken remains of a little girl.

I was off to the side waiting for someone to take my statement when one of the construction crew came over to complain to a cop next to me. He didn't want to lose a day's pay and shut down their work site. The man reeked of alcohol and a thinly veiled attempt to cover the odor with chewing gum.

God, I want a drink.

The thought was vehement and the craving for booze was like a starving animal clawing inside my belly. By the time I'd told the officers everything I knew, I only wanted to leave. I needed to get home and not stop to buy any liquor along the way. I did not call Maryanne's mother. I'd let the police do that. I just wanted to go home to Garrett and my loyal dog and annoying cat.

I pulled away from the curb and asked the Jeep's hands-free call system to call Garrett. The call went immediately to voicemail.

"Dammit."

I just remembered about his lost phone. I tried the landline at home, but it rang a few times before it too went to voicemail. If Garrett wasn't still sleeping, he was probably out replacing his phone. I thought about his banged-up face that he explained as an apprehension that got out of control, and my hands tightened on the steering wheel. Suddenly I wanted to be home just to look at his face and know he was okay. Normally I liked calling or texting him when I found a body. Just knowing he was my support system helped ground me.

"You're fine. You're good," I told myself.

Traffic was bad. I wanted a strong coffee to cover my need for a stiff drink but I didn't want to stop so I just focused on driving.

My heart sank when I pulled into my driveway nearly ninety minutes later. Garrett's car was gone. No doubt he was already at the store replacing his phone. I assured myself he wouldn't be gone long. As I stuck my key in the front door lock, I heard Preston's voice.

"Garrett forgot something when he went out."

I rolled my eyes hard and then turned with a smile pasted on my face that quickly faltered.

"Wookie?"

Preston had Wookie by the collar and released him. The dog lumbered happily over to me and licked my hand.

"What…how?" I was shaking my head as I gave the dog a pat.

"I guess he let him out in the backyard before he went out, and forgot the fence was coming down."

I'd forgotten to tell Garrett about the fence coming down today but then my face scrunched up and I slowly shook my head.

"He wouldn't just let Wookie out and forget him outside."

"Don't know what happened then." Preston shrugged.

"Thanks so much for making sure he was okay," I said, offering a genuine smile this time. "I'd hate to have him get loose in the neighborhood. He's used to being on a farm."

"No problem."

"Thanks again." Anxious to get inside now, I opened the door and hustled Wookie in and gave Preston another thank you as I closed the door behind me.

Almost immediately Wookie headed toward the family room and I noticed the patio door was open at least a foot.

"Wookie, stop!" I shouted and, reluctantly, the dog sat and looked over his shoulder at me. He would've walked right back outside and joined the workers who were taking down the fence. I'm sure they would be thrilled to once again have an enthusiastic, hundred-thirty-pound Rottweiler join them.

I walked over, closed and locked the patio door and then frantically looked around. Fluffy was sitting in the kitchen sink, just his head visible while he gave me a derisive glare. At least the cat was still inside. Wookie accompanied me as I did a quick check of the rest of the house. The blankets were tossed aside as if Garrett had just recently climbed out of the covers. The clothes he'd come home in were in a crumpled heap next to his hamper, which was also uncharacteristic. Neither of us were slobs but I was the messier one. I walked down the hall to the den and found paperwork strewn across his previously clean desktop but there was no sign of Garrett and no sign we'd had a break-in.

"So weird…"

I checked the counter for a note but there was nothing saying "Gone to the store. Be right back" in his serious, hard scribble. The note I'd left him lay where I'd placed it, with the pen beside it. Maybe Preston was right, and Garrett was so distracted he let Wookie out and then forgot him outside when he left the house.

If I was talking about anyone else, that would be a definite possibility, but this was FBI agent Garrett Pierce we were talking about here. The same man who was known to pitch a fit if I took Wookie for a walk down the street and forgot to set the house alarm. He'd left a back door to the house wide open.

"Maybe that pounding his face took scrambled his brain." I said it as a joke but my voice in the quiet house held no humor.

I was beginning to think he'd had some kind of emergency that caused him to bolt out of the house without even remembering Wookie outside or pausing to leave me a note. The scenario scared the crap out of me and I felt panic creeping a cold finger up my spine.

I kept checking my phone, hoping Garrett had his new phone and sent me a message, but none arrived.

Every time there was a notification of an email or message from Tracey I jumped. After a couple hours I was debating calling the police or trying to see if I could reach anyone working with him at the Bureau. He'd mentioned recently a change in coworkers. I wouldn't even know who to ask for at the Seattle office. A half dozen times I picked up my phone to make a call and just as many times I put it back down. With no sign of a break-in, nobody was going to jump up and down to declare Garrett Pierce missing just because he'd left the house without leaving his girlfriend a note.

"You're all worked up for nothing." Wookie came over and nudged my hand with his head. "Right, boy?"

I put my headphones in and walked around the house humming to myself and blasting uplifting music. I finished cleaning out my winter clothes and replacing them with summer stuff. Then I scrubbed every inch of the bathroom until it shone. I was tired and hungry when I returned to the kitchen. I was also beginning to get a little ticked off with Garrett. Between the worry, the anger began to bubble. *There's no excuse for not leaving a note. I mean it takes less than a couple seconds!*

I made myself a peanut butter sandwich, glanced at the clock on my phone and realized I'd been home for nearly five hours.

As I was cursing the lack of messages from Garrett, the phone rang in my hand and it was Tracey.

"Sorry. I can't talk," I told her.

"I'm thinking of going back to green," she said, ignoring my statement. "What do you think?"

"Green? As in green hair?" I dragged a hand through my own bleached locks. "Seriously. I don't care."

"You don't have to be snippy." Her voice was hurt.

"Look, Garrett's missing and I'm a wreck."

"Missing? As in missing missing or late coming home from work? Have you called the police? Do you want me to come over and help you look for him?"

"He's not a misplaced sock," I snapped. Then exhaled slowly. "Sorry. Oh God, I don't know what to do. I don't know if I'm worrying for nothing or if something is really wrong. He's been acting so weird and—" I stopped short and a relieved gasp burst from my lips. "Never mind. He's home."

I burst into a wide grin at the sight of his car pulling up the driveway.

"Great! Go give that man heck for scaring you," Tracey said. "That is so not cool!"

I grunted something about calling her back later and then disconnected the call.

Garrett walked in through the side door. I was prepared to wrap my arms around his neck and cover him with kisses while also giving him heck for scaring me. But he had his phone pressed to his ear and the fury in his voice stopped me cold.

"You owe me!" he shouted into the phone as he slammed the door shut behind him. "And when I get there, you'd better have the information I need."

He stabbed the off button and jammed the phone

into his jeans before glancing up and seeming startled to see me.

"I was worried." I tried unsuccessfully to keep the reproach out of my voice. "I went to Seattle and found the body of a girl and, when I got back, the neighbor brought Wookie over. The back door was wide open and—"

"I let him out and then got an important call. Guess I was distracted. Sorry." He moved to walk past me, and I put a hand on his arm to stop him.

"And you didn't leave me a note or call me? You've been gone hours. Is everything okay?"

He sighed and then pulled me into a brief hug. "You're right. I should've called or at least left you a note. Sorry, sweetheart. It's just this case." He kissed the top of my head and then walked toward the bedroom and I followed him.

"The one involving your brother-in-law? Is everything okay? I mean, obviously it's not by the sound of that phone call, but is Sid okay?"

At first, he didn't reply other than to open our closet, take out a duffel bag and begin jamming clothes in it. I thought briefly about the emerald ring in the box above his head. I needed to check to see if it belonged to his deceased wife and, if not, I needed to ask him about his intentions. Of course, now was definitely not the time to bring it up but, eventually, we needed to have a conversation about it if it was intended for me.

Garrett looked over at me while he grabbed a light jacket off a hanger and stuffed it into the bag. "Sid is in over his head with some bad people." He brought the bag out of the closet and went to the dresser. "I'm going to try and help him out."

"Sure. He's your, um, family. You owe it to him to help. I can see that."

"I don't owe it to *him*." Garrett opened a drawer and grabbed a handful of T-shirts. "I owe it to Faith."

The mention of his dead wife's name again hit me in that tender spot of my heart and seemed to suck the air out of my lungs.

"Oh. Um. I get that." I swallowed and then nodded vigorously. "Of course, I do." I watched as he continued to pack. "I take it that helping Sid means you're going away?" I frowned as he grabbed spare socks and boxers and stuffed them into the bag. "And for longer than one night?"

"I don't know how long I'll be. I'm hoping it'll be only a day or two at most but I'm not sure. I've gotta put this case to rest and—" He looked up at me and frowned. "And I can't do it from here."

Wookie came into the room and walked over to rest with his head on top of Garrett's bag.

"I'm not the only one who misses you when you're gone." I was trying to lighten things up because I'd never seen him this tense.

"Don't." Garrett's face suddenly twisted into an angry snarl and he pointed a finger at me. "I can't handle you making me feel guilty right now on top of everything else!"

My jaw dropped as he picked up his bag and rushed past me down the hall toward his office. I started to follow, ready to heatedly protest and ramp his biting words into a full-fledged fight but, instead,

I snapped my mouth shut and willed myself to remain calm. This was about the case. He was stressed. It was not about me. Although it sure felt personal.

I walked out of the bedroom and went to the kitchen. My hands shook with emotion. Garrett had never used an angry tone with me. I shooed Fluffy off the counter and was pouring myself a glass of juice that I really didn't even want while I listened to Garrett slam drawers in his office. After a few minutes, he came into the kitchen. He walked to the side door and dropped his duffel bag there. I was leaning a hip casually against the counter and sipping my juice. He walked over to me and pulled me close.

"I'm sorry." He bent and exhaled against my neck as he hugged me hard. "I love you. Please just give me a few days to get this sorted and then you and I will go away. Maybe we'll go back to that beach house on the Oregon coast and we'll do nothing but eat…" He kissed my neck. "And stay in bed all day long."

"I'd like that." I felt the tension melt between us. "I love you too."

He kissed me on the mouth long and slow until I wished I could drag him back to the bedroom where we could obliterate all the tension between us. Then he pulled his lips from mine and I could tell by the reluctant look on his face that he really didn't want to go. I tenderly touched the swelling on his cheek and lightly traced the gray that was spreading at his temples. He leaned in and kissed me again before he stepped away.

"Gotta go." He reached into his pocket and held

up his new phone as he shoved his feet into his shoes. "I've got a new number since the old one may have been compromised. I'll text you so that you have it."

"Okay." I followed him to the door. "Be safe."

"Always." He offered me a crooked smile over his shoulder as he headed out the door.

Watching his car pull out of the driveway, I realized he hadn't said a word in reaction to my finding the body of Maryanne. Usually he'd ask questions surrounding my own feelings in a situation like that but, today, he was wrapped up with what was happening with Sid.

His old family.

That thought slipped into my head, quickly followed by an urge to have a drink.

Just keep busy.

Wookie was at the patio doors, growling deep in his throat. The workers were hauling away the fence boards that were torn down. The men glanced over at me and one waved as I closed the blinds to block Wookie's view.

I rubbed the dog's head. "How about a run?"

I snapped the leash on his collar and headed out the door. Preston was out in his front drive, talking to the fence guys loading up the old boards. They both glanced my way as I took off with Wookie at a dead run in the opposite direction.

Garrett told me when we moved in that I didn't need to be friends with the neighbors, I just needed to be polite. In that moment I'd reminded him about the first time we met. He came to my small trailer on my grandparents' farm, and I pointed a shotgun at him and only allowed him inside once he said the purpose of his business as a federal agent. So being neighborly wasn't my strong suit.

When we returned from our run, both of us panting from the exertion, there was no avoiding our neighbors, who were sitting on the front stoop scrolling through their phones. Today's board shorts were turquoise for Phil and yellow for Preston, who was also wearing the same faded yellow T-shirt with the broken lightning bolt logo. Wookie happily lumbered over to him and betrayed me by licking Phil's hand enthusiastically.

"He doesn't usually take to strangers," I said, still trying to catch my breath as I walked over.

"He has a way with dogs." Preston hooked his thumb to indicate his partner.

Phil sheepishly pulled a dog treat from his front pocket. "It's bribery." He handed the snack to Wookie, who snarfed the kibble in one loud chomp. "I speak dog."

That made me laugh in spite of myself and I called Wookie over and we headed back inside our house. I hadn't even kicked off my runners yet when Preston was at my door. I cursed under my breath before I answered it.

"Phil sent me over here to borrow two eggs."

"Eggs?" I blinked at him for a second as if this was a foreign word, then nodded in embarrassment. "If we have eggs, they're yours. Garrett does most of the grocery shopping and most of the cooking too. When left on my own, I usually have soup or popcorn."

Sheesh, he didn't need to know that.

I headed to the kitchen and Preston waited for me inside the front door, patting Wookie's head. The dog was snuffling his pocket, hoping he also had treats in his pockets.

"Do you use your alarm?" He pointed to the alarm panel.

"All the time," I said. "Garrett loses his mind if I don't."

"I keep telling Phil we should use our alarm all the time, but he only ever remembers to set it at night before we go to bed. Break-ins happen during the day too." When I didn't reply he babbled on. "I love that your house is still all original."

And now he wanted to make small talk. Another thing I wasn't very good at. I glanced over at him to see if he was sincere in his compliment about keeping the house original or if it was a dig. The house was still vintage because Garrett hadn't had the time and I didn't have the energy or desire to make a change. I shoved things around inside the fridge until I finally found the carton of eggs.

"At our old house we started off with one renovation and that snowballed until, before you knew it, the entire house from floor to ceiling had been replaced. By the time we were done, there was only one original light fixture and everything else had gone modern. Sucked the character out of the house, you know?"

By now I was standing in front of him showing him the open carton of eggs which had exactly two left. "You're in luck."

"Oh my God, are you sure? I don't want to take your last two eggs. I'll just go to the store."

His dismay was comical as if he was committing some kind of neighborly crime.

"Take them." I shoved the carton into his hands. "Garrett's gone out of town for a couple days and he's the big breakfast eater. I'm more of a toast person."

Again. Too much info.

"He's out of town a lot, huh?"

"Is your T-shirt from some grunge band?" I changed the subject by pointing to the broken lightning bolt symbol on his chest. "It looks so familiar."

He laughed then, a loud raucous sound that filled the room. "I wish it was from some cool band and then maybe Phil wouldn't always be threatening to toss it! All my old T-shirts and my cool car. He hates both. I wear it for working around the house, mostly because Phil won't let me wear it in public. I probably would've trashed the shirt a couple years ago, but it's become a bone of contention between us. The more Phil wants me to toss it, the more I want to hang on to it. I think I picked it up at a convention or something."

"What is it that you do?" I asked.

He hesitated, and I had the awful feeling I was supposed to know the answer to this question. Probably he'd already told me, and I'd completely not paid attention like usual.

"Sales." He held up the carton. "Thanks so much for your last two eggs. I'll be sure to replace them right away." He opened the door and stepped out.

"You saved my dog from running away so I think

we can call it even." I stepped forward to close the door behind him. "In fact, I probably owe you a few dozen. I'd hate to lose Wookie."

"I love his name," he said as he walked away. "We need to have a movie night, right? All four of us."

I'd sooner remove my eyeballs with a spoon.

"See you later," I shouted and closed the door.

"You are a suck-up." I pointed a finger at Wookie. "There was a time when nobody could get near my trailer without you threatening to rip their ass off and now you can be bought by a biscuit or two." I clucked my tongue. "You're getting soft."

Wookie made a whining noise that could've been agreement and then he went to his plush dog bed.

After I showered, I shrugged into sweatpants and a T-shirt and brought my laptop in front of the television. Later that evening Tracey called and mentioned excitedly that she saw on the news about Maryanne being found in a dumpster.

"That was you, right? You found her! Good for you!" she exclaimed.

"Thanks. I'm glad to bring closure for her mom but I'm not exactly throwing a party over here."

"Oh yeah, of course it's pretty sad, but it woulda been even sadder if you didn't find her, right?"

"Right," I admitted.

"You sound distracted. Are you and Garrett in the middle of something? Oh my God, did I catch you in the middle of…you know…"

A laugh burst from my lips. "If we were having sex, I can guarantee I would not have answered the phone."

She giggled a little and shared news that she'd gone out on another date with the guy she'd already seen a couple times. "I think you're right about just dating the one guy for now. He's kind of sweet." Then she added excitedly, "Oh, did you ask Garrett about the ring? Is it from his dead wife or is he going to propose to you?"

"Actually, he was hardly home a second, so that conversation will have to wait. He's gone away working. Hopefully only for a day or two but could be longer."

"We should do a girls' night then. Manicures. Do each other's hair. Watch sappy romcoms."

"It's like you don't even know me."

"Okay, I know all those things are my kind of thing and not yours." She laughed. "What are you doing for excitement while your man's away?"

"I'm just looking at my emails."

"Wow. You really know how to live it up."

"Well, I'd love to crack open a couple bottles of wine, chug them dry and then dance around the kitchen naked but, unfortunately, I gave up drinking." I licked my lips involuntarily at the thought of wine hitting the back of my throat.

"Nothing stopping you from dancing around naked. I highly recommend it, in fact."

"With my luck the neighbor would drop by." I clicked Delete on one of the dozens of spam emails in my inbox. "I'm going to make myself some popcorn for dinner, so I'll let you go."

"I just wanted to ask what you were doing on August third."

I rolled my eyes. "Tracey, I don't even know what I'm doing tomorrow, never mind months from now."

"Okay, well, I was just wondering if you think you could bring me to the hospital for my surgery or, even, like drive me home after or something and I could take a cab there. I just won't be able to drive because it's my right knee, so-o-o-o…"

"Oh-h-h! Yeah. Sure. Of course, I'll take you for your operation. Are you going to be okay to stay on your own afterward? Do you want to come and stay here?"

"I was thinking of asking my mom to come but she doesn't drive so that would be a pain in the ass." She paused. "Wookie is getting better with me, isn't he?"

Tracey had made pretty good strides with Wookie but having her stay here after surgery might be expecting a bit much.

"I could even stay with you," I offered. "We've got a few months to work out the details. Think about it and let me know."

"I appreciate it. Hey, I have an idea. I'm sure Garrett has some pictures of his dead wife and kid, right? You should just find one of those pictures of her and take a look at the ring on her hand."

"Wow. That's a really good idea."

"Don't sound so surprised. Underneath this pink hair there's a for-real brain, you know!"

We ended the call just as Wookie and Fluffy decided to brawl. The cat bolted down the hall and Wookie was hot on his trail.

"Wookie, stop!"

He screeched to a halt, skidding on the linoleum until he'd stopped with a thud against the wall, then offered me a reproachful look that said the cat started the altercation.

"I know." I walked over and patted Wookie's head. "Cats are mostly just assholes. Sorry, dude, but you can't just chase him around. Avoid him. You're bigger. Walk away."

I heard a crash in the office and ran down the hall where I found Fluffy on the bookcase and the picture of Garrett's son on the floor. The glass from the photo was smashed and shards were scattered across the room.

"Bad cat!" I exclaimed. "Argh! Why do you have to be like this?"

As I swept up the mess I had to lock Fluffy out of the den because he kept attacking the broom. And my feet. And the dust bunnies under the desk. Cats were a different kind of crazy.

The face of Garrett's son smiled up at me from the floor, causing my heart to squeeze a little. He had Garrett's kind eyes and it hurt me to know that my guy had once been a dad, and I was guessing he was a pretty good one.

I gingerly picked up the frame and shook the loose glass into the trash can under Garrett's desk. The dust and glass covered crumpled paper in the can and one paper caught my eye. The letterhead logo was the same broken lightning figure that was on Preston's shirt. I put the picture down on the desk and, avoiding the bits of broken glass, I pulled the sheet out, put it on the desk and smoothed it flat. It was some meaningless form letter advertising a percentage off for new customers. The company's name was Flash Imports Inc., and the catch phrase beneath the name read *International imports and exports*.

It felt awfully coincidental to see the logo so much that I now recognized it but, then again, I may have seen it a hundred times in my life and never realized it until now. I crumpled the letter again and dropped it back into the trash. I ran the vacuum to make sure I got all the glass and made a mental note to keep the door to the den closed from now on. Only two days ago Garrett's desk had been pristine, and the top drawer locked. Now the desk was littered with paperwork and... I tugged open the top drawer to find it empty except for a couple of pens and a few paperclips.

As I took the picture of his son and propped it on the bookshelf, my mind went to the ring. I felt a little guilty snooping, but I knew he had a picture of her around here somewhere and I did find it tucked between some books on the bookshelf. It was a family photo. He could've displayed it prominently, but he kept it tucked away. Maybe out of respect for me, or maybe because it was just too painful.

In the picture Garrett had no gray in his hair. His eyes were bright and his smile wide. He looked impossibly happy. Did he ever smile like that these days? It made my chest hurt. I brought the picture close to my face and looked hard. Garrett wore a plain gold band, like my father's that I wore now on a chain around my neck. My fingers went to the ring and gave it a familiar pat. Then my gaze traveled to

Faith's finger. She wore an emerald surrounded by diamonds. The ring I found in the box in our closet was hers.

I felt a small twist in my chest of something that might have been disappointment. That was silly because I didn't want Garrett to propose. Still, I admitted that part of me liked the idea of wearing a ring on my finger. What a contradiction! I tucked the picture back into its location and felt guilty as if I'd spied on something private not meant for my eyes. I left the den, carefully closing the door behind me.

The sun was going down and Garrett still hadn't sent me a message from his new number as promised. I had no way to reach him and, based on his already swollen face, he could be involved in a dangerous situation.

"He's working," I mumbled under my breath as I tossed a catnip mouse to Fluffy. "He'll call when he can."

Fluffy looked at the mouse with scorn, hopped onto the kitchen counter and sat next to the heavy pewter urn that contained my mother's remains.

"Don't you dare!" I reached for the spray bottle while Fluffy looked at me with a challenge in his eyes. Finally, he got up and sauntered across the counter to the far end to look out the kitchen window.

"Fine. You win," I told the cat. "But you leave Mom's ashes alone."

Wookie and I went to the sofa where I watched sitcoms, the dog's head in my lap. It was after midnight when I climbed into bed, placing my phone on the table next to me with the volume on the highest setting. My anxiety bounced painful memories of the past into my head and tossed in jagged half-truths about my current situation. Talking about things with Garrett, or even hearing his voice, would've helped but I tried to find comfort in a phone app that played mindfulness meditations to help me count down to sleep. My fingers played with my father's wedding band around my neck. It was a token of love given to a man I never met but it gave me comfort.

Even on the third round of the meditation segment, my mind was racing and overthinking. I was worried about Garrett's safety and, if I was being honest, I had to admit that the self-doubt demons were planting seeds of concern in my head about our relationship too. Garrett was hell-bent on helping his brother-in-law, Sid, and he was doing it for Faith. His wife. My man was now focused on people who were his family. How was I ever going to compete with that?

SIX

WHEN THE SUN pierced through the slats of the bedroom blinds I bolted upright and snatched up my phone. No missed messages from Garrett. No unanswered calls. The panic and nervousness that had sat heavy on my chest while I drifted off to sleep ramped up as I sat up in bed.

I soothed myself with reassurances that he was busy. For all I knew he was undercover and had been in stealth mode all night and unable to take a break to use his phone. The fact that he'd always managed to find a way to message or call me before only made matters worse.

A loud hiss and meow followed by Wookie's painful yelp had me out of bed and shuffling toward the kitchen.

"Listen up, kids." I stifled a yawn. "This behavior is beneath both of you." The cat took a swat at my feet. "Okay, maybe it's not beneath you," I admitted, giving Fluffy's ass a light tap with my hand. "But unless you want to find yourself locked up in separate bedrooms all day, you're going to have to learn to get along."

Wookie looked at me with sad why-did-you-have-to-bring-home-a-cat eyes. I made coffee, even though my nerves were already jangling. While the coffeemaker sputtered and spat I filled the animals' food and water dishes. I was just pouring coffee into my mug and sending up a silent prayer that someone new wasn't pounding on Garrett's face when a knock sounded at my door. I jumped so high, I sloshed hot coffee all over myself and the floor.

Cursing vividly, I went to the door and opened it only to have the alarm screech because I'd neglected to deactivate it first. Preston squished his face and covered his ears as I punched in the code. Both Wookie and Fluffy had taken off to their various beds for protection.

"Sorry," Preston said. "I know it's early, but I saw the lights come on and knew you were up, and I just wanted to bring you these." He thrust into my hands a dinner plate holding two large pieces of cake covered in plastic wrap. I took the plate and looked at him questioningly.

"My birthday was yesterday and Phil used your eggs to make my cake, so..." He shrugged. "He told me this was better than just returning your eggs."

"Oh." I looked down at the cake and then back up to him, trying to replace the annoyed look on my face with one that was more appreciative. "Tell Phil thanks and happy birthday."

"Was that my doing too?" He pointed to my coffee-soaked shirt.

"No worries," I said hastily, becoming aware that the oversized tee I wore to bed only covered my ass by about two inches.

I started to close the door, but he stopped it with

his hand and quickly added, "By the way, the new fence posts will go in today."

"Great," I added unenthusiastically. When he continued to hold the door open and just stare at me sheepishly I realized there was more. "You want money, right? Garrett said something about splitting the cost. Is that it?"

He looked relieved. "Yes, well, it doesn't have to be right away, of course. I mean I've already paid the workers the first draw and then the balance is due once they're done but, you know, whenever you get around to it is fine."

But he acted like whenever we got around to it meant right now so I got him to tell me the amount and I wrote down his information, so I could send him an etransfer.

"You'll have it in a few minutes," I promised.

Preston finally left, and I dropped the plate of cake onto the counter and went straight to my laptop and sent him the money. It was probably in his inbox before he even opened the door of his house. I didn't want to give him any excuse to come over again. The alarm company called to make sure everything was okay and I gave them the password to assure them I was just one of the hundreds of idiots they probably dealt with who set off their own alarms.

Wookie had snarfed his food, drunk enough water that his muzzle was still dripping, and was now standing looking expectantly at the back door wanting out.

"Ugh." I frowned. "Sorry, boy, still no fence so we'll go for a walk, okay?"

Of course that was okay. At the mere mention of the *W* word, Wookie bounded to the side door where his leash hung from a hook. I put on some jeans and runners, pocketed my cell, and hesitated. What if Garrett called the house while I was out? I mean, he almost always called my cell but the other day, when using someone else's phone to call, he'd called the landline for some reason.

I pinched my eyes shut and drew in a deep breath. "He's fine. He'll call my cell if I don't answer this line." I hated that he was putting me on edge like this for no reason. At least I hoped it was without cause.

I zipped up my windbreaker and snapped the leash onto Wookie's collar. When we stepped outside I locked the door behind me and took off at a dead run. I was driven by the need to get Wookie's pee break and exercise over with, so I could hurry back home and be next to the phone. Only when you're in a big hurry do you notice that your dog absolutely *must* pee on every single corner and blade of grass. He refused to move from one street to the next without a significant amount of sniffing and dribbling.

On our way back my phone rang in my pocket and I nearly dropped it in my haste to look at the screen only to see that it was Tracey.

"Can I call you back?" I said by way of a greeting. "I'm just out walking Wookie."

"Sure," she replied.

I hit the disconnect button and checked my texts to see if somehow a message had come in from Garrett without my noticing or a notification sound from an unknown number that could be him. Zilch. My stomach soured with nervousness as Wookie and I jogged the last block home.

Back inside, I kicked off my shoes and ran to check the home phone. No messages there either and no missed calls.

"You're acting like a crazy person." I drilled my fingers through my hair. "And you're talking to yourself so that proves it."

I set about cleaning up the earlier spilled coffee and that led to a need to wipe the counters and that dominoed into a cleaning of all the cupboards inside and out. My tiny single-wide trailer might not have been so pretty, but it was definitely an easier space to keep clean. After an hour my phone pinged a message from Tracey asking if I was back from my walk. I'd completely forgotten to call her back.

"Sorry," I told her when she answered. "I had a bit of a coffee mess I needed to get to."

"No problem. Hey, I know that you're just starting to get back into your dowsing thing and you said you were only going to go super slow and take easy cases because of your mental health and all that…"

"Yeah? But?" I prompted.

"Well, I have this friend. That guy I'm seeing…"

"He has a body he needs found?"

"Yeah, it just came up last night. His brother has been missing for a while."

I rolled my eyes so hard I gave myself an immediate headache. "Tracey." I fought to keep my voice even because I was already annoyed. "C'mon…don't tell me you volunteered me to find the remains for some guy just so you could get screwed?"

"I take offense to that," she said evenly.

"Well…" I exhaled. "Sorry. I'm stressed."

"If you must know, we've already been to bed and it was afterward that this came up so…"

Great. My dowsing abilities were a post-coital discussion. That made me feel a ton better.

"Obviously, you don't have to do it if you don't want to. Seriously," she insisted. "I made him zero promises. It just sounded like exactly your speed right now."

"Oh really." I rubbed the crease between my eyebrows with the tip of my finger. "What exactly is my speed?"

"A simple case really. His brother, who had an intellectual disability, wandered away from their home when he was little. Their farm area had flooded during the spring runoff, and he was presumed drowned in the creek that backs onto their property. Water levels were high that spring but even after the water receded the only things ever recovered were his favorite book bag that he took with him everywhere and one shoe. His body never turned up. Anyway, Craig was mentioning how it would mean a lot to his mother if she could have something to bury, even though it's been a dozen years."

Damn. That was kind of my speed now. She was right. But I needed to be home for Garrett. "Look…"

"You're right," Tracey blurted. "It's a lot to ask. I never told him you'd do it. Swear to God."

"I don't know…" I started giving excuses about housework and Wookie and Fluffy fighting and wanting to stick around home.

"Something's wrong," Tracey sounded worried. "I can hear it in your voice."

"I just haven't heard from Garrett. He always texts or calls me when he's working. It's really unlike him."

"I'm coming over."

"No. You don't have to."

"Give me fifteen minutes. Actually, make it half an hour because I need to shower."

Ninety minutes later she showed up. I was convinced she'd changed her mind about coming at all and I was okay with that because I was too busy making mental notes detailing all the reasons why Garrett might not have called yet. The number one reason on that list was because he was dead, so I began a new list of plausible and nonfatal reasons he hadn't called, and that list was making me feel a lot better.

Wookie barked, which meant that I had to lock the dog in my bedroom because otherwise Tracey wouldn't come inside. Eventually, if Wookie remained calm and not jumpy and Tracey remained centered and not anxious, we could try a reunion in the living room. Tracey showed up carrying fancy coffees and a box of cupcakes.

"I wasn't aware we were having a party." I peeked inside the bakery box at four chocolate cupcakes with towering icing in pale pastel shades.

"You're stressed and that calls for caffeine and sugar."

"There's already chocolate cake from the neighbors that I haven't touched." I pointed to the plate on the kitchen counter.

Tracey kicked off her flats and thrust into my

hands some kind of espresso-based coffee with whipped cream and caramel drizzle.

"I'm almost positive that the last thing I need is caffeine and sugar but thanks." I took a sip and nodded. "Delicious but I probably won't sleep for a week."

"That's good, then you'll be wide awake and ready to read Garrett the riot act when he calls."

"True." I walked over to the sofa and slumped down. "It's this damn case he's on. That's why he hasn't called. It's personal so he's not thinking of anything else."

"Personal? How is that?" Tracey put the bakery box on the coffee table and sat in the chair next to the sofa. She adjusted the brace on her knee with a wince while waiting for me to answer.

"I can't talk about it."

"Really?" She snagged a cupcake with pale pink icing and handed it to me, then chose a light blue one for herself. "Like, who am I going to tell?"

"Anyone? Everyone?" I took a small bite of the cupcake which, for the record, tasted not nearly as satisfying as a glass of wine would at that moment.

"I'm insulted. We're besties. Anything you tell me goes in the vault."

"We're not teenagers, Tracey." I rubbed the back of my neck and felt the tight ligaments that held my stress. Dr. Chen said I needed to be open to a deeper friendship with Tracey. It wasn't that I didn't want to, it was just that I didn't know how. All my relationships had been abusive except for mine with Garrett. It was hard to trust. "Garrett hasn't even told me what's really going on except his brother-in-law, Sid, is involved with some company that's connected to some bad stuff and Garrett, of course, feels an obligation to help him."

"I didn't know he was close to her family."

"He isn't." I took another nibble of the cupcake and then put it down on the table. "But Garrett's a loyal guy and he feels he owes it to…you know."

"His dead wife."

"Faith." I cleared my throat. "Yeah. Her."

"I can see why you're upset."

I shook my head. "It's not that." Well it wasn't *just* that. "He always contacts me at night when he's away. The other night I didn't hear from him because his phone got damaged, but he ended up borrowing a phone and calling me on the landline."

"Landline? What are we, in the nineteen-sixties?"

"The point is, when he's overnight he calls or texts. The other day he came home with his face all busted up because of some altercation to do with this case so, you know, I'm worried."

"Have you tried—"

"Calling him? Yeah, that's the other part. His phone got lost or damaged the night his face took a pounding. Yesterday he replaced the phone and the number and said he'd text me, so I'd have his new contact number but…" I shrugged and blew out a breath.

"Are you thinking you should call the cops? File a missing person's report?"

I shook my head and suddenly felt silly. "He packed a bag. He flat-out told me he didn't know how long he'd be gone." I blew out a breath, remembering how angry he got when he thought I was trying to guilt him into staying. "You know what? He's fine. He's busy on a case and he told me he didn't know how long he'd be gone so it's crazy that I'm acting all bent out of shape just because he didn't call me the same day he left." Even though he always called. *Always*. I picked up my too-sweet coffee, took a swig and watched as Fluffy jumped into Tracey's lap and began purring.

"You're the only one that damn cat likes," I pointed out. "He hates me."

"He doesn't hate you." She stroked the cat from head to tail and he arched his back in pleasure. "He just misses his mom."

"Yeah, well, his mom was my mother too." I didn't want to get into that other, sordid story. "You know what, screw it, tell me again about your boyfriend's missing brother. I need the distraction."

"Not my boyfriend, just... Craig."

"You're sleeping with him."

"Trust me, there is zero sleeping involved."

I snorted at that.

"But I do kinda like him. He's a nice guy. It would be great if you could help him out."

Tracey turned in the chair to face me. She excitedly began to ramble, repeating what she'd told me earlier about Craig's brother going missing during the spring runoff flood and never finding the body. I asked her to find out the exact address of the property where it happened and the date. She fired off texts to Craig, and while we waited for a reply I told her I was getting Wookie out of the bedroom. Immediately, Tracey pulled her feet up on the coffee table as if Wookie was a little ankle biter instead of a hundred thirty-pound Rotty who could easily jump on the sofa and devour her if he had the inkling.

She became very still as Wookie bounded into the room.

"Go to your bed," I instructed.

Wookie glanced over at Tracey and growled.

"He wants to rip me apart," she whispered, visibly shaking and pale.

"No. He wants to rip the cat apart. He'd like to lick all the icing off your face though," I said, trying not to smile at her discomfort.

Wookie crawled into his bed across the room and dropped his head onto his paws to look at us with sad, pleading eyes.

"He's jealous of the cat?" Tracey asked, her voice still low and quiet.

"Yeah, they pretty much hate each other." I took my coffee cup, dumped the remaining whipped cream and coffee mixture into the sink, rinsed it and dropped it into the recycle bin. "For the record, Wookie's the one who's taking a beating. The cat is kicking his butt."

"We don't believe that for a second, do we?" she said in a baby voice as she stroked Fluffy. The cat's purrs intensified, probably just to annoy Wookie.

"You've come a long way," I said. "When we first met, you wouldn't come inside at all because I had a dog. Now you're sitting in the same room with him."

"Yeah." Although she was stroking the cat, her eyes never left Wookie. She'd come a long way, but she still didn't trust him.

"You know he's never bit anyone. Ever."

"You've said that a hundred times. I just don't wanna be the first."

There was no arguing with that. Her phone chimed, and she tore her eyes away from Wookie to read the message. "Craig is really excited. I've got all the information about their farm and the location of the creek. His mom is out of town visiting his aunt, but we can walk on the property all we want."

She read me the details of the location and I frowned.

"That's like a three-hour drive from here. Add in a few hours over there and another three hours back..." I chewed my lower lip.

"Don't worry. You'll have your phone with you the entire time, so Garrett will be able to reach you."

When I continued to hesitate she added, "You can't just sit around here making yourself crazy with worry when he's probably so nose-to-the-grindstone he's completely forgotten about calling."

"I guess you're right."

"And if he knew you sat around all day by the phone waiting for him that would make him feel bad."

I nodded, then got to my feet and clapped my hands. "I'm not going to sit around waiting for him to call me when he's probably tied up with work."

"That's the spirit."

I packed my backpack with water bottles and granola bars. A small squeak directed my attention back at Tracey. Wookie had gotten up from his bed and had walked over to her. She was frozen in terror.

"It's okay. He's only jealous of Fluffy," I said. The

cat was still in her lap and was now looking at the dog with annoyance. "You'd make Wookie feel a lot better if you'd pat his head."

"He'd feel better because he'd bite my hand off," Tracey said, her voice trembling.

"I can guarantee that's not going to happen."

I was about to call Wookie away from her when Fluffy hissed and swatted the dog's nose. Wookie yelped and skedaddled over to me for protection.

"Aw-w-w, poor baby." I rubbed Wookie's head and he ran off to drink from his water bowl.

"I can't believe Fluffy is such a badass." Tracey giggled.

"Evil. You're sitting there worried about Wookie while you're petting the real one who'd rip your face off." I waggled a finger at Tracey. "Plus, even when Fluffy sliced his nose just now, you notice Wookie did not retaliate. That dog is a friggin' saint."

Tracey didn't reply but she was watching Wookie with a lot less fear.

"Okay, I'm just going to take him out before we go." I snapped a leash on Wookie's collar. "The guys out back are building a new fence, so I can't just set him free or—"

"Or he might maul them?" Tracey got up and collected the cupcake box.

"No." I laughed. "Or he'll bother them until the next-door neighbor feeds him so many treats he becomes obese."

"I'm bringing the rest of the cupcakes for the road."

"Take the cake too. I'm going to forward the house phone to my cell," I said, picking up the handset.

"You're the only person I know who still even has a landline. I guess that's because Garrett is old."

"He's not old. Sure, he's over twenty years older than us," I pointed out. "But that doesn't make him old."

"But I bet you didn't have a landline before you moved in together."

"True. But he called me on it when his cell phone was broken, and he borrowed a phone from someone else."

"Probably the first and only call you'll get on that thing."

She was giggling about that but the gears in my mind were turning as I clicked through our caller ID log. Tracey was right. We had very few calls on this line and there it was…the number he used to call me when he didn't have his phone.

"Uh-oh. That look on your face reminds me of how Wookie probably looks at his next victim," Tracey said.

"What?" I looked up from the phone and then shook my head. "No…um… I just want to make a note of the number Garrett used to call me when he misplaced his phone." I took out my cell and made a note of the number.

"You should call that number if you're worried. It's probably a coworker, right? You just call them up and say, 'Hey, is Garrett with you? I'm trying to reach him.'"

"That makes me sound like a nagging wife or a worried mom tracking him down." But I admitted to myself that I wasn't above trying it if he didn't call soon. I finished punching in the code to forward the landline calls to my cell, then took Wookie outside to do his business.

After locking up and joining Tracey in the Jeep, she brought it up again.

"All I'm saying is that it wouldn't hurt you to call that person's number and let them know you haven't heard from him."

"I'll give it a few more hours," I told her, backing out of the driveway.

It was taking a lot out of me not to dial that person's number, but I kept thinking of the look on his face when he got angry. He'd pointed that angry finger in my face and raised his voice...

"I can't handle you making me feel guilty right now on top of everything else!"

If I hunted him down like a truant child, he'd probably blow his top and I'd feel stupid and hurt.

"He's an FBI agent working on a tricky case. The last thing he needs is a worried girlfriend tracking him down." I smiled over at her while we pulled away. "It'll be fine. Really."

"You need to tell your face that. Because that fake smile is scary as hell."

My heart was scared too, but I didn't want to admit that. "He'll call."

The words left my mouth but my heart didn't believe them.

SEVEN

AFTER STOPPING ONCE for coffee, another time because Tracey dumped a cupcake in her lap and we had icing everywhere, and two stops to find a washroom, we finally arrived at the farm where her boyfriend grew up. We entered the property following a long, rutted gravel road. When we pulled up to the old house, a large man was sitting on the bumper of his pickup.

"Oh!" Tracey exclaimed. "That's Craig. I told him we were making the drive, but I didn't expect him to show up. Sorry. That probably makes it awkward for you."

"Nope. I'm used to having the victim's families around when I search." I shrugged. "Might make it awkward for you since you never mentioned that your new boyfriend is old enough to be your dad and looks like Jay Cutler."

"Jay who?"

"The bodybuilder."

"Oh. Yeah, he has muscles." She smiled. "But he's not nearly as old as Garrett. He's only forty. And he's not my boyfriend. Just…a guy friend. Who's good in bed."

"Right."

We hopped out of the Jeep. Well, I hopped, and Craig rushed over to help Tracey, lifting her like she was a sack of feathers and tenderly placing her down on the ground as if she were made of glass. I grabbed my backpack and came around the other side of the vehicle.

"You're Julie Hall, right? I've heard so much about you." He thrust out a meaty hand. "I'm Craig. Thanks so much for doing this. It means a lot to me." His fist swallowed mine in an enthusiastic shake.

"You're welcome but I need to warn you that we may not find your brother. I'll try but…" I lifted my palms up. "There are no guarantees."

"Gotcha." He pointed his finger at me like a pistol and pulled the trigger. "I'm just glad my boo here convinced you to help."

"Boo?" I wiggled my eyebrows at Tracey, who blushed in reply.

We started walking toward the farmhouse, an old two-story in need of paint.

"My ma is going to lose her mind when she hears you were here. She followed all about your career in all the papers and she even sent you an email one time, but she never heard back." He held up his hand when I started to speak. "I know you probably get a gazillion requests, so you don't need to explain anything to me. I didn't tell her about you coming. This way, if you find my bro it'll be a nice surprise and, if you don't, no harm no foul, right?"

"Right." I liked that he was reasonable in his expectations. "Boo here already gave me a heads-up," I said, giving Tracey a smirk. "But why don't you tell me what happened to your brother in your own words."

"Sure."

We walked around the house and Craig pointed to the acreage at the back of the property.

"The creek that runs along the back of our land gets pretty fast and swollen in spring. Right now it's not bad but soon, once snow starts melting in the mountains, all the mountain runoff just goes whooshing through, and most years everything is A-okay. The creek level always rises in spring, but some years are worse than others. Every dozen years or so it overflows its banks, but the year Derek went missing most of the farm lands around here were underwater."

"And this happened…"

"Fifteen years ago, this month." His considerably large shoulders slumped. "Sometimes it feels like it was just yesterday."

"I'm sorry for your loss," I said automatically.

Tracey rubbed Craig's back until he continued with his story.

"I'd already left the farm and was working in Seattle. When Ma called and told me how bad the waters were getting, I organized some friends to come and do some sandbagging. The plan was to make a sandbag wall around the house in case the water got that high, and then I was going to take Ma and Derek back to Seattle to stay with me until the water receded."

I shifted my backpack from one shoulder to the other as we continued to walk down toward the creek.

"When we got here, Derek was inside watching

TV and Ma was in the house with him. She stayed inside with him and kept busy packing bags for her and Derek. Me and my friends dragged and piled up sandbags around the house for the better part of the afternoon. When we were done, and it was time to go, there was no sign of Derek."

"And you believe he wandered down to the creek and got swept away?"

The trickling creek looked hardly imposing. Right now, I could walk across and might worry about slipping on the rocks, but I'd barely get my ankles wet.

"Here's the thing about Derek," Craig said, coming to a stop. "He was nonverbal autistic, you know? And he was a boy all about his routines. He had his certain shows he watched every day and he liked to watch them in a certain order. He ate like maybe three different food combinations and his favorite of those was a grilled cheese sandwich with chocolate milk."

Craig's voice got soft and tender.

"On that day Ma, like most days, made him his grilled cheese sandwich with the crusts cut off and cut into triangles, just like always, and Derek ate it in front of his favorite cartoon while she packed. Derek liked to go down to the creek every day and get rocks. He had a collection of small pebbles. To us, they looked like any old piece of gravel you'd find on the side of the road, you know? But when he found one in a special shape or if it had a little bit of sparkle, he saved it." He sighed and looked dreamy as he grabbed Tracey's hand and gave it a squeeze. "Ma gave me Derek's box of rocks to hold on to. She just couldn't stand to see them in the house anymore."

I waited patiently for him to continue.

"We figure that me and the guys were bagging out front of the house and Ma was in her bedroom packing up when Derek decided to go down to the creek to look for rocks. He'd been warned not to but…" He blew out a breath. "He wasn't always great at listening, and when he was focused on something he was really, really fixated on that thing."

We were all quiet as we stood on the edge of the slow moving trickle of a creek about a dozen feet wide. Hard to believe that it could rise and become treacherous rapids, but I'd seen it happen.

"That's so horrible," Tracey said, once again patting Craig's back. He leaned in and gave her a grateful one-arm hug.

"And searchers were brought in, of course," I said.

"Yeah. We searched for days. Weeks even. Us and everyone around these parts, but all that was ever found was one of his shoes and his bright blue Pokémon book bag that he used to put his rocks in. Even once the water had gone back down to normal we had people out looking for him every day but…" He shook his head. "No sign of him anywhere. Police said he probably washed right into the river and even though they dragged and searched where the creek opens up a few miles down, they had no luck."

"How horrible," Tracey murmured.

And even though it really was terrible, my mind was more focused on finding him now.

"How old was Derek? And how big was he?"

"He was eleven. Would've been twelve a few weeks later." Craig scratched his head. "Maybe four foot ten and eighty pounds."

I put down my pack and pulled out my dowsing rods. Shielding my eyes with my hand, I looked as far down the creek as I could in the direction the water was flowing. "How deep did the water get here?"

"Deep. The house is on a bit of a rise, as you can see." He waved his hand toward the house. "Water got to a few feet of where we were sandbagging around the house and it was moving fast. Derek went missing just a day or two before the water crested. If I had to guess, I'd say our field—and every farm between here and the mouth of the river two miles away—was under a good six or seven feet of fast-moving water. Of course the creek itself was a raging river of probably twice that deep."

I nodded. "And how quickly did it recede?"

He shook his head then. "It took weeks before it was back to normal but a number of days before it was off most of the farmland."

"Okay, I'm going for a walk." I had my rods in my hands and hoisted my pack onto my back.

"We'll come along," Craig said, stepping up alongside me.

"No." I looked at Tracey. "You two might as well stay here. Rest your knee." When she started to protest I quickly added, "Keep your cell phone on and I'll call if I need anything, or if I've found anything."

Craig looked so hopeful that I finally had to add, "You know, fifteen years is a really long time.

There's a very good chance I won't find your brother. I just don't want you to get your hopes up, okay?"

"Oh sure. I know that." He nodded vigorously.

"But she's gonna try her damnedest, right?" Tracey put a small hand on one of his huge biceps.

"I am."

With that, I set out, following the creek with my dowsing rods held out in front of me. A crow swooped and cawed, and a little farther I frightened a brown bunny that took off into the tall weeds. I started thinking about Garrett. The songbirds were chirping, and the creek was babbling, but my head was filled with what-if scenarios that were a horror movie. Dr. Chen taught me how to deal with those sticky, dark, quicksand thoughts by replacing bad thoughts with good. I substituted the idea that Garrett was trapped in the wreckage of his car somewhere with an image of him looking tired as he typed up reports in his Seattle office. I swapped the image of Garrett in a hospital bed bandaged from head to toe with the visual of him waving off fellow agents and telling them he was heading home. I replaced the fear that Garrett was in trouble, with the idea that his phone was turned off and he was so busy wrapping up this case, he'd completely forgotten to message me. Finally, in my mind, I had a happier thought of him stopping on his way home to get all my favorite foods to make us a great barbecue dinner tonight.

I was smiling at that daydream as I trudged alongside the winding creek bed and nearly slipped on a wet rock. Glancing over my shoulder, I couldn't even see the farm where I started. Straight ahead the stream continued to meander with acres of farmland stretching on either side. A fat fly buzzed my face and I swatted at it, nearly poking myself in the eye with one of my rods.

I took a break, sitting on a rock on the edge of the creek, and pulled out a water bottle from my pack. I took a long drink and arched my back in a stretch as I gave the situation more thought. If Derek had been in the water, within days or weeks of his drowning he would've washed up somewhere. This brook emptied into a busy river about a mile from where I was now and, sure, the body could've traveled far, but bodies rarely stayed at the bottom of a river for long.

I covered my eyes with my hands and surveyed the farmland around me. All of this would've been underwater. He could've washed up in any number of the fields around me. The only problem with that idea was that these were working farms, and I doubted these fields had done anything other than produce wheat in all the years since that flood. Even now, the fields had already been planted and soon wheat shoots would stretch toward the sun. Farmers around here planted and harvested and cared for their land and they knew their neighbors. They would've been on the lookout for Derek's body as the water receded.

Still, I decided to make my way a dozen yards up field, so I walked through the recently planted rows, careful not to step on the precious seedlings. The land from Craig's farm sloped away at a gentle incline. The higher elevation of the house had saved it from flooding. As I walked between the rows, my mind drifted to my farm upbringing. Dropped off at my grandparents' farm by my mother, I'd been left to be raised by my grandparents. My grandmother was a vicious woman who got kicks from physically torturing and mentally tormenting me.

"No!" I spit the word out loud to stop the thoughts in their tracks and startled a murder of crows from a nearby tree.

"Sorry, guys." I mumbled the apology to the birds and sidestepped a puddle on the edge of the field.

Just as I stepped away from the puddle, my rods trembled and swung ever so slightly to my left.

The movement was lackadaisical, and someone else observing the slight rotation might consider it the result of a light breeze or a turn of my wrist, but I knew differently.

There was definitely a body here.

And from my practicing, the mild twitch of the rods felt right around that fifteen-year timeline. I followed the light but compelling tug of the rods across the rows in the field for a few yards until the dark farmed soil ended. A grassy ditch lay between the cultivated land, with a sheet of old rotted plywood on the ground. Once I got closer, my dowsing rods languidly crossed over indicating a body. The leisurely, hesitant movement meaning it was not a recent death.

"Here you are," I whispered. "I'm sorry it's taken so long, Derek."

I nudged the plywood with the toe of my runner. I knew immediately what I was looking at was an old water well. We'd had a few of these on my farm growing up. They weren't permanently capped and decommissioned, like they should be, but, instead, just had some kind of covering on top so you didn't fall in. I'm guessing that when Craig's brother was swept away in the flood waters, that the cover on this old well had also been moved away. The little boy's body dropped into the well and the farmer, without thinking much of it, would've just placed another piece of wood on top of it once the water receded.

My phone chimed in my back pocket and I whipped it out, disappointed to see the person texting was Tracey and not Garrett. She asked how things were going. I didn't reply right away. Instead, I sat down in the soft grass next to the well and placed my shaking hands on my thighs. Finding Craig's brother had been a slight distraction but worrying about Garrett was making me jumpy. I made up my mind that once I was home I'd call the Bureau office or, at least, try the number he'd used to call our landline. Unless, of course, he called or messaged me before.

"Please let him call me." My spoken prayer was whipped away by the spring breeze.

After a few moments taking in deep, calming breaths and steadying my heart, I called Tracey and told her I was certain I'd found Derek's body on a neighboring farm.

"In an old well," I told her. "Tell Craig to call the authorities. It's going to take me half an hour to walk back."

I could hear Craig peppering her with questions in the background as I ended the call. Before I could slip my phone back in my pocket a text came in.

Bad cell service. I'll call soon, Sweet pea. Love you.

Garrett! My heart leaped into my throat. Immediately I hit call on the number that came in, but it went straight to an automated voicemail, so I texted back.

Glad you're safe! I've been worried. Love you tons!

I stared at the phone hoping for the dot dot dot meaning he was replying but none came. I sent another message.

Call when you can. xoxo

Still no reply but I could feel a squeeze of relief in my chest. My nerves had been pinging for no reason. A burst of laughter left my lips as I reread the message; giggling at the use of *Sweet pea* as a nickname. Something new and silly but I'd take it.

"He's okay," I told myself as I walked on. I would've liked to hear his voice but he'd reached out and said the service was bad.

By the time I was close to Tracey and Craig I'd pulled my phone out of my pocket a half dozen times to reread Garrett's message and my head had picked apart every single word of his text. My thoughts kept getting hung up on *Sweet pea*. He'd never called me that before and I couldn't imagine him even saying the word out loud. It was crazy of me to obsess over the word.

"You're being stupid," I muttered under my breath as I reached Tracey.

"Craig's out front." She pointed behind her with her thumb. "Cops just got here."

I nodded and wordlessly dropped my pack on the ground, fished out a bottle of water and finished it.

"You okay?" She tilted her head at me.

"Yeah. I heard from Garrett. He's in a bad cell area."

"Oh good!" She put a hand on my shoulder. "You were worried for nothin' and now you went and solved another mystery. It's a red-letter day for you!"

"Right."

Sweet pea.

I cleared my throat and nodded a chin in the direction of the front of the house. "How'd he take it?"

"He got teary, you know? And then he just hugged me hard and thanked me." She rolled her eyes. "As if I've done anything at all."

"You got it started," I told her.

An officer was walking back toward us with Craig towering above him. I gave the police the information and location of the well.

"So, you opened up the well cap and you saw the body in there?" the officer asked me.

"No. I didn't open it and I didn't see it."

He made a bulldog scrunched-up face and drew in a deep breath through his nose. I could tell he didn't believe there was an actual body so before he could say anything else I told him about my dowsing.

"Check with your boss, if you need to. He'll have heard of me."

"Yeah," Tracey burst in. "Everyone's heard of her. She finds bodies all the time. Have you been living under a friggin' rock?"

"Easy." I put a hand on her arm. "The officer here

is just doing his job, and he doesn't want to walk with me to look in a well for no reason." I turned to Craig, who still had a deer-in-the-headlights look about him. "You've got a couple of good flashlights in the house? Could you go get them?"

Craig ran off to get the flashlights and Tracey tagged along.

The officer stood looking at me with derision. "I've heard of you. Of course I have. Just thought it wasn't true." When my only response was to shrug he added, "There'd better be a friggin' body down that well."

"Yeah, because nothing makes your day more than finding a dead kid, right?"

He looked away from me then with his arms crossed. As soon as Craig reappeared I tucked the flashlights into my pack and we all set off back in the direction I'd come. I led the way, followed by the cop, and then Tracey and Craig brought up the rear. Tracey's brace made it hard for her to keep up, but she insisted on following along. It was completely quiet except for our feet crunching on the dried grass. Instead of walking in the fields, we kept to the edge of the creek. Before long we were trudging down into the ditch. I pulled out a flashlight, handed it to the officer and pointed a few feet ahead to the old well.

"You going to help?" he asked.

"Nope. That's why you make the big bucks."

He snorted and mumbled something unpleasant under his breath. Craig pulled up alongside him and together they hoisted the damp, rotted sheet of plywood off the well.

Tracey was panting next to me and I told her to sit. I knew her knee was killing her. She shouldn't've walked all this way.

The officer crouched down on his haunches, shone the flashlight down the hole and leaned in.

"I don't see nuthin' except rancid water and—" The officer stopped himself short and then grunted. "Some kind of clothes or somethin'…"

"Pokémon!" Craig announced. "Derek's favorite yellow Pokémon shirt. He loved to wear it. Oh God." He gulped in air, stumbled toward Tracey and sat down hard on the ground next to her. "He's really down there."

"There. There." Tracey took his hand as Craig leaned his considerably large head on her shoulder and sobbed quietly.

"Let's not get ahead of ourselves." The officer got to his feet and dusted off his pants. "Could be just some junk down there and—"

"You go ahead and do what you gotta do to figure that out," I told him. "Call in whoever you gotta call. We're heading back."

"I wanna stay," Craig said on a hiccup. "You can go, and thank you so much for everything." He got to his feet and took my hands and shook them and then decided that wasn't enough and crushed me in a bear hug. "Thank you. I'll drive Tracey home if she wants to stay too."

She nodded at me to leave her and told me she'd call me later. I slowly walked back to the farm, grateful to leave it behind me.

By the time I reached my Jeep I was sweating and

out of breath. I'd jogged the last little bit of the trip and was glad to climb inside my vehicle, start it up and let the vent blow cold air in my face. I headed down the road and was a few miles out when I saw a marked police car coming from the opposite direction. I'd found a body today. I'd given someone closure. And Garrett had messaged me too.

So why did I feel like crap?

I drank another water as I drove and before long needed to make a restroom break. Once I was back in the Jeep I pulled out my phone and stared hard at Garrett's message.

All the words felt wrong. I told myself he was obviously stressed, and I needed to cut him some slack. Even though there'd been no reply to my last two responses to him, I sent another.

Hope you're ok. Love you xo.

I stared at the words to make sure they sent and, once I was sure they'd traveled across the ether to their destination, I headed for home. Before long I was pulling into my driveway and, at the same time, Preston pulled up into his drive, revving his fancy sports car. Phil came out of the house to greet him and they both smiled and waved at me.

I smiled and waved back through gritted teeth.

As I made my way to the door I noticed Wookie's face in the picture window. He was howling at me like I'd been gone a week, which was odd.

"He sure missed you today," Phil said with a laugh. "They've got the fence up and it's even stained. C'mon around out back and take a look. I think you'll absolutely love it."

Absolutely love seemed like powerful words to describe my feelings about a fence. I murmured some kind of "maybe later" to them and let myself inside the house.

Wookie bounded over and jumped, putting his feet on my chest.

"What the hell, boy, you're soaked! You been playing in your water bowl?" Even as the words left my mouth, my feet were sopping up water. A small spring of water was coming from under the kitchen sink and had spread to the living room and soaked the carpet where I stood.

"Oh no!"

I sloshed over to the kitchen with Wookie on my heels and met Fluffy's furious glare from his perch on the counter. Flinging the cabinet doors open, I stared at the pipe where water was pouring. There didn't seem to be any way to turn it off. I straightened, looked around the drenched kitchen and living room and cursed vividly as I tried to come up with what to do. I knew there'd be a shutoff somewhere to the entire house but where? I could feel a bubble of panic in my throat that could be quenched with wine.

"Dammit," I growled.

Making my way back to the front door I stepped outside and waved my arms at Phil and Preston.

"Help! I seem to have a bit of a flood here... I don't know where the shutoff is."

Both men ran inside, pausing only to leave their shoes at the front door before they took over. Preston sloshed over to the back hall while Phil made his way to look under the sink. After a couple minutes of chaotic shouting between them, the water stopped flowing and we all met back in the living room, where Wookie was bounding around thinking this was the best day at the beach he'd ever had. Fluffy hissed and puffed up angrily from the kitchen counter.

"Good news is that the water didn't reach the back hall or bedrooms," Preston announced. "Bad news is you've got a huge mess."

"Call your insurance company." Phil slicked his hand through the tangled mess on top of his head. "They'll take care of it."

"Right," I nodded. "Insurance company."

"Happened to our place a couple years ago when we were on vacation," Phil said. "Luckily my mother was checking on the house and found the mess before it made too much damage. We just stayed away an extra two weeks until everything could get sorted."

"An extra *two* weeks?"

At the pained look in my eyes, they both started telling me that it would be okay and they offered for me, Garrett and the creatures to stay with them until it all got sorted. I thanked them profusely for their help but told them not to worry because I had plenty of options of places to stay. A blatant lie.

My phone rang as I was seeing them to the door. "Oh look, that's Garrett now, he'll know what to do." I answered the call. "Hold on just a second, honey." And then said to the neighbors, "Thank you both so-o-o much. Really!" and all but shoved them out the door.

Putting the phone back to my ear I said, "Sorry about that, Tracey."

"You're welcome, *honey*. Everything okay?"

"No." I exhaled a high-pitched, near hysterical giggle. "I seem to have had a bit of a flood here at the house. I've gotta find our insurance papers and—and…" I took a step and skidded along the wet carpet, nearly falling on my ass. "Sorry, I've gotta go."

I ended the call.

I wrangled Fluffy and received a deep scratch for my troubles as I dumped him into my bedroom, and then took Wookie to the den and brought some towels in to dry off his feet. Over the next few hours emergency restoration workers showed up with equipment to suck up the water, and giant fans to dry things out. An insurance adjuster also arrived and his face was so pinched it looked like it might implode on itself.

I took lots of pictures with my phone and sent them all to Garrett. It was a dumbass move since the last thing he needed when dealing with a difficult case was news of a crisis at home. But that was too bad. I needed him and I found myself resentful that he was unavailable.

Tracey showed up on my doorstep after I ignored a couple of her texts.

"You okay?" She pulled me into a tight hug.

"I'm fine. It's just a little water." I nodded and forced a smile. "I'm all good," I repeated as if I said it enough times it would make it so. "Keep your shoes on if you're coming in. It's no longer ankle deep but still wet."

"What happened?" She whistled as she looked

around at the fans that were each the size of a large child.

"Some kind of pipe gave way under the kitchen sink."

"Did you get a hold of Garrett?"

"No." I pointed to the floor. "And you know what? He's the one that wanted this house. I said it was too old and too close to neighbors, but he said it's got good bones." I snorted. "Apparently good bones mean that the plumbing is garbage." I surprised myself with the venom in my voice. "I'd offer you coffee or tea or water but, hey, there's no water to the house until they fix the plumbing and who knows how long that will be?" I dragged a hand through my hair.

"The insurance will cover this, right?"

"Yes, but first we'll have to pay the huge deductible."

At least that part wasn't such a worry. I'd made a profit selling the house I bought with my inheritance, and Garrett made a good living. Between the two of us we had ample savings set aside to tackle the home renovations on this fixer upper, but we'd planned on doing it at our leisure.

"Gather up that mutt and cat. You're coming to stay with me."

I burst out laughing because the thought of me, Wookie and Fluffy staying in Tracey's tiny one bedroom was hilarious. "Thanks, but no. The motel up near the Walmart is okay with pets and I've already booked a room there for a couple days."

"I get it, you're Miss Independent."

I'd never relied on someone before, that was true.

When you'd been raised with abuse you learned that the only person you could ever really trust was yourself. And even that wasn't always true.

"I really want a drink."

I realized I'd said the words out loud when I saw the alarmed look on Tracey's face. "Don't freak. I'm not going to run to the store and bring home the entire wine aisle."

But I wanted to. Desperately. I licked my lips at the thought. "I'm fine."

"You are so *not* fine. If you won't come stay with me, at least let me help you pack up everything you need and help you get to the motel."

I had to admit that it was easier with two people and soon I had Fluffy in the crate and Wookie in the back seat with a large duffel bag, my backpack and all the animals' needs, and we were driving to the motel with Tracey following behind us. Once we were all settled in the motel room, Tracey went and got us burgers from a nearby fast-food place.

We sat around the small table in the room while Wookie chewed his favorite rope in the corner and Fluffy kneaded the bed, trying to get comfortable. Tracey told me about how what was left of Craig's brother's body had been pulled from the well and how grateful his mother was to finally have something to bury.

"The farmer who owns the property isn't the same one who had it all those years ago when Derek went missing but he said that there'd always just been a piece of wood covering the well as long as he'd had the property."

Decommissioned wells were a hazard, but few farmers wanted to incur the expense of having them properly filled and capped.

"Are you even listening to me?" Tracey asked.

"Yeah." I slurped noisily from the Coke in my cup. "I'm glad Craig's family got closure." I crumpled up my greasy burger wrapper and two-pointed it into the trash. "Does Craig call you any nicknames?"

Her eyebrows went up.

"Like what?"

"You know…like honey, or sweetheart, muffin… things like that."

"He calls me *boo*, remember?"

"Oh yeah." I smirked.

"And he also calls me baby sometimes." She tilted her head at me. "Why?"

I pulled out my phone. "This is the text I got from Garrett." I cleared my throat. "'Bad cell service where I am. I'll call soon, Sweet pea. Love you.'" I put the phone down. "He's never called me *Sweet pea*. Ever."

"So?" She shrugged. "He's stressed, tired and working too hard. If you hate that name, tell him to call you sweet cheeks instead, or honeybunch, or sex beast."

"Yeah." I drummed my fingers on the table. "He never replied to any of my responses."

"He said he was in a bad cell area."

I nodded.

She picked up my phone and scrolled through the messages to Garrett. I didn't stop her, but I felt myself blush.

"You thought sending him umpteen pictures of your flooded house was the best route to go?"

"He's a rescuer. It's what he does…"

We looked at each other and burst out laughing at the silliness of it all. Then I grew serious and sighed.

"I think that if I don't hear from him by tomorrow, I'm going to call the number he used to reach me on the landline and check in with whoever he's working with to make sure he's okay. I know he said he was out of cell range but still…something feels wrong." Then I cringed. "Do you think that's crossing the line?"

"You're asking a person who once threw a surprise birthday party for a guy I'd dated twice. I'm not the best person to ask about boundary lines." She smiled and then slowly nodded. "You know what? Do it. Call that person. Garrett wouldn't be pissed. I mean, if it was you who was MIA he'd be tracking you down like a hound dog."

"You're right. He would."

Fluffy leaped from the hotel bed onto Wookie's back with a loud hiss. The dog jumped up and growled, causing Tracey to jump onto her chair and scream.

After I'd separated the animals by placing the stupid cat in his kennel, I looked at Tracey.

"If you really want to do me a big favor, you'll take this annoying hairball back to your place until I can get back into my house."

"Really? I'd love to have little Mr. Fluffikins with me!"

"He's like a gang member carrying a switchblade." I held out my wrist to show the deep scratch he'd given me at the house. "You're welcome to him and I'll pay you back for all the bandages you'll need to buy."

A few minutes later Tracey's car was loaded with litterbox, food and Fluffy, along with a couple of toy mice. I waved goodbye to her as she drove out of the motel parking lot.

When I returned to the room, Wookie was in the center of the bed, looking very pleased with himself.

"Don't get your hopes up. It's temporary."

An uneasy quiet settled over the room, broken only by Wookie's noisily licking himself. I opened my laptop but couldn't bring myself to look at emails requesting help finding loved ones' remains. I'd had enough of that today. I turned on the television and climbed onto the bed, nudging Wookie's considerable form over to give me room. As a mindless sitcom played on, I scrolled through my phone and stared hard at Garrett's earlier message as if the longer I stared at it the better I'd feel.

When I woke up at dawn, the TV was still on and I had a kink in my neck from being awkwardly slumped over in the bed. The first thing I did was snatch up my phone. No new message or missed calls from Garrett. My heart squeezed painfully with worry.

I sent him a quick text.

Wookie and I are staying at a motel while they clean up the flood at the house. Fluffy is bunking with Tracey. Love you.

Wookie was on his hind legs, standing and nosing through the motel drapes to get a look out the window. I snapped a picture of the dog and sent it to Garrett.

The parking area of the motel was surrounded by a cedar hedge except for a small grassy lawn area off to one side. I took Wookie to the green area to pee and while he found the perfect spot I went through my phone and found the number Garrett used to call the landline. Chewing my lower lip, I toyed with the idea of sending a text to the person and asking about Garrett. All I wanted to know was that he was okay and working. That's it.

Once we were back inside the room and I'd given Wookie kibble and fresh water in his bowl I still couldn't shake the idea of contacting this person.

"Screw it." I hit Call on the number. I panicked as soon as the number rang in my ear but it was really early so it would probably go to voicemail. I was surprised when a female voice sounded in my ear.

"Hello?"

"Hi. This is Julie Hall. Garrett Pierce's, um, girlfriend. He called me from this number the other day so that's why I have it…" I took in a quick breath and then blurted, "Sorry to bother you. I know Garrett's working a case, but I'm just calling to check on him because it's unusual for him not to call."

"Garrett's not working a case," the woman said with derision. "He was put on leave."

I mumbled something about being sorry for bothering her and then disconnected. My mind raced to list the lies he'd told me.

If he wasn't working, where the hell was he?

EIGHT

AFTER I HUNG up my phone rang immediately in my hand. It was the woman I'd just been talking to.

"Look, obviously I made an incorrect assumption," I said hastily. No matter what Garrett was doing, I didn't want to get him in trouble.

"We should meet and talk in person," she said.

"That's not necessary"

"I think it is. Tell me where you are, and I'll come to you."

"I don't even know who you are."

"I'm Agent Karla Powel. Garrett and I were working this case together until I went on maternity leave. I'm worried about him too."

It was the concern in her voice that did it. I gave her the name and address of the motel and she said she'd be here within the hour.

While I waited I showered and brushed my teeth. The reflection that stared back at me had dark circles and a look of fear. I made myself some crappy coffee from the tiny pot in the room and forced myself to eat some trail mix I kept in my dowsing go bag.

Even though I was expecting her, I still jumped out of my skin when a knock sounded on my door almost exactly an hour later. Wookie growled but I hushed him as I opened the door.

Karla Powel was beautiful; tall, dark skinned with a prominent baby bump and a look that said she could kill me where I stood if I messed with her.

"Are you alone?"

"Yes." Wookie growled from the bed. "Well, except for my dog. Do you want coffee?" I asked her as she stepped inside.

"No." She grabbed a chair at the tiny table in the corner and lowered herself into it.

"You're probably wondering why I'm staying here rather than at home. It's because—"

"You had a water issue at your house. I know." When I looked at her in question she added, "I drove by the house last night hoping to see Garrett's car there and I saw a plumber and restoration company's vehicles parked in the driveway and your Jeep was gone."

My mouth opened and closed a couple of times before I could get the words out. "But why would you—"

"I was hoping that once he was told he was on leave, he'd just go off for a few days to clear his head. But I have a feeling he's meddling in this case. I had no way to reach him. I guess he changed his number when he got his new phone."

"You were checking up on him because…?"

"He'd taken this case personally. I was worried he wasn't going to back off even though he was ordered to." She rubbed her hand on her pregnant belly and narrowed her eyes at me. "And I'm guessing you never even knew he was put on leave."

"He came home a couple nights ago. He'd been

roughed up and said his phone was damaged." I chewed my lip at the memory of his swollen face. "He told me he was put on leave because his brother-in-law, Sid, was involved with a company that was part of your investigation."

"That's more than he should've told anyone." Her eyebrows went up but then she regarded me seriously. "Obviously he trusts you."

"Well, of course he—"

"Before you get your bra all twisted, not every agent has a significant other who can keep their tongue under control." She shook her head. "My guy, for example, couldn't keep a secret if his life depended on it." Her phone rang then, and she smiled at it. "Just a second," she told me and took the call, which was brief. Afterward she smiled. "That was my OBGYN, Dr. B, calling to confirm the date of my cesarean."

"That's exciting."

"Yes, it is." She smiled as she said it but then her face got hard again. "What I'm going to tell you stays between us. I was never here. We never talked, okay?"

I nodded.

She took a deep breath and I could see she was weighing information in her mind. Finally, she began to speak. "Garrett and I were working together with other agents investigating a sudden increase in heroin coming into the Port of Seattle. Of course, the Bureau isn't working alone on this. The FBI was working with local authorities, the DEA and CBP regarding TOC."

"CBP? TOC?" It was hard for me to keep all the acronyms straight.

"Customs and Border Protection and Transnational Organized Crime." She paused. "TOC is when it became our baby."

"Right, because FBI deals with organized crime."

She nodded. "We knew that certain container ships were bringing in heroin from Mexico. Couple months ago, we uncovered three hundred packages of heroin, Mexican Mud, with a street value of nearly four million dollars inside a container filled with knickknacks and crap most likely designated for dollar stores. The import company bringing this trash in was Flash Imports Inc."

The hairs on the back of my neck prickled at the name. The meaningless crumpled paper I found in Garrett's garbage had that name on it.

Agent Powel kept talking. "The shipment was traced to a new kid on the block that we'd been watching for some time because of their link to money laundering and human trafficking: the Flores Cartel. Our informants in Seattle told us they were going to become big players in Mexican Mud. We knew they were involved in drugs but had no idea they'd reached such a big scale. Anyway..." She patted her belly. "I was off on maternity leave and was mostly doing desk work researching the ins and outs of this Flores gang, so I gave Garrett a list of all the employees at Flash Imports, so he can check them out."

"And Garrett saw his brother-in-law's name on the list."

"No." She shook her head. "His name wasn't on

the list. I don't know why but Garrett found out he worked there when he dug deeper into some of the other coworkers."

"Garrett must've freaked when he realized his brother-in-law was working there."

"Yeah, I kept telling him that just because he worked there didn't mean he was hanging with the drug cartel but Garrett was like a dog with a bone. He just kept digging."

"He never really talked about—" I searched for a word besides *family* "—his past life so I'm not familiar with them. Did he find out his brother-in-law had gone bad?"

"Look, nothing I dug up implicated Sid in any way. He looked like an honest, hardworking guy. You know he even lived with Garrett and Faith when they first got married. Sid's her baby brother, right? Garrett told me all about it. Said he gave him a letter of recommendation to get him set up in a good job and everything. Of course, we're talking a decade ago."

"Oh." I swallowed a lump in my throat. "He never told me anything about him."

"Garrett being Garrett wanted to be the hero. He should've left well enough alone, but I'm sure he thought he could just show up and warn Sid about these bad dudes in the Flores Cartel and maybe try and rescue him." She shook her head. "Right before I left for maternity leave he went to the higher-ups and admitted his connection so of course they pulled him. He must've known that would happen, but he was still pissed." She sighed.

"So, is he okay? I'm worried because he…" I

stopped myself short. I didn't want him to lose his job if everyone believed he was on leave. "I'm just worried because he, um, is obviously upset."

"You think he's investigating this on his own. That's why you reached out to me." She pointed a finger in my face. "Don't lie."

"Garrett has more integrity in his little finger than most people I've ever met. He'd never do anything wrong. If he was told to stay out of the investigation, I'm sure that's what he's doing. It's like you said. He's probably just trying to keep Sid safe and away from the cartel."

"Yeah, but he's also loyal as a good old dog, right?"

"I just want him to be safe. I mean, he sent me a text saying he was okay, just out of cell range but… I don't know. The message felt off."

"Show me."

When I hesitated, she tilted her head. "Look, I may be on mat leave but Garrett's still my partner and I've got his best interest at heart. If he's doing something he shouldn't be, I might be able to give him a nudge before he's in too deep."

"I don't want him getting in trouble. For all I know, he is taking some time just to clear his head and, sure, he might be looking out for Sid but that doesn't mean he'd do anything to jeopardize the investigation."

I opened the text messages from Garrett and handed my phone over to her.

Since he'd texted me from a brand-new number, the only message from him was his text to me followed by my reply and the pictures of our flooded house.

Agent Powel read his text out loud. "'Bad cell service where I am. I'll call soon, Sweet pea. Love you.'" A fleeting angry look crossed her face as she glanced at the message. "This the only number you have for him?"

I nodded.

"So, no other messages from, say, Sid's number or anyone else's?"

I shook my head.

"Did he ever talk to you about the new shipment of Mexican Mud expected to come in to Tacoma? Did he ever mention an important date?"

"No. Of course not."

She took out her own phone and made a note of Garrett's new phone number. Then she shrugged as she handed the phone back. "That's not bad. Sounds like he's just keeping his head down."

"He's never called me *Sweet pea*. Not ever." Those words sounded lame even to me.

"*Sweet pea*, huh?" Something flashed across her face and was gone. "I'm a strong believer in gut. I'm not saying *Sweet pea* is code or anything but, if you tell me honest to God you feel in the pit of your stomach something is wrong, then I'm going to do a little digging and see what I can find out on the QT."

I closed my eyes and licked my lips. I thought hard but I didn't have to think long. "If you could do some digging, I'd really appreciate it."

She gave a sharp nod, then got to her feet surprisingly quick for a woman so pregnant.

"I'll see what I can find out. In the meantime, you hear from him or he comes home, you need to tell me, okay?" She twisted her neck from one side to the other, cracking it. "I'm going stir-crazy waiting for this kid to pop but that doesn't mean I want to spin my wheels for nothing. Keep me in the loop or I can't help you. If you hear anything from him, or anyone else, about where he might be, you've gotta let me know. It's the only way I can protect him, got it?"

"Okay. Sure."

She opened the door and as she was leaving she turned around.

"Just one more thing. Garrett Pierce is the most honest guy I know, and he loves you. We didn't talk lots about our personal lives but, when he mentioned your name, I could hear the love." Wookie had joined us at the door and she reached and patted his head with a smile. "I'm telling you this because I don't want you to think anything bad because he may have gone off to check stuff out on his own. I'm sure it'll all work out fine. You don't have to go storming all over trying to find him. He'll return home good as gold once he's ready."

But her eyes looked over my shoulder when she spoke like someone who didn't believe her own words and, instead of feeling reassured, I was more nervous than ever.

I watched from the door as Agent Karla Powel climbed into a snazzy pearl-gray Lexus sedan and took off. Then I brought out my laptop and connected to the motel Wi-Fi. I wanted to know everything I could find out about this person Garrett was so determined to help.

Sid Klein was active on social media. He was good-looking in that way that said he was a player and didn't care who knew it. An attractive thirty-something guy with short dark hair whose profile pictures showed him all businessy in a suit and tie. Meanwhile most of his online posts were all about partying with friends and cuddling up to sexy young women. I saved a few pictures of him to my phone. An hour later, I knew he lived in the Bellevue area of Seattle, and I had the name of his drycleaner, the address of a pub he liked to frequent for happy hour, and the location of his favorite fishing hole. It took a bit more digging to come up with his home address.

I pulled on sweats and a T-shirt and took Wookie for a quick run. The day was shaping up to be a warm one for April and we were both panting by the time we reached a park at the end of the street where the motel sat just off I-5. Several other dog owners were also walking their dogs in the park and Wookie tried to make time with a German shepherd and shied away from a four-pound Yorkie with an attitude. A new park meant Wookie was determined to leave his mark on every single tree and blade of grass but finally his bladder was empty, and I ran him back to the motel.

I kept my phone only inches away in case Garrett called or texted while I filled up Wookie's bowls and planned out my day. When my phone rang my heart sank to see it was Tracey.

"Hey," I answered sounding less enthusiastic than I should.

"Still no word, huh?"

"No." I wanted to change the subject. "How's the cat?"

"Aw-w-w he is just so good." She said to Fluffy in a singsong voice, "You're a precious widdle kittie, aren't you?" Then to me, "Can you hear him purring on my lap? His purrs are so loud!"

"Can't believe he's sitting on your lap. The one and only time he sat on mine was to rake my face with his claws."

"He's just a precious angel. Aren't you, cutie-pie?"

"Huh." I was glad things were working out with Fluffy, but it made me wonder why the stupid cat didn't like me, considering I was the one who took him in when my mom died. "And how is Craig doing?"

"We're taking some time apart." Her tone was casual, like it was no big deal. "I told him he needed to be with his mom and process the finding of his brother."

"Wow. That's really mature of you."

I snagged some jeans and a T-shirt from my bag on the floor and started to dress.

"Yeah, well, his mom was grateful, of course. She was just gushing about how if it wasn't for me getting you to help find him she never would've been able to put her boy properly to rest and then she kept going on and on about having you over for dinner, but I knew that was not your thing."

"Yeah, definitely not my thing."

"So, I told him to go spend time with his mom and I'll talk to him in a few weeks or something. I'm headed to work now and thought I'd see if you wanted to grab a bite later."

"I dunno. Maybe." I sat on the edge of the bed and ran my hand through my damp hair. "I have to go into Seattle for a bit, but give me a shout when you're off work."

"What are you doing in the city?"

"Just checking on a few things…" I kept it vague. I didn't want her to know I was going to be snooping around after Garrett's brother-in-law. "I'll talk to you later."

Wookie had slurped up some water, eaten some kibble and was now curled up at the foot of the bed. I went over and rubbed his head.

"Be good while I'm gone."

I refilled my water bottle from the sink and snatched up my backpack and purse. Once on I-5 I tried to relax but it was the morning rush so traffic was snarled. The drive to Seattle shouldn't ever take as long as it did but I'd learned long ago not to stress out about the inevitable bumper-to-bumper experience. My mind wanted to drift to worst-case scenarios regarding Garrett, but I did some deep breathing exercises and put on a self-help audio book. While the narrator's voice droned on about the importance of mindfulness and meditation to process trauma, I drummed my fingers nervously on the steering wheel.

Traffic came to a standstill near Exit 177. I knew from another time there was a little store just off the exit that had a well-stocked wine section. There was also a beautiful little park with a view of a lake. Once, when I was a different person, I'd bought a couple of bottles and drunk them in my car while staring at the lake. I could do that now and forget all about being worried about Garrett.

"He'd never know," I murmured to myself, staring longingly at the exit ahead.

Just then a horn honked behind me. Traffic had begun to move. I gave my head a quick shake and accelerated past the exit and turned up the volume on the self-help book.

Before long I was on 520 crossing Lake Washington into the area of Bellevue. When I stopped for gas, I entered the address I'd found for Sid Klein into my GPS. I asked myself what I'd do if I saw Garrett's sedan parked in the driveway. I had to admit that I'd probably accelerate right on by because this was beginning to feel a lot like I was checking up on my boyfriend. Even though it was from a place of anxiety and worry for his well-being, it still felt wrong.

The neighborhood had older traditional homes on large lots with long front drives. Anyone who knew anything about Seattle real estate wasn't fooled into thinking the pale yellow two-story with the green shutters was for the working middle class. Homes anywhere around here would start at two million. My research into Sid Klein had told me he held a management position with Flash Imports, but he'd been there less than a couple years. Long enough to afford this house?

"Maybe he won the lottery."

Obviously, this brother-in-law who lived with Garrett and his wife ten or so years ago and needed help getting a job at the time had done well for himself. Or else he was in debt up to his eyeballs. Who was I to judge?

I drove by a couple times, slowing a little in front of the house. There were no cars in the driveway, but it had a double garage, so someone could still be home.

I turned around at the end of the street while I thought about what to do.

"To hell with being discreet."

I pulled right into the driveway and parked my Jeep on the far side of the garage. If someone was home maybe I should consider trying to pull myself off as a friend of Garrett's dead wife, but she was close to Garrett's age so that made it ridiculous. I would've been in my teens when she died.

I walked up the sidewalk to the front door, past blossoming cherry trees humming with happy bees. The air was saccharine with the scent of the blooms. It was getting warm and my T-shirt clung to my back as I broke out in a nervous sweat. My finger hesitated only briefly before I took a deep breath and rang the doorbell. I listened hard but couldn't hear any sounds on the other side of the door. No footsteps as they padded to see who was here and no sound of breathing on the other side of the thick double doors. Just in case, I offered a friendly smile to the peephole, but nobody answered even after a second ring.

"Damn."

Turning around, I headed back toward my car but

then changed my mind and walked past the Jeep and around the corner, where I entered the gate on the side of the garage that opened into the backyard. The yard was vast—an acre of grass that needed mowing and cherry trees pink with blossoms. In the far corner of the yard a large garden shed had been built to resemble a gingerbread cottage.

Staying firmly against the house, I kept my body close to the cool brick. When I got to the first window I stood on tiptoe and peeked inside. Through the slats in the blinds I could make out an office area that was in complete disarray. Paperwork was strewn everywhere, an old pizza box sat in the middle of the desk with congealed cheese the only remnants. Sid Klein was obviously a slob. I kept walking. French doors at the back of the house were off a large cedar deck.

As I approached the deck, the doors suddenly burst open and a young woman flew out the door and took off like her ass was on fire. Without even thinking, I raced after her. She struggled with the latch at the gate on the far side of the house, and I reached her before she could open it. She whipped around, her hands slapping and scratching at me like a cornered animal.

We were about the same age and size, but I was stronger and had more experience at fighting for my life. I ducked as she went for my face, grabbed her by the waist and butted my forehead hard against her face. Her nose exploded and when her hands went to her nose, I grabbed her by the knees and took her down. Her body hit the aggregate walkway hard and

I straddled her body, pinning her arms with my knees and sitting on her chest. The cloying aroma of an expensive floral perfume wafted up to me.

She started to scream, and I covered her mouth with my hands.

"Relax! I'm just looking for someone."

She was maybe mid-twenties with waist-length blond hair and cornflower-blue eyes that were wild with fury.

"If you promise not to scream, I'll take my hands off your mouth," I told her.

She didn't move. She didn't even blink.

"Nod if you understand," I told her.

She gave a sharp nod and I took my hands off her mouth but kept my position pinning her to the ground.

"You friggin' broke my nose!" she hissed. "Sid's not here. I came looking for him too. Place has been trashed. He's gone."

"Trashed?" I wasn't expecting that. "Did someone break in?"

"Yes." She attempted to wiggle out from under me. "Get off me."

I hesitated and then rolled off her and helped her to her feet.

"Show me." I nodded toward the house.

She whipped her hair over a shoulder to expose a tiny dragonfly tattoo on her collarbone. As we walked into the house, she pinched her nose to stop the gushing blood.

"Who are you?" I asked.

She grabbed a stack of fast-food napkins off the kitchen counter and held them to her face.

"I could ask you the same question." When I didn't reply she said, "I'm Meg." I looked at her questioningly and she rolled her eyes. "Sid's girlfriend. Duh."

"Oh."

"Well, who are you? Have you ever even met Sid?"

"No, I—"

"You're just sneaking around the house, peeking in windows at the butt-crack of eleven in the friggin' morning and then assaulting me?" she sneered. "I should call the cops."

"If there was a break-in then, yes, you should." I took a look around the place and let out a low whistle as I followed Meg through the house. Kitchen drawers were emptied onto the floor, furniture had been overturned, sofa cushions had been slashed. "Holy shit," I muttered under my breath. "Why haven't you called the police?"

Meg snorted as she picked up a slashed sofa cushion, tossed it on the couch and sat on it. "Yeah, right. I'll do that. I'll just call the police." Again, with the eye roll.

"Well, yeah. That's what you do when people break into your house," I said slowly as if speaking to a small child.

She reached for a purse on the end table, pulled out a pack of smokes and lit a cigarette.

"Who are you? And what do you want?" she asked, her voice nasally as she'd rolled up tissue and stuffed it into her nostrils. She tossed her thick long mane over a shoulder. "Wait a second, are you Sid's side chick?"

She looked amused, rather than jealous at the thought.

"I'm Julie Hall. My boyfriend is Sid's brother-in-law."

"His dead sister's husband? The FBI guy? Wow. He's like a hundred years old."

"No, he's not." I blew out a raspberry and blushed at my childishness.

"Are you a fed too?" She narrowed her gaze and looked me over with renewed interest.

"Of course not." As I glanced around the finely furnished sitting room that now looked like a flop house, I put my hands on my hips and shook my head. "Seriously. Did you call the police already? Do you want me to do it?"

"No police." She angrily wagged a finger at me. "Don't even think about it. You want to screw over both Sid and Garrett? You think whoever did this is going to be scared away because the popo show up here and dust for fingerprints? Give your head a shake."

"You obviously believe Garrett and Sid are together. Where do you think they could be?"

"Who cares?" Her gaze was suddenly hard. "I'm sure they're tucked away somewhere they can be useful."

"What the hell does that mean?"

"Look, all I know is you and I are both here and they're not." She winced as she picked a small stone out of a scrape on her knee that she'd received when we tussled in the yard. "Yesterday was my birthday. You wanna know how I spent my day? Alone." She blew out a puff of smoke then added sadly, "I ordered a friggin' pizza and ate it by myself."

"Happy birthday." I grabbed a seat in a recliner that had a crisscross pattern of slash marks in the cushion.

"Thanks." She smiled sweetly at me, then looked around for an ashtray and, when she couldn't find one, picked up a beer bottle from the floor and flicked her ash into it. "You worry too much. I'm sure Sid and your guy are going to be just fine. Go home and do…" She waved a hand at me. "Do whatever it is you do? I bet you're a bookkeeper. You've got that kind of look about you."

"A bookkeeper, huh?" I changed the subject away from me. "What's really going on? Is it drugs? Is Sid mixed up with that cartel?"

"What do you know about a cartel?" Her eyebrows went up as a smile played on her lips.

"I read about it in online," I admitted. "Is that why you don't want the police called?"

"What Sid does is his own business. I'm not in charge of him. Sure, I have a key for his place and can come and go because we've been together a while, but I'm not his mom or something."

"I call bullshit. If you're not wanting to call the cops it's because you know Sid is up to no good and that's why he'd be angrier about the police being here than about the place being tossed."

She shrugged, dragged deep on the cigarette, then

dropped it in the beer bottle where it made a wet sizzle in the remaining dregs of beer at the bottom.

"What if they didn't find what they were looking for?" I asked. "What's to stop these people from coming back and grabbing you just to get Sid's attention?"

She seemed unconcerned. "Well then…" She got to her feet and flicked her long hair. "Guess I better get outta here."

"Tell the truth, is Sid working for that Mexican cartel?" I demanded.

"You know what?" She planted hands on her hips. "You've got a pretty big mouth for some FBI agent's young piece of tail. You should watch yourself. That kind of talk is liable to get you killed."

I called after her as she walked away, "You might be happy to just leave here, but I want to find Garrett and I'm not stopping until I do."

"If you know what's good for you, you'll go back home and wait for your man like a good girl. It would be much safer."

"This house is worth what? A couple million minimum, right? And that rock on your finger has at least a two-carat diamond."

"Two-point-five." She turned around to hold her hand up so that the ring sparkled in my face. "And it's not even an engagement ring. Only a promise ring and that's why I'm wearing it on my right hand."

"Right. Sid is some low-level executive at an import-export firm. I guess we know where the real money is coming from."

She just kept walking.

"I know you're scared but—"

"If you're smart, you'd be the scared one."

"I just want to find Garrett and make sure he's safe!" I followed her as she walked toward the door that entered the garage, but she just shook her head. Finally, I stopped her as she was almost out the door by putting a hand on her shoulder. "At least give me your number so if I find them I can let you know."

She thought about that for a second and then shrugged. "Why not."

We exchanged cell numbers and I had her text me while she stood there to make sure she didn't give me a fake number. In the garage there was a black Lamborghini and a newer pale yellow VW bug convertible. I made a mental note of her license plate as she climbed into the VW, backed it down the driveway and drove off.

As soon as Meg was out of there, I started going through the house. I took pictures of the destruction in every room. It takes a considerable amount of time and energy to diligently toss and slash a house that's about five thousand square feet. Either one guy spent a helluva long time here, or, more likely, an entire gang of guys tossed it. At first, I thought maybe someone was looking for something here but as I went from room to room I got the impression that this was a scare tactic. They wanted to send a clear message to Sid that they could get to his house and get to him too. That also meant they could get to Garrett. I shuddered.

A guest bedroom upstairs remained pristine except for a slight tussle of the bedding. The room smelled distinctly of Meg's flowery perfume. In the guest bathroom I was struck by the stark contrast to the bathroom counter.

"Holy crap."

I kicked over a drugstore bag on the floor, and hair stuff spilled onto the floor. One end of the marble counter held a tidy array of expensive makeup palettes and brushes. The other end was littered with balls of tinfoil, a pipe, spoon and discarded needles.

"That's why she didn't want to call the cops," I frowned and shook my head. "Meg's armpit deep in heroin herself and she's definitely been staying here."

But why would she be in the spare room instead of sleeping in his bed? A visit to the master bedroom gave me the answer. The king-sized mattress was shredded, a large armoire was toppled over, and a wall mirror had been shattered.

There was only one reason Meg would've stayed here. She was pretty sure that whoever tossed the place was not coming back but she was confident that Sid would find his way home. If Sid could make it back here, then so could my guy. I wondered if Garrett had squirrelled Sid away somewhere until all this blew over. That sounded exactly like something he'd do. That way he wouldn't be involved in the case but would still be loyal to his dead wife's memory.

I headed back downstairs and walked through to the den off the living room. There were power cords where a laptop probably normally sat. Flash Imports Inc. letterhead was scattered over the floor and crumpled notes rolled out of the overturned trash. I unfolded a few of the notes with chicken scratch in what I assumed was Sid's own handwriting.

One of the crumpled sheets had Garrett's old telephone number scratched onto it. I swallowed nervously as I looked through the rest of the balled-up pages but there were so many it would take too long. I didn't want to be standing here when who-ever trashed this house came back to see if Sid had returned. I walked back to the kitchen and found a discarded grocery sack and used it to collect all the notes. I'd take them back to the motel and read through them to see if they offered any clues.

A cordless landline phone was on the floor next to the desk. I picked it up and took down the time and day of every call that had come in for the past week, storing them on my phone. Then I checked the outgoing calls and there was Garrett's number again. Twice in the past week.

"Damn, Garrett, what did you step into?"

Before I left the den, I gave the room a quick look to see if I'd missed anything. A door in the corner was slightly ajar. I stepped around an overturned bookcase to get to the door.

It opened into a small two-piece bathroom. On the tile floor was a sticky puddle of blood.

I found myself praying that the blood didn't be-long to Garrett.

NINE

THE SIGHT OF the blood motivated me to call in reinforcements. I texted Agent Karla Powel that I was
at Sid's house. I gave her an update about the girlfriend, Meg, and the state of the house. I fired off
every picture I'd taken of the house. The last one I
sent was a close-up of the bloody mess in the den.

She called me immediately.

"I can't believe it!" she exclaimed when I answered. "I didn't even know Sid had a girlfriend. Is
this Meg person still there?"

I told her Meg had gone and gave a description
of the VW she drove away in and the license plate.

"That crazy bitch," she said. "I'll take care of it.
Get out of there."

I had no idea how long it would take before the
guys in suits descended on the house, so I ran out to
my car, dropped the grocery bag filled with papers
onto the passenger seat and took off.

I was half a block away when Agent Powel's own
gray Lexus whizzed by me, coming from the opposite direction. She'd obviously been very close by.

My anxiety was ratcheting up every time I thought
of the puddle of blood in the bathroom and Garrett's
involvement with Sid. It wasn't just the fact that he
was dealing with a dangerous drug cartel. That was

his usual job and he was careful as well as highly intelligent. Sure, the job came with an element of risk, but I'd never seen Garrett take any chances. Now I was worried all clear thinking was going out the window since he was in rescue mode. He was hot on this case because he needed to save Sid in the name of his dead wife. I was anxious that Garrett would take unnecessary risks to help this guy and I hoped with all that was inside me that the blood at Sid's house wasn't his.

My stomach was growling with need so I pulled into a drive-thru and got a burger and a Coke. Then I drove to a corner of the lot and, while I ate, I carefully smoothed out every wrinkled piece of paper in the grocery sack and tried to make out each scrawled word and doodle that Sid had taken the time to scratch out.

After I had all the sheets of paper sitting in a pile in my lap I went over them again. Most of the notes were phone numbers and doodles. Tracey called me as I was holding a sheet that only said *4-26 Burke*, circled half a dozen times as if those numbers and that name were super important.

"I'm just finishing up my shift," she said. "Got time to grab lunch?"

"Still in Seattle." I picked up the next sheet and held it up in the same way.

"I can wait until you're back. We can try out that new diner on—"

"Just ate."

"Oh." There was a pause. "You okay? You sound, um, preoccupied. And bitchy. But mostly distracted."

"Sorry." I put the paper down and rubbed my eyes.

"I guess I'll drive back soon. Just one more thing I want to check. I just grabbed a burger but I'll have a coffee while you eat."

She gave me the crossroads for the diner where she wanted to meet, and I asked her to allow me extra time because I had something I wanted to do in Seattle, plus I wanted to go back to the motel to walk Wookie and change out of my jeans, which I'd torn tackling Meg.

I entered Burke Avenue into my GPS and took a drive toward the Green Lake area. There was no number 426 and no apartment four at twenty-six. It was a hunch that turned out to be useless, so I just pointed my Jeep back toward the motel. Wookie was excited to see me. I felt bad keeping him locked up in a motel all day, but I knew he'd only be sleeping like he did all day at home. I took him for a hard run and let him add his scent on every light post down the road and back again. When we returned to the room, he drank from his water dish until his muzzle was all slobbery and then we played tug of war with his rope toy until he hopped back up on the bed and decided to nap. I left him a chew bone and promised I wouldn't be too long.

In all honesty, I had no desire whatsoever to go meet Tracey. I wanted to be alone with my thoughts and theories on where Garrett might be, but I kept remembering what Dr. Chen told me about maintaining close relationships to keep myself from going bonkers. I knew that on any given day I was only an ounce of alcohol or one bad, post-traumatic stress-induced episode away from hospitalization. I'd learned to make a conscious effort when it came to my mental health. Even though today the only thing I wanted to do was run myself ragged searching for Garrett to make sure that he was safe, I needed to do something else. I could feel my anxiety about him increasing and I hoped Agent Powel was also beating the bushes trying to find him. In the meantime, meeting with Tracey would be a great way to distract my mind from the edge of panic. At least that was the plan but the minute we were sitting across from each other I spilled the beans on what I'd discovered.

"Oh my God! So, his house was ransacked, and his girlfriend is firing the ack ack gun!"

"The what?"

"Shooting smack." Tracey made a motion about jabbing her arm with a needle. "You think Sid's doing it too? Maybe Garrett took him away to get him to detox? What else did you find there?"

Tracey leaned in as I told the story of the notes I took and the puddle of blood in the bathroom.

"I feel like this brother-in-law, Sid, is a sack of trash." She sat back and shook her head. "Your man is literally running around trying to save the ass of a man hooked up with a dangerous drug cartel. Why would he do that?"

"Well, I don't know for sure that *is* what he's doing but if it is, it's because Garrett has powerful loyalties. And he wouldn't be doing it for Sid. He's doing it for her."

"His dead wife."

"Yes." I nodded and licked my lips. "Faith." I said her name on a whisper. I didn't feel like I had the right to even speak the woman's name out loud.

Tracey ordered a soup and sandwich combo and insisted I at least have pie to go with my coffee. "So, you figure Sid is in up to his neck in smuggling drugs?"

"His lifestyle doesn't look like a middle management exec at an import company. I did some online searches and it looks like he'd be making a good income; maybe one hundred thousand a year. But his house is two and a half mil and the diamond on his girlfriend's finger is a few carats and it's not even an engagement ring. She called it a friggin' promise ring! What's he promising? To keep her in as much heroin as she can handle until she's dead?" I shook my head. "Sid's social media accounts are exotic trips, fancy cars and expensive scotch. He's living wa-a-ay beyond his income."

We sat in quiet a few minutes, both scrolling on our phones until the waitress brought our food. The lemon meringue pie looked delicious, but I couldn't choke down more than a bite. My thoughts kept returning to all the blood in Sid's bathroom.

"I wonder how Sid explains his fancy lifestyle to his coworkers," Tracey mumbled through a bite of her sandwich.

My fork dropped noisily onto the table and I pushed my plate of pie away.

"What?" she asked. "Why are you looking at me like that?"

"His work. God, I should've called his office!" After a few taps on my phone to locate the phone number I called Flash Imports and asked to speak to Sid Klein. "They're putting me through to his office," I whispered to Tracey who gave me a thumbs-up.

A receptionist answered, "Mr. Klein's office, how may I help you?"

"I'd like to speak to Mr. Klein, please?"

"Mr. Klein is out of the office at the moment, whom may I say is calling?"

"I'm with the Seattle Police Department and I need to speak to Mr. Klein about an urgent matter," I said all business like.

Tracey choked a little on her sandwich.

"I'm sorry, Officer, but Mr. Klein has been on leave for a number of weeks. He took time off due to a death in the family. Would you like his cell phone number?"

"One moment." I dug a pen and paper from my purse. "Yes, give it to me."

I jotted down the number and thanked her for her time but stopped just before she was about to hang up.

"Is there anyone at the office who is a personal friend to Mr. Klein? Someone who associates with him outside of work?"

"Well…" Her voice trailed off, thinking. "He sometimes goes for drinks after work with Mr. Mayer."

"And Mr. Mayer's first name is?"

"Jerry." She added, "But he left early today. I saw him leave a few minutes ago. Would you like me to connect you to his department so that you can leave a message for him?"

"Not at this time. Thank you for your help." I ended the call and immediately dialed the cell phone number she gave for Sid. It went straight to his voicemail and I hung up. Then I scrolled through my phone.

"Did you just impersonate a police officer?"

Tracey whispered, leaning across the table and waving a sandwich in my face. "That's not cool. You can get in so much trouble for that kind of stuff. The only time it's okay is if you're dressed like a cop for Halloween and that's only because the costumes for that are all slutty and the badge is plastic."

I held up my phone showing a picture on Sid's Facebook page. It was a photo of Sid and his co-worker, Jerry Mayer, having a pint at a pub not far from their office.

"Feel like going for a drink?" I asked her.

"No." Tracey shook her head. "And neither should you."

I signaled the waitress for our check. "I'm not going off the wagon here. But if this Jerry Mayer guy has left work early for the day and maybe stopped to have a drink, I wouldn't mind picking his brain about Sid. If they're buddies, there's a good chance he knows what he's up to. Maybe he even knows where he's hiding with Garrett."

"That's a lot of ifs and maybes," Tracey griped. "Like maybe this Jerry guy is also into the drugs and hooked up with smuggling and we're going to die trying to talk to him."

"We're not going to question the guy in a dark alley. That's why meeting him in a public place like the bar near his work is a good idea."

Tracey wrapped the last half of her sandwich in a napkin as we paid the bill and within a few minutes we were headed south to Seattle. Tracey left her car at the diner while I drove. I had her look up the address of the pub and put it in the GPS and then I fielded a couple of calls about the repairs at the house. I'd given Preston and Phil a spare key and they were more than happy to let in all the trades needed to get the job done, and both men had sent me texted updates throughout the day. At this point, I didn't care about the house. My only thought was about Garrett's safety.

I drove as fast as traffic would allow and soon we pulled into a lot on the side of the pub. I positioned my Jeep to back into a spot next to a newer red Jaguar convertible.

"You're going to want to get out of the car before I back in."

"Oh my God, half this lot is empty, why the hell would you park next to some guy's Jag?" Tracey opened her door and started to climb out.

"Because that's Jerry Mayer's car. I saw pictures of Sid and him leaning on it on the day he bought it. He's not going to be able to get into his car unless I let him."

"Wow. You're hard core." Tracey nodded with appreciation.

Once Tracey got out, I slowly backed in so close to the driver's side of the Jag that he'd either have to climb in from the passenger side or use a can opener to get inside. Satisfied with my parking job, I put the Jeep in park and killed the engine.

"I can't tell if you're smart or crazy," Tracey said as we crossed the parking lot to the pub.

"The good news is—" I put an arm around her shoulder "—it's possible to be both."

Tracey sighed as she limped along with her knee brace. "Show me his picture again so I know who I'm looking for."

Earlier I'd taken a screenshot of Sid and Jerry Mayer together. I pulled up the photo and handed my phone to Tracey. She expanded the picture so Jerry's face was enlarged. He looked to be in his forties with a shaved head, neatly trimmed goatee and hard brown eyes.

"He looks mean," she grumped as she handed me back my phone. "What's our plan? Are we just going up to him and saying 'Hey, I hear your bestie is doing the tango with a Mexican drug cartel, care to share how that makes you feel?'"

I laughed and shook my head because I had no idea how to play this. "Just follow my lead, okay?"

Inside the dimly lit bar the smell nearly knocked me off my feet. I stopped short and Tracey bumped into me. That musky aroma of alcohol and fried food slammed me back to every bar I'd ever had the misfortune of nearly passing out in. I took in a jagged breath while doing a quick scan of the premises.

Garrett. This is about Garrett.

The thought helped me refocus.

"You okay?"

I gave Tracey a quick nod.

Jerry was easy to spot, balanced on a barstool and leaning an arm on the back of the stool next to him where a tall brunette sipped a martini. I beelined in that direction and took up the stool on the other side of him and Tracey got up next to me.

The urge to tell the bartender to fill me a wineglass and keep the drinks coming was a powerful demon on my shoulder but I ordered a club soda with lime and Tracey asked for the same. I wanted to tell her she was okay to drink around me, but I'd be lying. I was grateful she didn't ask.

"What now?" Tracey mouthed to me as she brought her glass to her mouth.

"We wait," I whispered.

Jerry had his back to us with his full focus on the girl beside him. He had a beer glass half-filled with Blue Moon and a slice of orange bobbed around inside it. When the brunette was done with her drink he quickly ordered her a refill, and when she excused herself to use the restroom, I took the opportunity to get his attention.

"Jerry Mayer, is that you?" I gave his arm a playful punch. "I was just telling my friend that it looked like you."

He turned on his stool to face me and offered a confused smile while trying to remember who I was.

"I'm Julie." I flashed him a bright smile that was all teeth. "I'm a friend of Meg's."

"Meg?"

"Sid's girlfriend."

He tilted his head and looked at me hard.

"You probably don't remember me," I said quickly. "We met months ago at some party."

"I'm Tracey." Tracey leaned around the front of me and stuck out her hand.

"Nice to meet you," he said taking her hand automatically and giving it a quick grasp.

"Speaking of Sid," I said. "You don't happen to know where he is, do you? I called him days ago and he hasn't called me back."

"That right?" Jerry picked up his glass and took

a long drink from his beer. "Sid does whatever he wants. I think he's off work because of a death in the family or something." He shrugged. "I'm sure Meg would know. You should ask her."

The brunette was on her way back, carefully putting one high-heeled foot in front of the other in a deliberate way to try to hide how drunk she really was. I recognized that walk. Hell, I had perfected it at one time.

"Yeah, I talked to Meg this morning, but she's really pissed about Sid missing her birthday. It ended up being just the two of us eating pizza because she didn't hear from him."

"That right." He didn't seem too concerned.

"Yeah, missing your girl's birthday…" I shook my head. "That's pretty cold."

"Really cold," Tracey piped up from behind me. He shrugged again.

"What Sid does and doesn't do with his girl is none of my concern, right? I've got my own life." He turned his stool back to focus on his date.

This wasn't going nearly as well as I'd hoped. Before he got too involved with his girl again I put a hand on his shoulder and said to his back, "You know what might be helpful? If *you* were to give Sid a call. In fact, why don't you call him right now. He's not taking my calls or Meg's, but I bet he'd pick up for you."

He ignored me except to shrug off my hand. Then he pulled a knot of cash out of his pocket and left a bunch of twenties on the bar as he got to his feet. While the brunette complained about not yet finishing her drink, he took her by the elbow and helped her off her stool and told her they were leaving.

I waited until he was almost out the door before I said anything to Tracey. "Damn. I was hoping he'd tell us where Sid was." I rubbed the back of my neck. "It sounded like a good idea in my head."

"Are we following him?" Tracey asked, getting to her feet. "We should definitely follow him."

"We've got time."

She followed me out the door and from across the lot we could see Jerry waving his arms in the air and cursing at my Jeep. The brunette was already in the passenger seat but, even though he'd squeezed his body between my Jeep and his car, there was no way he was going to be able to open his door. As we walked closer, he came out between the two vehicles and glared.

"Is this your friggin' Jeep?" And then threw his hands in the air. "Of course it is. You'd better move it as in NOW."

"I don't know if I have my keys." I made a show of patting the pockets of my jeans and then turned to Tracey. "Have you seen my keys? Maybe I left them in the bar. You know what would help? If you told me where I could find Sid. I bet I could find my keys then and—"

Abruptly he was on me and I found myself pinned against the hood of my car with a revolver pressed into my stomach. I heard Tracey's sharp intake of breath only a few inches away.

"I know who you are, Julie," he snarled in my face and spittle hit my nose. "I got a call the second after you left Sid's place this morning." He pressed the gun harder into my stomach and I cringed. "The guys who got hold of Sid came for him because your FBI boyfriend was nosing around."

"The Flores Cartel?" I asked on a gasp as he leaned his face up to mine.

"There's no way I'm talking to you, and if you come near me again, it's not going to be Mateo Flores's henchmen you're gonna have to worry about, got it?" He pushed the nose of the gun hard against my ribs. "First thing I'd do is kill your friend. Then I'd have some fun with you and send pictures of that fun to your boyfriend. You want that?"

I swallowed thickly and shook my head.

He pushed off me then and took a step back.

"I'm gonna give you to the count of ten to get your car out of this lot."

I scrambled into the car and Tracey, because she couldn't climb in on the passenger side, hopped into the back seat on my side. We were out of the lot and around the corner before he could count to eight.

"I may have peed myself," Tracey whimpered.

I didn't reply until we were a few blocks away and I'd pulled behind a convenience store. When I took my hands off the wheel, they were shaking.

"That may not have been my smartest moment," I admitted as Tracey climbed back into the front passenger seat.

"You think?" She punched me in the shoulder. "You are not Garrett! You are not with the FBI and you don't even have a gun!"

"I'm a pretty good shot with a rifle," I said trying to lighten the moment but my voice cracked as sorrow washed over me.

"Oh he-e-ey…" Tracey leaned over the console and gave me a half hug. "He'll be okay."

"You don't know that." I sniffed.

"No, but I believe it. He's a big, tough FBI guy, right? He's got this."

They were just words, but they did help.

"Okay. Thanks."

It took a while to compose myself. Tracey walked into the convenience store and came back with slushies and Doritos. After a blast of sugar and salt, I took a deep breath and started the Jeep.

"Why don't you let me drive?" she offered.

"I'm fine," I told her with a quick smile that belied that horrible ache of fear and sadness in my chest.

By the time we were back on I-5 headed north I concentrated only on driving. Traffic wasn't as bad as it usually was but a couple of times I could've sworn a dark Escalade was following me. Although it was a few cars back, whenever I changed lanes, so did he. I was getting paranoid. Thankfully, by the time we arrived at the diner where Tracey had left her car, there was no sign of the Escalade.

"If you feel like company, I can swing by the motel later and even stay the night," Tracey offered as she climbed out.

The thought of me sharing a bed with her and Wookie made me chuckle.

"Wookie would try and sleep between us and you'd have a heart attack right there." I offered her a tense smile. "Thanks, but I'm good. Go home to

Fluffy. He's probably shredded every piece of furniture in your house and knocked anything of value off the counters."

"He's a good cat. Just misunderstood."

When I got back to my motel room, Wookie was excited to see me. I took him for a long slow walk and told him about my day. He wasn't at all judgmental about the fact that I pulled a stupid move and almost got myself and Tracey shot. That's the good thing about having a dog. I tossed a tennis ball for him for about half an hour. Neither of us were looking forward to going back to the motel but it was starting to rain.

In the room I gave Wookie a lengthy belly rub and ear scratch as I told him about how worried I was about Garrett and he licked my hands to comfort me. I was tossing his stuffed rabbit around for him when my cell phone rang. It was Preston. I didn't want to deal with the house or my neighbors but, still, I made myself take the call.

"Hi, how are things on the home front?"

"Good. Great," he said. "Thought I'd call with an update."

Hurray.

"All the carpet and lino have been pulled out of the kitchen and living room. I remember Garrett saying something about you guys wanting to switch to hardwood."

"Yeah, we'd talked about doing that eventually."

"Well, now is eventually." He laughed. "The insurance will pay for the amount it would've cost to replace what was there, so you'd only be paying the difference for the upgrade. Much cheaper to do it now than in a couple years down the road when you'd have to get everything ripped up again."

"That makes sense but, honest, I'm a little busy right now so—"

"I know, and I guess Garrett's still away on business, right?"

"Yes."

"Right. Well, I got the flooring guy to leave you a few samples on the counter. Maybe you can send Garrett pictures and the two of you can decide that way. If the wood is in stock, I'm sure they can get it in lickety split."

"Yeah. Sure." I dragged a hand through my hair. "I'll come by first thing in the morning and take a look. Thanks."

"No problem. Also, I'm going to be out of town for the next couple days myself, but I've got Phil watching your place."

There was an awkward pause where Preston was probably wanting me to ask him about where he was going but I really wasn't interested. "Okay. Thanks, for everything. I really do appreciate all you've done."

"Just being a good neighbor," he said. "By the way, when you hear from Garrett tell him to give me a call. There's something I want to talk to him about."

You're not the only one.

"Sure."

I tried to watch some TV, but my heart and head hurt. I got an angry text from Agent Powel telling me to stop snooping or I was going to hurt her ability to track down Garrett. She informed me that another agent had been in the pub and had seen me

and Tracey chatting up Jerry Mayer. Obviously that
agent hadn't seen Jerry threaten us in the back parking lot or Agent Karla Powel would've mentioned it.

I apologized for doing what I shouldn't, but I
didn't tell her I'd stop. If I was missing, Garrett
wouldn't stop searching for me. If I was gone, he'd
be tearing up the entire state with his bare hands
and running around with guns blazing. My hands
tightened into fists and Wookie sauntered over and
shoved his well-chewed rope onto my lap.

"Thanks, boy." I rubbed Wookie's head and we
curled up on the bed together while a sitcom played
too loud on the television.

I nodded off briefly and woke up with my neck
stiff and Wookie growling low in his throat. New
motel neighbors were coming and going from their
room, opening and closing their door repeatedly with
a slam, and Wookie had a strong opinion about that.
It was close to midnight, but now I was wide awake.

"How about a car ride, boy?"

He was off the bed and at the motel door in a
heartbeat and I smiled as I slipped on my runners
and grabbed his leash.

My house was only a few minutes away and
Wookie began to whine as we got closer. He knew
we were going home. I hated to disappoint him that
it was only for a few minutes to look at floor samples. I pulled up in the driveway, and my headlights
illuminated the exterior of the house and created
long-fingered shadows from the shrubs to the door.
I looked longingly at the spot where Garrett would

normally park his car. I ached with worry for him and I missed being home.

It was late and dark. Suburbia was so quiet you could hear the crunch of my feet on the aggregate sidewalk and Wookie's panting breath as his feet padded alongside me.

The turn of the dead bolt echoed inside and when we entered, the loud hum of half a dozen industrial-sized fans were an assault. All the furniture had been taken from the living room and kitchen and piled in the back rooms so workers could take out the flooring. My feet sounded loud walking on the plywood to the kitchen counter where I could see the floor samples.

Wookie hesitated at the door, then ran from one room to the next, squeezing his considerable girth between the chairs and tables stacked neatly in the hall. He whined at the door to the den. He was look-ing for Garrett and it gave my chest a painful squeeze.

Six wood samples were spread out on the kitchen counter and it felt like a formidable task to choose one. If Garrett were here I'd have him choose be-cause he would have a definite opinion. I didn't want to make this decision except for one point; the quicker the flooring happened, the sooner I could be back home. And when Garrett came home, I didn't want him returning to this disaster. I might not be able to protect my man from whatever was happen-ing to him, but at least I could give him a comfort-able place to come home to.

I snapped a picture of all the samples and sent the photos in a text to Garrett. He wasn't going to reply to that message, like he hadn't to any of my others.

But at this point it felt like a diary to send him my messages. A one-sided conversation that took the weight off my mind.

I texted: I wish you were here. And regretted it the second the message went because it sounded weak and like we were on separate vacations instead of me here worrying that he was held captive somewhere or on the run with a brother-in-law connected to a drug cartel. Still, I sent another: I love you. I'm scared. And, even though it sounded like a whine, it was true.

With a sigh I picked up each sample of wood flooring and stared at it hard. As I looked at the samples, I tried to imagine each of them covering the area beneath my feet.

Too dark.

Too light.

Too knotted.

Quickly I eliminated half and then traced the other three with the tips of my fingers.

"What do you think?" I asked Garrett as if he stood in the echoey room with me.

Somewhere in the neighborhood a car door slammed, and an engine started, and the sound was muffled by the loud hum of the fans in the rooms around me.

I eliminated another sample and now was down to two: Nevada Maple and Ginger Oak.

Wookie jogged out of the back hall and was growling low in his throat

"What do you think, boy?" I grabbed the two wood samples and lowered them to mid-thigh. "Can you choose which one Daddy would like?"

At my singsong tone Wookie jogged over and licked one of the samples.

"Nevada Maple it is!" I proclaimed, giving him a scratch behind his ears. "Now if Garrett hates it, I'll tell him you're the one to blame."

I stacked all the other samples off to the side, took a pen and paper out of the drawer and left a note that simply said *This one*.

After one last look around the empty kitchen and living room, I tenderly touched the pewter urn holding my mom's ashes with a sigh and told Wookie it was time to go. I would've liked to just bring him to our bedroom, but the workers were scheduled to be back at the house first thing in the morning and I didn't want to have to deal with them.

"Only a few more days, boy," I promised Wookie as we headed out the door. "Then we'll all be home again. Even that dumb cat."

We stepped out the door, and I turned my key in the dead bolt. From the corner of my vision, a bright glow startled me. I turned and was alarmed at the sight of my Jeep. Bright golden flames three feet high licked the hood of my vehicle.

"Holy shi—"

There was a roaring *whoosh* and the entire car was engulfed.

TEN

THE LIGHTS IN the neighboring houses began to flicker on at the sound of emergency vehicles, who all seemed to arrive at the house at once. I brought Wookie in, then stepped back outside to watch the responders deal with the flames. Wookie howled and barked at the window, desperately wanting to be part of the action. Firefighters surrounded the vehicle and extinguished the blaze quickly. My mind was trying to wrap itself around the fact that I'd been in that vehicle only a few minutes earlier.

"Oh my God, what happened? Are you okay?" Phil had come up behind me.

"I don't know what happened." I blinked in shock. "I'm okay. My car, on the other hand, is fried." I glanced over at his concerned face. "So sorry to wake you up."

"Preston told me to keep an eye on the place since you haven't been staying at the house. When I saw all the fire trucks here, I freaked out." He covered his face briefly with his hands and blew out a breath. "I thought maybe some kind of equipment in the house caught fire. I'm just glad nobody was hurt, and your house is okay."

Preston and Phil were good guys. I was going to have to try to be nicer to my neighbors.

"I've never seen a vehicle just go up in flames like that," he said.

"Me either." I couldn't believe how calm my voice sounded when my heart was racing.

We stood shoulder-to-shoulder and watched the firefighters and police circle the vehicle. I wrapped my arms around myself and shivered in the cool night air.

"I'm being a horrible neighbor," Phil said. "Do you want to come to my place while they deal with this? I could fix you a drink?" Then he hit his forehead with the palm of his hand and quickly added, "Sorry. You don't drink. Duh."

And now I was remembering why being neighborly didn't come naturally to me. I didn't like the fact that everyone knew my business. My struggle with alcohol was mine and I liked to be the one to pick and choose who got to be part of that knowledge. The fact that Garrett had shared that with Phil and Preston irked me.

"How about a smoothie?" he asked.

Was smoothie the proper beverage to console an alcoholic when their vehicle exploded in their driveway? I stifled a stupid giggle and covered it up with a cough.

"Thanks," I told him. "But I'm really exhausted. Wookie and I are just going to call a cab and go back to the motel as soon as they're finished up there."

"I could drive you. And Wookie. I love dogs." He beamed.

Ugh. Just leave me alone.

"Um. Okay. Sure." He was obviously desperate to be helpful and I would need a ride. "That's very kind of you. I'll come knock on your door when everything is done here."

He started to walk away but when an officer and firefighter approached, he changed his mind and took a step closer.

"Found a jerry can in the ditch beside your vehicle," the firefighter reported, indicating behind him with his thumb.

"Appears your entire vehicle was doused with gas, inside and out," the officer finished.

He raised his eyebrows and waited expectantly for me to make some kind of shocked sound but that was done by Phil who, at first, clutched his hands together and muttered, "Oh good Lord!" Then reached to put a reassuring hand on my shoulder. Phil excused himself to go back to his house and left me to "deal with things."

"Someone poured gas on my Jeep? Are you sure?" I asked the officer and firefighter who'd joined him. "I mean…why would anyone…"

As I tried to wrap my head around what they were saying, I explained to them about the burst pipe in my kitchen.

"A burst pipe and now this, huh?" The firefighter gave me a sympathetic look.

"Yeah, I've been staying at a motel a couple blocks away during repairs. I got a call from my neighbor Preston—" I nodded next door "—saying there were floor samples left here for me to choose. I couldn't sleep so Wookie and I—" I pointed to my dog still barking out the window "—decided to come and look at those samples. We were inside the house

less than ten minutes. When we came back out…"
I pointed to the charcoaled carcass of my Jeep and
bit my lip to keep in a strangled sob. "I'm sorry…
I'm a little overwhelmed. I don't know what to say."

My mind was racing. This felt like a definite
warning. But was it directed at me, or Garrett? While
the vehicle was still blazing I'd snapped a picture
with my phone but stopped myself from sending it
to Garrett. No matter what, he didn't need the added
stress that I might be in danger. I did send the picture to Agent Powel.

The officer asked me a lot of questions but, in
the end, he concluded that it might have just been
neighborhood thugs.

"The high school was vandalized, and the dumpster set on fire last week," he explained as if the two
must be connected. "Could be some idjits were walking by with a jerry can and took it upon themselves
to just light up your Jeep."

I was slowly nodding as if that was completely plausible. I didn't launch into the fact that my boyfriend
was a federal agent hunting a drug cartel because that
information was going to be far beyond his pay scale.

Agent Karla Powel tried to call me, but I declined
the phone call. I texted her that I'd call her in a few
minutes.

It seemed to take forever for everyone to take care
of the scene. In the end my poor Jeep sat in a blackened puddle, and the grass on either side of the driveway was singed black. I went inside and spent a few
minutes doing breathing exercises to calm down before snapping a leash on Wookie and heading to Phil's.

He opened the door before I could even knock. He was either eager to drive me back to the motel or, like me, wanted to put the horrid night behind him and go back to bed.

"I really appreciate this," I told him as I crammed my one-hundred-thirty pound dog into the back seat of his compact car.

"No bother at all. The least I can do. Preston told me to keep an eye on things." He started up the car. "He's going to absolutely die when he hears what happened."

Yes, I imagined my continued misfortune would make quite the discussion.

"So vandals, huh?" he asked.

"What?" I frowned at him as he backed out of his driveway.

"I overheard the police say there'd been some vandalism at the school and they think they targeted your car. I'm going to have to tell everyone in the neighborhood to be extra cautious from now on."

"Right."

"Do we even have a neighborhood watch?" he asked, and I replied that I had no idea.

The drive to the motel was short but strained since Phil was talking nonstop as if he was afraid to allow a silence between us. "I'm sure once I tell Preston about this he'll want me to reassure you that we'll make sure nothing like that happens around your place again."

How on earth were they going to do that? "I don't think you can have an eye on my place twenty-four-seven and I really don't expect you to." As we pulled up in front of the motel I added, "And I bet Preston is going to be thrilled that it was my Jeep and not his Alfa Romeo Spider."

"Ha!" Phil made a face. "I hate that car." He turned to me and put his car in park. "Don't you worry. We're going to be vigilant. Preston has most of the neighbors on an email list and I'm sure by the time he's back in town he'll have people so worked up nobody will be sleeping."

Yeah that sounded like the way to go. Get the entire neighborhood all freaked out. I should probably have a talk with Preston before this gets blown out of proportion. "When does Preston get back again from—?"

"Portland. Tomorrow night."

"Okay. Thanks for driving me, Phil." I stifled a yawn as I opened the door.

"No problem. Did you manage to choose the wood flooring you wanted?"

"Yes. I left a note for the contractor."

"Too bad the workers didn't have the samples ready when Garrett was at the house this morning, but he was in and gone before any of the contractors showed."

"What?" I'd been about to climb out of the car but now I turned and put a hand on Phil's arm. "Garrett was at the house this morning?"

"Yes." His chatty smile had vanished. "Didn't you know? It was early, like around sunrise. I got up to get a glass of water then decided to make tea and when I plugged in the kettle right by the window I saw him."

"You actually saw him?" I squeezed his arm hard and he yanked it away.

"Yeah. I saw him. He ran into the house, but he was only inside for a few seconds. I know that because the kettle hadn't even boiled yet and he was running back to his car and backing out of the driveway before my water boiled." He frowned. "What's wrong?"

"Nothing." I shook my head. "His phone, um, hasn't been working and so I wasn't able to reach him. Was he alone?"

Phil squished his face in concentration. "There may have been someone in the passenger seat. Honestly, I couldn't get a clear view of the car because our rhododendron is just starting to bloom and—"

"Thanks again for giving us a ride and, of course, for watching the house." I climbed out of the car.

"No problem and I don't want you to worry. I know it can be frustrating when our guys are away on business," Phil said. "Sometimes when Preston is away he's in a bad area and I can't get hold of him for days. Just last month I needed his opinion on—"

"Thank you, Phil," I interrupted as I opened the door to the back seat for Wookie. "You've been a big help. Do me a favor and if you see Garrett again could you give me a call? It's important."

"Sure." He nodded seriously. "Absolutely."

Phil was rambling about keeping an eagle eye out for all activity on the street when I offered him a half wave and walked to my motel room door. Inside, Wookie jumped onto the bed, circled and then collapsed.

My head was reeling with the fact that Garrett had come by the house that very morning. He would've seen the disarray—the flooring torn up, the giant fans drying out the damp rooms. More important, he would've seen I wasn't there, would've been able to deduce why, and still didn't reach out. I sat on the edge of the bed and tried to wrap my head around what could possibly be going on, and nothing I came up with made sense except I knew for certain now that something was terribly wrong.

I dozed fitfully throughout the night, and the next morning I woke up with a jolt. A loud noise startled me, and I looked around the room, trying to orient myself to my surroundings. I was still dressed in the same clothes and with my shoes on as if I'd keeled over from exhaustion mid-thought. I was on my feet and gasping when a bang sounded again. Wookie growled and barked once. It was with relief that I realized the people in the room next door were coming and going from their room and slamming the door as they went.

"It's okay," I told Wookie, drawing a deep breath in myself.

I dug my phone out of my pocket, disappointed once again to see there were no messages or calls from Garrett but there'd been a few texts from Agent Powel. I'd promised to call her back after sending her a picture of the inferno engulfing my Jeep but never did.

I called her now. "Sorry I didn't call back," I told her as a greeting.

"You can't just send me a picture of your friggin' car on fire and then not tell me what the hell's going on!" she shouted.

"Yeah…sorry." I dragged my fingers through my hair and got to my feet. Wookie was at the door and wanted out. "I went to the house to look at hardwood samples. When I came out, my Jeep was blazing."

I snapped a leash on Wookie's collar and pocketed the motel key.

"You went to look at flooring samples in the middle of the goddam night?"

"It wasn't the middle of the night." I started walking across the motel parking lot. "It was just before twelve. I couldn't sleep. Excuse me if I've been a little stressed. You may have heard that my FBI boyfriend is missing. Or not." I sighed, thinking about Garrett being at the house and not trying to reach out to me or even leave me a note. "I don't even know what's going on."

Wookie peed long and hard at the first patch of grass he could find on the side of the lot. Silence stretched on while I waited for Agent Powel to reply.

"Hello?" I thought maybe we'd been disconnected.

"I'm here. Just trying to figure out if you're crazy or stupid."

"Look," I bit back. "I do not appreciate the insults. Something is definitely wrong! There is no way Garrett would go this long without contacting me unless someone or something was making it impossible for him to do that."

"Yeah, yeah, I get it." I heard her blow out a breath. "Do me a favor and just back off, okay? Your little visit to Jerry Mayer almost blew the cover off our agents in the bar. Just stop your constant poking around. It's only making this harder."

A squirrel ran up a nearby tree and Wookie nearly yanked my arm out of the socket trying to chase it.

He was barking like a lunatic and Agent Powel got sick of trying to talk above him, so she shouted into the phone that she'd talk to me later. I hadn't even told her that Garrett had been spotted going back home yesterday morning. I wondered if she already knew.

My phone was low on juice so I did a halfhearted jog around the block with Wookie and then headed back to the motel. While my phone was plugged in I made a call to my insurance company and tried to explain what happened to the Jeep. The person on the phone seemed pretty shocked that my vehicle was torched. He wasn't the only one.

Once that was dealt with I texted Tracey.

Can you drive me to a rental car place this morning?

Sure. What's up with the Jeep?

I replied by sending her a picture of it in flames.

Holy shit!

She called then, and I gave her the abbreviated version.

"I don't like this one bit," she said. "Garrett is missing, some guy pulled a gun on you and now you have your car blown up! What the hell is going on?"

I wish I knew the answer.

While I waited for Tracey to arrive I sent a text to Meg.

Did you hear from Sid?

But there was no reply. When Tracey arrived to pick me up she rapped twice on the door to the motel room. Wookie barked in reply and I looked through the peephole to confirm it was her.

I opened the door and stepped outside. I was surprised to see Craig sitting in the front passenger seat of her little car. He looked like a giant in the small car.

"Craig?" I turned to her in question. "I thought you two were on a break?"

"I got lonely." She shrugged. "And he offered to come over and make me breakfast. Who doesn't like a man who will drive over just to fix you a meal?"

Garrett made the best breakfasts in the world. The thought caused a painful ache in my chest.

She leaned in and sniffed me.

"Why do you smell like barbecue?"

"I haven't showered, and I slept in these clothes. That's the smell of my Jeep going boom." She brought me into a hug and patted my back and I added, "The neighbor said Garrett came home yesterday. He said he saw him run in the house and was only there for a couple minutes before leaving again. Why would he do that and not leave me a note or call me?"

"I don't know." She squeezed me harder. "It'll be okay. He'll come home. You'll get a new vehicle. Your house will be fixed, and everything will be perfect."

"Thanks." I took a deep breath and extricated myself from her tight embrace. "I hope you're right."

I climbed into the back seat of the car and told Tracey where to take me.

"Hope you don't mind me saying," Craig said, "but I think you should just let the authorities find your boyfriend before you get yourself killed."

"You told him?" I glared at Tracey.

"Sorry, my defenses were weakened by French toast and bacon." She smiled at me in the rearview mirror.

"Thank you for your opinion, Craig." I bit off each syllable with as much restrained anger as I could muster. "If the person missing was Tracey here, I have a feeling you wouldn't be so happy to sit back and let others handle it."

"You're right." He bobbed his head and reached for Tracey's hand. "I'd be turning over every boulder to try and find her."

"Aw-w-w." Tracey grinned at him.

Oh brother.

My stomach growled loudly as we pulled up to the car rental building.

"I heard that." Craig turned in the front seat to regard me. "Follow us back to Tracey's and I'll whip you up something great."

"I appreciate the lift, but no thanks. I've got things I need to do."

I walked into the car rental office and a few minutes and a ton of paperwork later, I was walking out the door with keys to a new midsized car. Tracey and Craig were still there. She rolled down her window and I approached.

"Yes?"

"We just wanted to say we're behind you one hundred percent. If you need backup, we'll be there for you. Where are you going today? We'll be your wingmen."

"Thanks." I straightened. "I'm just going to go back to the house and talk to the contractors. I don't have any desire to get shot at or blown up today but, if I change my mind, I'll let you know."

"Oh." Tracey frowned in disappointment.

"Call us if you need anything," Craig said, leaning forward to give me two thumbs up.

"I will," I promised.

After I climbed inside the dark gray rental car, I spent a few minutes acquainting myself with the buttons and dials before I started it up. I hated the way it handled, not that it was bad, just that it wasn't my Jeep. I was too low to the ground and there were too many buttons that weren't like the ones I was used to. But it would serve the purpose.

I pulled into the driveway of my house and all that remained was a huge sooty spot on the driveway where my Jeep once was and the blackened grass on the sides. A few different construction vehicles were parked on the street in front of the house, and the doors and windows were open. From inside I could hear workers talking loudly to each other over the sound of power tools.

When I walked inside, a guy whose clothes were like a camo experiment in dried paint turned off the power vac he was using and walked up to me.

"Can I help you?"

"I'm Julie. This is my house."

"Right." He wiped his hands on his jeans and offered one to me. "Sorry, we were told to keep an eye out for strangers wanting to come inside. Apparently, there was some trouble last night."

"Yeah. Thanks." I took a breath. "Speaking of that, my boyfriend supposedly came by really early yesterday morning before any of you were here. He didn't happen to leave a note or anything, did he?"

The guy frowned and shook his head. "We did see your note about the flooring though, and the order has already been placed. It's super easy now. Flooring will be here in the next couple days and then wham, bam it'll be installed and you're in like Flynn."

"Thanks. Don't mind me." I sidestepped around him. "I've just got some paperwork I have to take care of in the back."

"Cool." He bobbed his head in a nod, then flipped the switch on his shop vac again.

It occurred to me as I was squeezing between the furniture in the hall that with all the workers coming and going, a note from Garrett could easily have gone missing. But he was a smart guy. He would've seen the state of the house and not left a message out in the open.

I scooted around the sofa standing on end outside the den, and went into Garrett's office. If he'd been here, maybe he left me a message, a clue or a trail of friggin' breadcrumbs here.

The first thing I noticed was that drawers of his desk weren't closed all the way, which struck me as odd. I was the one who lazily only half closed a drawer, and Garrett was the one who'd come behind me and nudge drawers the rest of the way shut. It was one of those quirky little things in a relationship that you discover when living with someone. But Phil had said Garrett was in a hurry.

I sat in his chair and, one by one, opened the drawers all the way and looked inside. Paperwork and all kinds of writing utensils that were normally neatly stacked were tossed about. I started at the top drawer and carefully moved the writing utensils and notepads around. I did the same with the next drawers, but nothing appeared to be added or removed. But when I tried to close the bottom drawer, it was jammed and wouldn't close all the way. After removing a large stack of paper, I saw a handgun was angled in the back corner, blocking the drawer from closing. Odd. Garrett kept his weapons in a gun safe. Never in his desk.

Licking my lips, I gently brought the gun out and tucked it into my waistband and pulled my shirt over the bulge. He'd obviously meant for me to find it. On top of loose papers in the drawer was a small fluorescent pink sticky note. A note in Garrett's handwriting said:

Don't contact me on my phone. Don't look for me. Trust no one!

My hands shook as I peeled the note from the paperwork and held it to my heart.

"Hey, I just wanted—"

I let out a small *eep*! when the voice sounded behind me.

"Sorry, didn't mean to scare you." A worker covered in dried paint looked sheepish in the doorway.

"No problem." I cleared my throat as I stuffed,

the note in the front pocket of my jeans. "Just deep in thought."

"Yeah, well, wanted to let you know that I heard your flooring will actually be ready for pickup later today. We'll be installing it tomorrow."

"That's great. Thanks." I picked up a large note-pad on Garrett's desk as if that was what I'd come for. "Well, I'm all done here so I'll leave you to it."

I followed him out of the room. Outside I hesitated because my eyes were frantically looking for my Jeep until my brain adjusted and reminded me the Jeep was ash. I was walking to the rental car when Phil came out of his house and jogged over to me.

"Your Jeep got hauled away by the tow company at the crack of dawn." He grinned at me. "In case you were wondering."

"Okay. Thanks. Yeah, I came by just to check on that and—" *Trust no one* "—to make sure the work-ers saw my note about the hardwood. And, good news, it's in stock and might be installed tomorrow."

"That's great!" He was eying the notepad I still had in my hand.

I held it up to him. "The thing about motels is that they only give you a tiny message pad, so I figured I'd grab this while I was here. Going to write out my ideas about other renovations. You know, maybe it's time to do the bathrooms too."

"Hey, if you ever want to come inside our place and get some ideas, then you're welcome to. The previous owners did an amazing job of the bath-room renos."

"Thanks. Sure." I nodded and smiled stupidly as I

walked around the car and opened the driver's door. "I'll definitely take you up on that."

He was still standing at the curb staring after me as I pulled away and drove off down the street.

Back at the motel I shoved the handgun into my backpack and took the tiny pink sticky note out of my pocket and stuck it to the front of the notepad. I stared at it hard.

"Oh God, Garrett, what is going on?"

I pinched my eyes shut but still the tears slipped beneath my lashes. Wookie came over and placed his muzzle on my lap and I sobbed quietly as I rubbed his thick head.

My phone rang, and it was Agent Powel.

"Just wanted to give you an update," she said. "I talked to the other agents working the Flores Cartel investigation and they say they have eyes on every person remotely connected to drug trafficking in the area, including all connections at Flash Imports."

"So, they're looking out for Garrett then? They'll call you if they spot him?"

"It's tricky." She paused, and I could hear her starting up her car followed by a moment when her phone switched over to her Bluetooth. "I know you're worried, but I don't want to throw him under the bus, know what I mean?"

"No. I don't know what you mean." I rubbed the last tears from my eyes. "He could be in trouble… he… I don't know. He could need help."

"He's supposed to be on leave from this case, right? If he's just doing some quiet checking on his own because of family loyalty, or if he's just got Sid squirreled away keeping him safe for now, I don't want to get him in trouble over that. So I'm not putting up red flags all over screaming to other agents to go looking for Garrett Pierce, got it?"

I wanted to argue and scream that I wanted every agent on the lookout for Garrett and finding him to bring him home.

Trust no one!

Did that message also mean his partner? I doubted it but it could mean any other fed she might be in contact with so I needed to agree with her method.

"Okay." I sighed. "I get it."

"Good. I've gotta run. Damn baby is kicking me in the kidneys and I've gotta pee like a damn racehorse."

The call ended before I could respond.

My stomach was aching but I realized with some food and coffee I might be able to form a clearer plan of action. I tore off a couple sheets from the notepad, leaving Garrett's sticky note message on the bigger sheet and put both and a pen in my purse. I left the room telling Wookie I wouldn't be long. As a shortcut to a restaurant around the corner, I angled across the parking lot and cut between a break in the tall cedar hedge.

I chose a booth in a far corner. The waitress arrived with a menu and proceeded to tell me the specials, but I cut her off.

"Coffee, two eggs over easy, bacon and toast." Then added, "Please and thanks."

She hurried off to take care of that and I waited until she returned with my coffee before I took the papers out of my purse. I stared again at Garrett's note warning me not to contact him by phone or trust anyone. Again I felt my heart pound but I calmed it with deep breaths as I smoothed out the notepaper I'd torn off from the pad.

Garrett was a heavy writer and I could feel the indentation from whatever his last notes had been. My eyes went immediately to a word on the center of the page that looked an awful lot like the words *sweet pea*. I held the note up to the light. The various indents and scribbles were illegible, but that word had been written all in block letters and underlined. I got out my phone and entered *sweet pea* into the search.

The first thing to come up were, of course, sweet pea flowers. A few minutes later I'd read all about the climbing plant and how it was in the genus Lathyrus and originally from Italy. Nothing of interest but I did pause when I read a bit about the seeds being toxic. I highly doubted that Garrett was being poisoned by sweet pea seeds, but I scribbled a note on the papers nonetheless.

Next thing on my internet search was that sweet pea was a Benjamin Moore paint color that was kind of a putrid green.

"Not on my decorating list." I wrote it down on the paper anyway.

Next, I entered sweet pea and the Seattle area but there were no streets with that name. One by one I jotted down company names that had sweet pea in the title. There was a surprising number including a photography studio, a preschool and a pediatric dental clinic. In each case, I clicked on the websites to see if there were any clues.

The waitress delivered my food and I mumbled a thank-you and mindlessly ate while I continued my search. I felt like I'd searched every damn *sweet* and *pea* and *sweet pea* thing in Seattle but, unfortunately, none of the sites opened onto a page with a flash video showing the Flores Cartel smiling at the camera.

Which made me think…

I renewed my search typing in *sweet pea* and *Flores*.

Immediately a website came up for a tree nursery in the small city of Wenatchee a couple hours away. Wenatchee was known as the apple capital of the world so *sweet pea* was a bit of an odd name. I clicked through to the website to find out why my search linked to this company. On the About Us page was a list of workers. Beside each photo was a name and description of their duties at the nursery. A Josephine was listed as the treasurer but there was no last name and no photo of her. The very last name on the page had only a blank box where a photo should have been. The person was described as the owner and operator of the Sweet Pea Nursery.

My blood chilled in my veins as I said his name out loud.

Mateo Flores. The head of the Flores Cartel.

ELEVEN

I WAS QUICKLY on my feet and nearly knocked over the waitress who'd come to clear my plates.

"Sorry." I dug out some bills and handed them to her before she could even hand me the bill and then I was out the door.

My mind was focused on only one thing. I needed to get to Wenatchee and visit this Sweet Pea Nursery and I needed to do it like yesterday. Again I cut through the tall cedar hedge that surrounded the motel parking lot but then I stopped short. A stocky man with a ball cap was staring inside my rental car. He approached the motel and peered inside the window of my room and I took a step back so I was hidden behind the hedge but could keep an eye on him from between the branches. I put my hand over my mouth to keep from screaming. Even from where I stood I could hear Wookie's snarling attack bark.

"Go right ahead," I whispered. "Break in and we'll see how much meat Wookie can rip off your ass."

The man craned his neck to get a good look between the drapes to see inside my room, then he turned and took out a cell phone. He snapped a picture of the room number on the door and turned to take a picture of my rental car parked directly in front of the door. He even leaned close to take a picture of the license plate. My throat grew dry with fear.

The man began to walk in my direction across the lot and I scrambled back a few feet, panicked that he might have spotted me. As he got closer I got a good look at his face—brown skin, a crooked nose and a spider tattoo on his neck. I was just about to turn on my heel and run when he changed the direction of his walk and headed toward an older black Honda Civic. The car had a long scrape that ran all along the passenger side.

While he walked with his back to me, I got out my own phone and, making sure the volume was off so he wouldn't hear the click, I snapped a number of pictures of him and his car. Unfortunately, with the ball cap pulled down low over his eyes the only thing I could say was that he was a stocky guy with brownish skin and a spider tattoo. I tried to get a picture of his plate as he pulled out of the lot, but he was gone too fast.

Resisting the urge to run immediately across the lot toward my room, I forced myself to wait until a full two minutes had passed. As soon as that time was up, I raced across the lot. My key card wouldn't work the first couple times I tried to unlock the door because my hands were shaking so hard, but I finally got the door to the motel room open.

Wookie jumped all over me. He was thrilled to have me back from breakfast, but I had no time for fun or to give him the attention he craved. Someone was following and tracking me, and it was probably the person who blew up my Jeep.

"We're moving, boy," I told him as I began to fling things into my large duffel bag.

Within five minutes I had the car loaded with Wookie and his gear as well as my duffel bag and dowsing backpack. I hooked the Do Not Disturb notice on the motel room door and made sure the drapes to the room were closed tight and the TV was turned on with the volume just high enough it could be heard from outside. I didn't check out. For as long as possible I wanted whoever was stalking me to think I was still staying at this motel.

I accelerated out of the lot and onto the main street. First stop was the car rental place where I told the young woman working the counter that I wanted a different vehicle.

"But you just got it a couple hours ago. You don't like the car?"

"If you don't mind, I'd like something different. An SUV if you have one. I'm just used to driving something bigger." My smile was polite, but I tapped my fingers impatiently on the counter.

She shrugged and snapped her gum as she clicked a few things on her screen. "It's going to cost you more money. Your insurance only covers a basic compact or mid-sized car for one week until you can buy something else after a collision."

I didn't tell her my Jeep was blown up, not involved in an accident.

"That's fine." I gave her another pleasant smile. "I really appreciate your help because I'm kind of in a hurry."

She shrugged again.

It took ten minutes for her to put me into a white mid-sized SUV. When she opened the vehicle, I pronounced it suitable and immediately began transferring all the gear from the car to the SUV. That gear included Wookie.

"Our pet policy says you have to make sure you vacuum the vehicle before you return it. Any pet hair and we'll have to charge you a cleaning fee."

"I didn't have a chance to vacuum this one." I nodded to the car. "Charge me if you need to. But I'll be sure to clean this one once I'm done." I snatched the keys for the SUV from her hand. "Thanks. Have a good day."

I'd tossed my backpack up front with me and, as I drove onto the main street, I dumped its contents all over the passenger seat. I snagged my Mariners ball cap and put it on my head, carefully tucking my blond hair under the cap, and put on my sunglasses. It was the best disguise I could come up with on such short notice, but it would have to do.

It was going to take me nearly two and a half hours to get to Wenatchee, and that was plenty of time to think. Unfortunately, most of my thinking was worst-case scenarios. I tried to focus on the positive. Garrett was alive. At least he was alive yesterday when he'd left me a note to warn me. That was reassuring so I'd keep that in mind.

I licked my lips and tried to relax. It occurred to me that I was about to rush into a situation that I knew little about, and my recklessness could end up putting Garrett in more danger. My entire body was taut with fear.

"I'm okay," I told myself, and Wookie whined from the back seat as if even he didn't believe it.

The highway was forested on either side and about halfway there I took a turn onto a dirt road and pulled my vehicle behind some trees. I let Wookie out to sniff and pee and put a water bowl out for him. Part of me was screaming that I had no time for this and should hurry back on the road, but the sane voice inside told me I needed to clear my head before I lost it completely.

I had barely a signal out here but with patience and moving around to search out a bar or two of service, I managed to look up what I wanted; pictures in various news sources of the Flores Cartel and their henchmen. Enlarging pictures, I got a good look at Mateo Flores, the head of the cartel—good-looking in a cocky way, mid-forties, fit, thin mustache. A newspaper reported Flores had a penchant for sports cars and was known to give one as a gift to his informers. I immediately thought about the red Jaguar convertible driven by Jerry Mayer.

In the news article one of his muscled thugs caught my eye. I recognized him as the guy who'd been looking for me at the motel. He was called La Araña. Spider. That made sense given the spider tattoo on his neck. Every article I could find listed the man as a suspect in numerous murders. If Flores wanted someone gone, La Araña took care of it.

My anxiety was bad. Every inch of my body was vibrating with nerves. While Wookie chased a squirrel up a nearby tree I closed my eyes and drew in deep, cleansing breaths. In through my nose and out through my mouth. And again. I consciously un-clenched my fists and relaxed my jaw, so my teeth were no longer clenched.

Everything is okay.

You are safe.

Garrett is safe.

Even in my mind, the words stumbled.

I wanted a drink so bad. A sweet little guzzle to make all this bad go away.

Over and over I repeated positive thoughts until, finally, my hands stopped shaking and I felt a little calmer. Wookie sauntered over and slurped noisily from his water bowl and then put his dripping nose against my legs.

"Ew-w-w." I chuckled. "Thanks for that, you big goof."

I gave him a chew treat and returned him to the back seat of the SUV. Before I hit the road again I formulated a tentative plan. My phone chimed quickly in succession as two text messages rolled in.

The first message from neighbor Preston was: Great flooring choice!

A picture followed showing about half the living room already had the new hardwood installed. Nevada Maple had been a great way to go.

His second text said: So sorry to hear about your Jeep! What the hell happened there?? You coming by today to look at the floor?

I hesitated in sending my reply because I suddenly recalled the T-shirt he was wearing with the broken lightning bolt on it. The one for Flash Imports.

Trust no one.

Garrett's words screamed in my head as I sent my vague reply: Working today but I hope to stop by later. Thanks for the pic!

Preston sent me a smiling emoji that felt evil and mocking. What if he was one of the bad guys and I'd given him an actual key to our house? I thought of Phil and Preston and their exuberant neighborliness and couldn't imagine either of them hurting us.

Another text sounded just as I was about to start the car.

I'm working til 4. How bout dinner?

I wanted to call Tracey and tell her everything that was going on. I wanted to warn her to stay away from the motel and not to go by my house and not to call or message me until this was all over because I'd dragged her too far into this situation. I'd already put her in danger once by bringing her to that pub. I wouldn't make that mistake again. I could only hope that if she just stayed away from me she'd be safe.

Garrett's back and he's great!! I'm meeting him in… I thought for a second then finished… Seattle. We're going to have a few days together.

Tracey was quick to reply.

Awesome!! Don't worry about Fluffy. I'll keep him as long as you want.

Thanks. Talk in a couple days.

She sent me a thumbs-up and a hugging emoji and

my bottom lip quivered just a bit. Maybe I should've told her to go into hiding but if anyone was watching her too, I wanted it to look like her actions were normal and I had to believe the only danger she'd be in was if she was with me. I closed my eyes and crossed my fingers that big muscled Craig was also staying close by and keeping her safe.

I'd plugged the address of the Sweet Pea Nursery into the GPS and it was now indicating I was arriving at my destination on my right. I slowed to just below the speed limit and coasted by. The area was surrounded with tree orchards, and the property itself had three massive steel buildings probably used for storage. Even from the road I could see several security cameras at the entrances so approaching would not go unnoticed. A small paved parking lot out front had some vehicles in it and a long drive that went around back had a semitruck exiting.

"Now what?" I murmured as I accelerated past. Wookie woofed as if in reply.

I continued driving until I reached a town about a half hour farther down the road. After a moment's thought, I entered a store and picked up a couple blankets and some food and water. I vaguely remembered searching for a drowning victim at a lake nearby. After a quick search of the location on my phone, I headed to a somewhat secluded campground.

"We're probably sleeping in the car tonight," I told Wookie as I put the vehicle in park. "It'll be like camping."

It had been a long time since I'd gone camping.

Another lifetime ago with a monster I once considered family. I shuddered at the dark thoughts as they tried to envelop me. With a clap of my hands and a loud clearing of my throat, I tried to refocus.

It was still getting quite cold at night but, with the blankets, we'd be warm enough and, if needed, I could start the vehicle. The Sweet Pea Nursery website said it stayed open until eight o'clock. It was nearly that now. My plan was to wait until late tonight and then go and see if I could do a little investigating around the facilities. The massive warehouses on the property could hide just about anything—thousands of pounds of Mexican Mud heroin or an FBI officer and his wayward brother-in-law.

"Let's go for a walk."

At the W word, Wookie was whining with excitement and he happily bounded out of the vehicle. We took the narrow path down to the lake. A crisp breeze came off the water, bringing the damp wooded scents of forest and marsh. Wookie found a stick nearly as big as he was to play with and, while I watched him, I talked out loud to myself.

"Garrett's okay. He wrote me a note to warn me not to message him maybe because someone has his phone."

His earlier text to me calling me *Sweet pea* and the etching of the word into his notepad made me believe I was definitely on the right track by searching this nursery.

I picked up a smaller stick and threw it for Wookie to fetch. He was thrilled with the game and more than happy to put it on repeat until my arm was exhausted.

The sun sank down across the lake and the air grew chilled. My phone chimed an incoming text from Agent Karla Powel asking if I'd heard anything more from Garrett. I hesitated. When Garrett said to trust no one I'm sure he didn't include his very pregnant partner on maternity leave. Still, I reasoned that even if Agent Powel was helping as much as she could on the sidelines, she would not exactly be impressed to think I was planning on checking out a business owned by Mateo Flores. I sent her a simple 'no' in response.

I grabbed a blanket from the car and wrapped it around my shoulders as I sat on a nearby log. Wookie slumped at my feet, gnawing enthusiastically on his stick. When I started to feel overwhelmed, I covered my face with my hands.

"What does your gut say?" I asked myself. After a deep breath, my reply was, "It feels like he's not safe, and all I know is that if he's in danger, he needs my help."

I thought about Agent Powel again. Big as a house and ready to give birth any day. The fact that she'd been trying to keep an eye on Garrett since he was pulled from the case made it feel like she would be a safe person to turn to. There was no way I alone could stand up to a bunch of cartel henchmen if Garrett was being held at Sweet Pea. I made up my mind that, if needed, I'd call Agent Karla Powel and ask her to send reinforcements.

I sat with my eyes closed and tried to splice together everything I knew for fact, and those things I only felt in my gut. Somewhere in the middle of those two things was what I needed but it was still out of reach. A crisp breeze picked up, and even the blanket around my shoulders wasn't helping to keep away the chill.

"C'mon, boy."

We walked back to the vehicle with Wookie startling a rabbit out from a shrub and then losing it again a second later. I took out his bowls and let him take a long drink and eat some kibble. For myself, I took a muffin out of the convenience store sack and ate it while leaning against the car and staring up at the darkening sky. We climbed into the car and I started the motor to give us some heat. I gave Wookie one of the blankets on the back seat and took one to cover myself. We both immediately snuggled in. Once we had enough heat, I cut the engine and we sat in the still darkness of the woods and waited.

I dozed off and the sound of an incoming text jolted me awake. Fumbling for my phone I scanned the screen hopeful for a message from Garrett but it was Agent Powel.

Stopped by the motel but you're not there??

Her two question marks made it feel like a demand. It was nearly midnight. What excuse could I give her for not being there? And did she have information for me regarding Garrett? My fingers hovered over the letters on my phone while I struggled with a reply.

Wookie hurt his paw at the dog park. Had to find a 24 hour vet.

I hit Send on the fib hoping against hope that I really didn't need to be lying to this FBI agent. Praying she was on my side but not willing to risk it. I quickly added, Any news on Garrett?

Was she weighing the truthfulness behind my story about Wookie? Even without FBI connections it wouldn't take her long to figure out how many vet hospitals in that area were open twenty-four hours for emergencies. I was hoping it wasn't on her priority list to start checking. It felt like forever for her reply to come.

No. Things are heating up in the case. Can't get into it. Things might wrap soon.

Had she stopped by the motel near midnight just to tell me that? Or was she afraid to put anything in writing and would've told me more had I been there, or maybe just showed up to pick my brain and see what I knew. And by *wrap* did she mean the FBI was closing in on the case with the Flores Cartel? Did the heating up put Garrett in danger? I didn't even know how to reply to that because I had too many questions I knew she wouldn't answer. While I was still tossing her words around in my head she sent another message.

See you soon.

And I wasn't sure if that was a warning. Maybe she suspected I wasn't going to be back at the motel, so she was letting me know she would be checking on me. I tossed my phone to the passenger seat where it landed next to my dowsing rods and the muffin wrapper.

Before I went to investigate the Sweet Pea Nursery I needed to be sure I couldn't be identified. I climbed out of the vehicle and walked down the dark path to the lake, where I scooped up handfuls of clay-like muck which I used to smudge the license plates. I'd seen for myself that the nursery buildings had video surveillance. These cartel guys could easily have connections that could trace my plate back to the rental company and then to me. If they had Garrett, that would put him in more danger. I rinsed the dirt off my hands using a water bottle and wiped them dry on my jeans.

Wookie stirred in the back seat, sitting up and looking around as I started the engine and began to drive along the rutted gravel road that led out of the wooded area and onto the main road. After we'd driven a mile, Wookie settled back down, curling up onto the blanket on the back seat. As he softly snored I again picked up my Mariners cap and tucked my hair up inside. It was too dark for sunglasses but as we neared the Sweet Pea Nursery I pulled the brim of my hat down low and grabbed a bandana from my backpack. I tied the scarf around my face so that the only part of me visible were my eyes.

The large steel warehouses of the nursery loomed dark and foreboding in the night as I turned off to approach them from the main road. The front parking lot was completely empty. Staff and customers were long gone and tucked into their beds for the night. I drove around back to the massive paved lot that semitrucks must use for loading and transporting apples picked in the surrounding orchards. In the far corner of the lot was a single tractor trailer next to a massive pile of wood pallets. Behind the trailer and pallets was a long equipment shed. There were security lights and cameras in all the truck bays and worker entrances.

Wanting to keep my vehicle out of the view of the cameras as much as possible, I pulled my car behind the shed and angled it just enough so that I could get a view of the buildings but be out of range of the cameras. I killed my motor and familiarized myself with the area.

This was the loading area and no doubt these massive warehouses were filled with apples from the surrounding orchards and machinery to maintain the groves. Given that the nursery was owned by the Flores Cartel, there was a good chance the warehouses were also used to store heroin. I assumed the FBI had already figured that out.

The first thing that struck me was the sheer amount of security here. Every rollup door had at least two cameras. Each building also had an entrance door for employees on the side and, again, there were cameras. This was a place of business and so, of course, there'd be security but there weren't rogue apple pirates randomly breaking down the doors and stealing the crops. This was all about Mateo Flores and the drug cartel.

"Now what?"

I stared at the buildings and nervously chewed my lower lip. Suddenly I felt uncertain. I didn't have any tools with me that would help me break into one of these steel warehouses. The employee doors on

the sides looked solid as well. My own Jeep had a
basic tool kit in the trunk that was now melted but
I doubt I'd have much more than a jack in the back
of this rental. I had a handgun in the backpack but I
didn't want to use all my bullets shooting off a lock.

The equipment shed I was parked beside would
have tools and it probably wouldn't be alarmed. There
was a chance I could break the window of the shed
and climb inside to get whatever tool I might need to
pry open a steel door. It had small windows that might
allow me to be able to see inside. Maybe if I busted
the window I could even boost myself up and inside.

"What are you, a gymnast now?" I murmured
discouragingly.

I had to try. I had no choice. I might find information regarding Garrett. He might even be inside one
of these buildings. The thought made my throat go
dry. He'd rescued me a number of times and he would
never back down from a challenge if he thought I was
in danger. It was my turn.

I had my hand on the door to my SUV about
to open it when a convoy of vehicles sped into the
lot and pulled up behind the buildings. I doubted I
could be visible from where my car was located, but
still I sank lower in my seat while keeping my head
high enough to see. There were three dark high-end
sedans—a black Escalade and a couple of BMWs—
as well as one beat-up-looking black Honda Civic.
I covered my mouth and gasped. The Civic was the
car I'd seen at the motel.

I leaned forward with my eyes just above my dash.
Men climbed out of the cars and when their doors

slammed, Wookie growled low in his throat. I quickly ordered him to be quiet. I didn't need his growl to rev up to a bark and give away my position. As the men gathered outside their vehicles, I recognized one of the men immediately as Mateo Flores. All the men had their jackets wide open to reveal they were carrying handguns. La Araña, the stocky guy who visited my motel, had his gun in his hand and at the ready.

My hands grew slick with nervous sweat as Flores and La Araña entered the building while the other two men stood guard outside. There was no way I could approach the building without getting shot. I pulled the brim of my hat lower and pulled the scarf once again up over my face. It felt like forever before the doors to the building reopened. La Araña was exiting the building with a man held at gunpoint. When they stepped closer, I saw the man's hands were tied behind his back. They opened the door to one of the BMWs and, as they shoved him roughly into the back seat, the light in the car briefly illuminated the man's face. It was Garrett's brother-in-law, Sid Klein.

"Damn!"

The BMW started up and its headlights illuminated the building just as the door of the building opened again. Mateo Flores was coming out, and ahead of him was another man with hands tied behind his back. As they stepped up to the Escalade the head lamps shone brightly on them.

Terror breathed ice down the back of my neck. It was Garrett.

TWELVE

I WATCHED IN horror as Garrett was roughly shoved up against the Escalade, a large handgun pointed between his shoulder blades. At one point he turned and said something to Flores, and one of the bodyguards punched him hard in the stomach.

I bit my knuckle to stop from screaming. Even though I wanted to grab the gun from my pack, take aim and shoot Flores from across the parking lot, I was too far to get a good shot. I'd miss, and before I knew it, I'd be surrounded by four men with guns. As much as I wanted to jump out of my car and run to protect Garrett, I was no match for these thugs and we'd both end up dead.

Doubled over in pain, Garrett was forced into the back of the Escalade and soon all four vehicles were speeding out of the lot.

There was no way I could risk losing sight of where they were taking him. I waited only a few seconds before I fired up my SUV and rocketed after them. By the time I was on the road, the taillights of the other vehicles were far ahead of me. I kept back as far as I could without losing them, hoping not to draw their attention. My hands were white knuckled on the steering wheel as I followed them mile after mile toward Seattle. The city was at least a couple hours away.

I comforted myself by saying if they were going to kill Garrett and Sid, they could've done it more easily in the apple orchards or even behind those nursery buildings. There had to be a purpose for keeping both men alive until now and taking them toward the city.

After an hour it was getting more and more difficult to maintain a discreet distance and not lose the cars. Luckily there weren't many other vehicles on the road at this time of night but occasionally I allowed another car between myself and the evil convoy so as not to arouse suspicion. As we got closer to the more heavily populated areas, more cars were on the road even though it wasn't even two in the morning.

The stress of driving and the raging thoughts in my head caused my shoulders to ache with tension. Should I call the police? Agent Karla Powel? There was no way I could tackle this alone. I made up my mind that as soon as these vehicles arrived at their destination, I would call for help.

"As soon as I see where they're taking them, I'm going to call Agent Powel and she can send active agents to rescue them." I spoke between clenched teeth as my eyes burned with fatigue.

The beat-up Honda driven by La Araña abruptly slowed and, before I knew it, I was coming up behind him fast. I hit the brakes so that I could match his speed, but I was only a few yards behind him by the time I reacted. The driver leaned out of his window, pointed a gun in my direction, and multiple shots punched holes in my windshield and whistled past my head.

I braked and yanked on the steering wheel, causing the vehicle to overreact. Next thing I knew I was in the ditch and my vehicle was on its side and Wookie was howling.

Frantically, I scrambled to unbuckle my belt and climb out of the vehicle. I was convinced that the shooter had stopped and was going to join me in the ditch to finish me off. However, out of the car I could see all four vehicles rocketing down the road, their taillights disappearing in the distance.

"Damn!" I screamed into the wind and slammed my fist onto the vehicle.

Wookie was frantically barking in the back seat and, with the vehicle on its side, it took me a few minutes to release him. He leaped from the car and bounded around the tall grass in the ditch, obviously unhurt. I sat down in the damp weeds and sobbed into my hands. Seconds later a passing motorist spied me, pulled over and came to offer her help.

"You fall asleep at the wheel, or are you drunk?" the young woman asked, obviously not noticing the bullet holes in the windshield.

"Guess I dozed off," I admitted.

"Want me to call a wrecker?" she asked, absently rubbing Wookie's head when he came to greet her.

"I can do that if you wouldn't mind driving me to the nearest town?"

She hesitated, obviously weighing what she'd always been told about picking up wannabe serial killer hitchhikers.

"I'll give you fifty bucks for your trouble," I offered.

She quickly agreed. Together we hauled Wookie and all my belongings from the banged-up SUV. I had to scramble back inside to gather up my backpack from the passenger seat, pushing around inflated airbags to gather my dowsing rods and other supplies that had scattered onto the floor. The gun had rolled out of my pack and I gently tucked it back inside.

Fifteen minutes later I handed the girl fifty dollars after she helped bring my things out of her car and place them at the door of a roadside hotel. All I could think about was Garrett being dragged off to who knows where by those criminals. The last thing I wanted was to get a room at a hotel instead of following them, but I had no car and they were long gone. I needed to make a new plan.

Luckily the hotel had a dog-friendly room available on the main floor and soon Wookie was curled up on the queen-sized bed looking comfortable. I called the rental company and told them there'd been an accident with the SUV. After giving them information on where to find it, I cracked open my laptop and did more research on Flores. I needed to know the enemy.

When I tried to find a connection between Sweet Pea Nursery and Flash Imports, one name came up: a woman by the name of Josephine. The woman's name showed up as working at the nursery and as a consultant at Flash Imports. A little more research and I found a Josephine listed as a friend of Sid's on social media. However, her profile picture was a cat and I couldn't find any pictures of the woman's face. On Sid's page he'd mentioned her often but, again, no pictures. Whoever this woman was, there was a good chance she was the person who connected Sid Klein and Jerry Mayer to the cartel. Maybe she was the one who'd enlisted them into working to help Flores's gang smuggle the drugs into Washington.

My body ached from the vehicle accident. A final internet search showed there was a car rental company a mile from the motel, but it didn't open until eight in the morning. I'd be there as soon as it opened. I took a scalding hot shower and then crawled under the blankets with Wookie.

"Garrett, please be safe," I cried into my pillow. "I can't lose you. I just can't."

I fell asleep, my fingers gripped around my dad's wedding ring on the chain around my neck. I woke with a start as the sun pierced the drapes. Snatching up my phone I realized it was nearly seven-thirty. I filled Wookie's bowls and dressed while he ate. Then I took him for a quick run around the outside of the building before locking him in back in the hotel room and hanging up the Do Not Disturb sign.

"I won't be long," I told him, but he was already stretched out on the bed. He was adjusting much better than I was to this vagabond lifestyle.

With my hat on my head and my scarf around my neck, I grabbed a coffee in the lobby and set out to walk over to the car rental place a mile away. With every step I took I rehashed all that I knew so far. I was convinced that somewhere in my head lay the key to where Garrett might be stashed but I couldn't seem to unlock that knowledge.

With all the recent expenses I was hoping my credit

card wasn't maxed out, but everything seemed to go through without a hitch. The old man working the car rentals could only offer me a compact car. At this point I really didn't care because I'd formulated a plan.

As soon as I was inside the car I called Tracey's number.

"He-e-ey. Don't tell me you two love birds are done with your vacay already? I didn't expect to hear from you for days, girlfriend."

"I need you to do something for me."

At the seriousness in my tone her demeanor immediately changed. "Are you okay?"

"Yes. Are you working today?"

"I was just about to head to work now," she replied.

"Call in sick," I told her.

"Done."

I took a deep breath and explained exactly what I needed her to do. When I arrived back at the hotel I made my way into the breakfast room and put together a tray of food from the offerings included with my stay. I grabbed another coffee as well and brought the works back to my room. Wookie yawned and stretched when I opened the door.

"You're getting lazy," I told him.

He wagged his little Rottweiler nub of a tail.

"I'm joking." I patted his head. "You're a good boy."

His entire body wiggled then because maybe being a "good boy" meant he'd get some of the bacon off my plate. He was right. At first, I had no appetite but the minute I started to eat I became ravenous and was considering going back to the breakfast room for more when there was a knock at the room door. Wookie growled at the sound. I got up and glanced through the peephole and when I opened the door wide Wookie barked in delight at the sight of Tracey.

"Bed," I told Wookie and he reluctantly jumped onto the hotel bed instead of going over to greet Tracey like he wanted.

She grabbed me in a big hug.

"Tell me everything," she said, walking over to the corner table and taking a seat.

"First, do you have it?" I asked nervously.

She nodded, pulled a velvet jewelry box from her purse and handed it to me.

I popped it open and stared at the emerald-and-diamond wedding ring that had belonged to Garrett's deceased wife, Faith. Licking my lips nervously, I snapped the box shut again and put it aside on the table.

"Yeah, when I got to your place I had to get past your nosy neighbor first. Even though you sent him a text telling him I was coming by to get a ring I'd loaned you, he still made me show ID and everything. Who made him the king of the world? Look at me! Do I look like I'm capable of doing a B&E?" She pointed to her braced knee and indignantly blew a strand of hair out of her face. "He followed me around, watching me get the ring from the closet. This was the hard part because I seriously thought the man would not let me use the bathroom alone." She pulled a revolver out of her purse, holding it gingerly like it might explode at any second, and gently placed it on the table. "Who the hell keeps a handgun at the bottom of a box of maxipads!" She shook her head. "I guess we know who the hell does that—it's you!" She pointed a finger in my face. "Now tell me the truth. Where's Garrett? Why are you bunking in the middle of bloody nowhere? Why do you want his dead wife's ring? And a gun? What's going on? Oh my God, did you guys break up? Are you going to shoot him? Don't do it! No man is worth the jail time."

I put up my hands to stop her ranting. "That gun is for you. I already have one here for me."

"What?" She shook her head. "Nope. No way."

"I want you to have it, just in case…"

"What is going on?"

"I didn't tell you the truth. I told you Garrett was home and that everything was great, and we were going off to spend time together but that was all a lie."

Hurt spread across her face and was gone as Tracey folded her hands neatly on her lap and waited.

"I wanted to keep you safe." I explained to her about Flores's henchman La Araña showing up at the motel and about how I'd gone on the run after Garrett's message to trust no one. When I got to the part about sneaking around at the nursery only to discover Garrett and Sid being led away at gunpoint, Tracey's eyes grew big. When I told her about my new rental car being shot up and how I ended up at this motel, she gasped and grabbed my hands.

"Stop! This is bigger than you can handle. It's way bigger than your FBI agent boyfriend can handle, so you *know* it's way above your pay scale, got it?" She pulled out her phone. "We're calling the cops and telling them everything."

"No!" I snatched her phone from her hand and dropped it on the table next to the gun. Wookie raised his head from his paws curiously and then returned to a relaxed position as I lowered my voice. "When Garrett told me not to trust anybody he didn't say 'only trust the cops' or 'only trust the FBI.' He wouldn't have written that warning unless he believed I was truly on my own with this."

"You don't know that." Tracey shook her head. "Sounds to me like he wants you to hunker down and be safe, not go getting shot at trying to rescue his ass. Call that partner of his. You told me you were talking to some agent who worked with him. The pregnant one."

"I have been talking with her and even she is investigating this on the sly. Besides, she's due to have a C-section any day. She's not exactly going to be getting into shootouts with a drug cartel."

"Oh, and we are?" Tracey sputtered.

"Not *we* and, hopefully, not me either." I picked up the velvet jewelry box and cracked it open. My fingers shook a little as I plucked the emerald and diamond ring from its resting place. "I'm hoping that Faith will help us find Garrett." The words cracked as they left my throat.

"You're going to use it for pendulum dowsing." Tracey straightened. "That could work, right? I mean you said before that kind of dowsing only works for you if you're using an object that's important to them and if you're really connected to the person."

"Yeah." I shrugged. "But I'm not really connected

to Faith, am I?" I blew out a breath. "I just hope our mutual connection to Garrett will be enough."

I unclasped the necklace around my own neck, slid my dad's wedding ring off the chain and tucked it into a small pocket inside my backpack. Then I threaded Faith's wedding ring onto the chain and redid the clasp. With a deep breath I sat down facing south and began.

Holding the chain up above the small round table, I gently stilled it with my fingers and waited until it no longer moved.

"Show me your yes," I whispered.

The ring began to move back and forth slowly in a pendulum fashion from east to west. At first the movement was gentle and small but within a few seconds the left to right movement became more sure and deliberate. I could hear Tracey's breath coming hard and fast with amazement. I stopped the swaying ring and made it motionless once again.

"Show me your no."

The ring immediately swung away from me and then toward me, back and forth, north and south, increasing its momentum with every sway.

"Thank you."

Once again, I stopped the ring with my hand. I sucked in a deep breath through my nose and let it out slowly through my mouth.

"Is Garrett alive?" I choked on the words and bit my lip as I waited for the response.

Immediately the ring swung left to right indicating a yes, and a small whimper left my throat. Tracey reached and put a comforting hand on my shoulder as I stopped the ring.

"Can you help me find him?" I asked.

Again, the ring moved widely from east to west in a yes motion. A jagged breath that was half sob escaped my lips. I took the ring and held it close to my chest.

"You can only ask it yes and no, right?" Tracey tapped the table with her finger. "How are you ever going to find him that way?"

"I was doing some research before you came." I took out my phone and opened the list I made. "There are a number of locations that are connected to Sweet Pea Nursery, Mateo Flores and Flash Imports. They have warehouses, shipping containers, delivery locations, a boat..." I scrolled down the list. "And then there's all the staff. I've checked a lot of their social media pages and many of them have cottages and some even own acreage. For example, a woman named Josephine is friends with Sid Klein and Jerry Mayer on social media and there's a Josephine who works for both Sweet Pea Nursery and Flash Imports and lives in Tacoma right near a shipping container lot also connected to Mateo Flores."

"You're going to go through every single place on that list and ask the ring—um, Faith—to tell you whether Garrett's there?"

"Yes." I nodded solemnly. "And, if I have to, I'll make another list of a hundred more places or drag out a map and start friggin' listing every city and town in Washington State."

"In that case..." Tracey got to her feet. "Give me your room key. I'm going to go get us some coffee."

"There's a coffee machine in the breakfast room off the lobby."

"No, thanks. I'm going to get us a couple real coffees."

After she left the room I found myself talking to the ring as if it were Faith.

"I realize you and your son died when you were hit by a drunk driver," I whispered. "I know that if you and your son were still here, Garrett would be a happy family man. A husband. A father. And, no doubt, damn good at both. Now he's with me, a weirdo dowsing girl over twenty years younger who doesn't want marriage and is scared to death of the idea of having kids. I don't know why I'm telling you this except to say that I love him with my whole heart and, well, he loves me too. Maybe not as much as he loved you and his son because that must've been the world. Anyway…" I sighed as I clutched the ring tight in my hand. "I know you might, on some level, wish he was with you…wherever you are." I cleared my throat. "So, I want to say thank you so much for anything you can do to help me find him."

The ring began to feel quite warm in my hand as I held it up to begin asking more questions.

When Tracey returned to the room about a half hour later, she placed a paper coffee cup on the table in front of me. I took a sip and thanked her.

"How's it going?"

"So far not great but I'm only halfway through my list."

After another sip from the coffee I continued using the ring as a form of divination, hoping for a small miracle. I kept asking Faith my yes and no questions regarding locations and I was beginning to lose hope that the position was on my list. Faith, via the ring, also appeared to be getting impatient. When I asked about the Port of Tacoma, instead of swinging like a pendulum, the ring remained completely still.

"Is Garrett at the Port of Tacoma?" I repeated but, still, the ring did not move.

"Is that where the drug cartel is bringing in the heroin?" Tracey asked. "You think they'd bring him there? Why?"

"I suspect that the only reason they have for keeping Garrett alive, is to get him to tell them when the FBI suspects the next big drug haul is arriving, so they can change it to another time."

I also believed that if he didn't give them what they wanted, they'd kill him in a heartbeat. Probably they'd do that anyway, just as soon as they got what they wanted cleared through the port.

Again, I put out the question of whether Garrett was at the Port of Tacoma and I frowned at the ring as it hung unmoving suspended from the chain.

"That's a yes or no question, right? I mean he's either there, or he's not so why is there no response?" Tracey slurped noisily from her coffee. "Maybe she doesn't know. After all, she's dead. How much can a dead person know?"

"You're not helping." I frowned at her. An idea occurred to me and I carefully reworded my question.

"Is Garrett *near* the Port of Tacoma?"

The ring immediately swung wildly to indicate a yes and I squealed with happiness.

"Is he in the city of Tacoma?"

Again, the pendulum answered affirmatively.

"Let's go." I got to my feet.

"Now? To Tacoma?" Tracey got hurriedly to her feet as well. "But we don't even know where to go once we're there!"

"You're driving and I'm going to keep asking questions until we're there."

"Are you sure? You hate my driving." Tracey hobbled around, helping me gather up my belongings. "Do we have to bring him?" She nodded her chin toward Wookie.

"I'm checking out," I said. "I'm not going to leave my boy behind."

I snapped a leash on his collar and Wookie happily bustled past Tracey for the door. Tracey took a leap back when he approached but didn't scream or faint, which was a good sign. I suggested we load everything into her vehicle and drop off my rental car. She wasn't impressed about having Wookie in her back seat and grumbled something about him taking a chunk out of the back of her neck while she was driving on the highway.

"He's not a vampire," I told her impatiently.

"Yeah, maybe a werewolf though."

I left the car in the lot and used the key drop so I didn't have to get into a long conversation about it. Then I climbed into Tracey's car, putting my pack with the two guns and dowsing rods at my feet. I clutched Faith's ring, still on the chain, tightly in my fist. I was counting on narrowing down Garrett's location as we drove.

"Your job is to drive as fast as you can without getting a ticket and without getting us killed." I buckled up.

"Sure. No pressure at all," she muttered as she accelerated down the highway.

A couple times I had to tell her it wasn't necessary to ride another car's ass so close we were practically passengers in their back seat.

"It's not tailgating if I'm just encouraging them to drive in the slow lane," she explained.

It was exactly that kind of logic that made me not a fan of her driving. When we got close to the ports in Tacoma, I asked her to pull over so I could spend some time pendulum dowsing. I'd tried asking questions along the way but was no closer to finding out where Garrett was being held.

Tracey put gas in her car while I dangled the ring over my lap and asked more questions. Unfortunately, there was either no movement from the ring, or it was a negative response.

"So where are we headed?" Tracey asked when she climbed back in the car.

"I'm not sure." I scratched my head and directed her to pull over to a corner of the parking lot, so I could take Wookie out to pee. "I've been able to find out that Garrett is not right in the port, but he is somewhere in this area. That could be anywhere here. There's no way I can go through every stupid road in a sixty-mile radius."

As I walked Wookie along the greenbelt next to the gas station something occurred to me and I did a little more research on my phone.

"What about those lots where they store the containers that come off the ships?" I asked Tracey as Wookie hopped back into the car. "Hot damn." I leaned in the car and held up my phone so that Tracey could see what had caught my attention. "Flash Imports has a lot in East Tacoma where they sell, rent and provide storage for sea cans."

"Sea cans?" she asked.

"Yeah. Those giant shipping containers and crates that carry cargo. That would be the connection. That's why Flores needed Flash Imports. We should check the place out."

"Let's go," she said.

"I'm driving," I told her, walking around to the driver's side. "Your turn to ride shotgun."

"Don't say shotgun when you have guns in your backpack," Tracey said as she slid into the passenger seat. "Do you want me to put your pack in the back seat?"

"Um…" I started the car and just shook my head. "I'd feel better keeping all that within arm's length."

Tracey hoisted my unzipped backpack onto her lap and took out a granola bar and water bottle for herself. When a gun and my dowsing rods tumbled onto the floor at her feet she looked revolted at the idea of picking up either.

"Just leave them," I suggested.

I clasped the necklace around my neck with Faith's ring resting on my chest. My stomach was in knots. Tracey's car didn't have a GPS, so I entered the address of the Flash Imports' lot into my phone and followed the instructions. Our destination was only a couple miles from our current location. The street was mostly commercial lots. I slowed as I came upon the one with chain-link fencing and a small yellow sign with the broken lightning rod that was Flash Imports' logo. Abruptly I accelerated past the driveway.

"Wait!" Tracey whipped her head around. "Isn't that it? Wasn't that Garrett getting out of the car?"

"Yes!" As we'd gone by I'd seen Mateo Flores yanking Garrett out of the black Escalade in the driveway.

I pulled over when the street rounded a bend and we were out of sight. My breath was coming hard and fast.

"I don't know what to do! We can't just waltz in there with our guns. Those guys are all armed to the teeth."

"It's time to call in the Agent Powel chick. Even a pregnant FBI agent is better than just us," Tracey said.

I had to agree. I dialed Powel's number and listened to it ring before it finally went to voicemail. "Call me as soon as you can. It's urgent."

"So, I guess we wait?" Tracey asked.

I nodded but I hated the idea. I drummed my fingers nervously on the steering wheel. After five minutes staring at my phone I looked at Tracey.

"I can't just sit here. Maybe we should call the local police." I bit my lower lip. "But if a bunch of uniforms arrive with sirens blaring that could cause Flores and his guys to panic and kill Garrett and Sid."

"But we can't rescue Garrett on our own!"

"Maybe we can." I turned to face her as an idea percolated in my mind. "The delivery must be happening tonight. There is no other reason to bring them here. I'm guessing this is the place they'll store the heroin until it's moved to the streets. We're only a few miles from the port where it'll come in. The entire reason to keep Garrett and Sid around is to make sure that delivery clears the port and there's no interference from the FBI to stop it."

"I can't see Garrett helping these cartel guys bring heroin into the country." Tracey shook her head. "He has no reason to do that!"

"He told me he's doing this for Faith." My hand went briefly to her ring around my neck. "If they've threatened to kill Sid if he doesn't cooperate, that would be enough."

"And blowing up your car," Tracey whispered. "Sid isn't the only one they've told Garrett they'll hurt."

I nodded and swallowed the lump in my throat. "But after the delivery is made tonight, they won't have any reason to keep him alive."

"What can we do?"

"Give me a second." I squeezed my eyes shut while I thought it through. Finally, I turned to look at Tracey. "First, you need to drive back the way we came. They won't know you or your car so I'm just going to hunker down in the passenger seat until we've gone by. Drive slow enough that you can get a look at how many people you can see. Let me know once we're past. Then I want you to drive onto the main road and take a left onto the next street over.

We'll look to park the car at one of the businesses that back onto Flash Imports' lot. Hopefully we can see what's going on from there."

We switched positions so that Tracey was behind the wheel. I lowered the passenger seat to a reclining position and pulled my ball cap over my face as Tracey drove past slowly enough that she could look over but not so leisurely as to draw attention.

"There were a couple guys leaning against the Escalade," Tracey said. "Looked like armed muscle. There are so many rows of those metal containers that I couldn't tell if there are more guys between them."

I pulled my seat up once we were past. "I shouldn't have dragged you into this," I said as she drove on the main road and then took a left one street over from the Flash Imports' lot. "Find a place on this street that backs onto that lot and then leave me. I know you're going to hate this, but I'm going to ask you to take Wookie with you."

"No."

"I know you hate dogs, but I need both of you to be safe." I cleared my throat and added firmly, "Get Craig to help you with Wookie. I'm sure he wouldn't mind and—"

"It's not the dog." She glanced over her shoulder at Wookie. "Not just the dog. I'm not leaving you. I don't know what kind of crazy thing you're going to do, but I'm here for you. I can be your getaway driver, if nothing else."

I laughed nervously and pointed to a shuttered business up ahead. "That place looks perfect. It's shut down, so we shouldn't encounter any people coming and going from work. If we can park around back, we might be able to see into the Flash Imports' lot."

Tracey pulled around back of the small warehouse building, and sure enough the chain-link fence behind was shared between this closed company and Flash Imports. We had a clear view of the many rows of sea cans, and a wide aisle down the center of the rows allowed a view of the one-story office building where I suspected they were holding Sid and Garrett.

"Park over there." I pointed, and Tracey pulled the car behind an overflowing dumpster.

Since the business had been closed, people had taken to dumping debris behind the closed business. The stack of bagged trash and old mattresses would provide perfect cover. The Flash Imports' lot held maybe fifty sea can storage crates stacked two or three high. On the other side of the chain-link fencing, in the far corner of Flash Imports' lot, were a few expensive sports cars covered in tarps. That article I read said Mateo Flores was known to give expensive sports cars to people working with him. Like Jerry Mayer's Jaguar. Also like the black Lamborghini in Sid's garage. In the corner of the lot I could just make out the hood of a red Ferrari where the tarp had slipped up. The cars were parked neatly in a row alongside the fence that separated us.

"We passed a hardware store around the corner," I told Tracey as I climbed out of the car and took Wookie from the back seat. "Go and pick up some bolt cutters, kerosene and a couple lighters."

"What are you going to use that stuff for?"

"A distraction." My stomach rolled with tension. "Please hurry."

As she pulled away, I slung my pack over one shoulder and led Wookie to the farthest corner behind the dumpster. He lifted his leg and marked his territory, then just looked up at me, panting happily as if this was the most natural thing in the world to be hiding behind a dilapidated building and sneaking behind a dumpster. I gave him a chew treat and he plopped himself down on the asphalt to gnaw happily on it.

I heard voices and Wookie began to growl.

"Quiet," I ordered.

I leaned in and, from between the piles of trash, I could see a dozen yards into the Flash Imports' lot. Mateo Flores was in front of the office building waving his hands and talking angrily to his thugs. There was no sign of Garrett or Sid and I assumed they were still inside the building.

The group of men began walking to a different end of the lot with Flores leading the way. I began to follow along my side of the fence, keeping hidden behind the trash. Abruptly I felt movement in my backpack. With an uneasy feeling I brought the pack around my front and looked inside. Just as Tracey was driving into the parking lot, I pulled out my dowsing rods, which tugged immediately to my left.

There was a body in the Flash Imports' lot.

I could only pray the dead person wasn't Garrett.

THIRTEEN

"No-o-o," I SOBBED.

Wookie licked the back of my leg and whined.

"What's wrong?" Tracey asked, coming up beside me, dropping her bag of purchases at my feet and placing a hand on my arm.

I nodded to the dowsing rods in my hands.

"Someone's dead. What if it's him?" My breath hitched. "What if we're too late?"

"It's *not* him." Tracey came around front of me and gave my shoulders a hard shake. "It's definitely not Garrett."

"You don't know that." I sniffed.

"Yes. I do. I'm magic." She hugged me briefly. "And if you don't believe me, ask the damn ring around your neck."

Her matter-of-fact statement gave me a jolt. I sat down on the gritty gravel parking lot and unclasped the necklace from around my neck.

"I can't do it." I clenched the ring in my fist and shook my head. "I can't ask Faith if Garrett is dead."

Wookie licked my face and slumped down next to me.

"It's not him," Tracey said but I heard the fear in her voice. "Maybe it's Sid or Flores. Start by asking that!"

"It's not Flores. I just saw him…" With a deep breath I hung the necklace in front of me and stilled it with my hand. "I'm sorry, Faith. Is it your brother? Is it Sid that's dead?"

The necklace immediately moved to indicate a no, and fear gripped me because I knew what I had to ask next.

"Is it Garrett?" I asked, my voice barely above a whisper. "Is he dead?"

Again, the necklace swung wildly in a no. I threw back my head and exhaled loudly.

"Thank God."

"I told you," Tracey said, her voice giddy with relief.

The wind was picking up and it was growing chilly. Tracey ran to her car and put on a hoodie, I followed her.

"Okay…" I got to my feet and clasped the necklace back around my neck. "Garrett and Sid are hidden away somewhere inside this fence along with some dead guy." I picked up the bolt cutters. "We're cutting our way in and then setting a distraction."

"We are?"

Tracey sounded anxious, but I had no time to reassure her now. Snipping the wire fencing was slow going but eventually I was able to cut an L-shaped opening of just over three feet high, which would be big enough for me to climb through.

"Now what?" Tracey asked nervously.

"I'm going in to start looking for Garrett and Sid," I told her, my voice low as I placed a hand on her arm. "I'm going to leave Wookie here. You okay with that?"

She glanced at Wookie, who was sitting with his head cocked at the sound of his name.

"Sure. No problem." Tracey gave me a tight smile.

"Okay. Good."

I took out the container of kerosene she'd bought and poured it very carefully into an empty pop bottle I found near the dumpster. Then I stuffed my bandana into the bottle like a wick.

"Give me a few minutes. When I'm ready, I'll send you a text saying 'go.' When you get that message, light this sucker and toss it over the fence in the corner over there." I pointed. "Be careful. You don't want to slosh any on yourself, okay? Just aim to get it right there onto the Ferrari." I pointed to the covered sports car. "Can you do that?"

Her eyes grew huge with uncertainty.

"You're magic, remember?" I grabbed both her hands in mine and gave them a light squeeze.

She nodded. "Yeah. I can do it."

I took out the handguns and put one in the waistband of my jeans and handed her the other.

"I've never even held a gun before." She shrank away.

"This is only in case of an emergency, okay?" I forced her to look while I gave her a quick lesson on the weapon and then I placed it in her hands. I grabbed my dowsing rods and headed toward the fence.

"Julie? What happens if I don't hear from you?"

I licked my lips and considered my answer. "If

you haven't heard from me in ten minutes, light it anyway."

She nodded but I could see the fear in her eyes.

I turned to Wookie. "Stay, boy."

He sat obediently but his eyes were worried too.

I squeezed through the opening I'd cut in the fence and walked as fast as I could toward the first row of shipping crates. Each of the sea can shipping containers was about forty feet long and over eight feet high. Some rows had three stacked on top of each other, so it was like hiding behind a narrow building. I waited behind the first row then looked carefully around the corner and quickly ran toward the next row.

My dowsing rods moved, wanting to pull me to the right. There was a body in one of these containers, but that would have to wait. According to Faith and my pendulum dowsing, the dead person wasn't Garrett or Sid so for now I didn't care. The pull was intense though, and I was beginning to regret bringing the rods with me because I needed my hands free in case I needed to use my gun. When I reached the last row of sea can crates I knew I was close to the building where I'd seen Garrett and Sid taken. Suddenly, I heard a vehicle start up.

"Oh no!" I muttered.

Certain I'd missed my chance to save Garrett and Sid, I risked being seen by craning my neck around the corner. Mateo Flores had started his Escalade, and with his window rolled down, was talking to La Araña. The rear windows were so darkly tinted

I couldn't see if Flores had Garrett and Sid in the back seat or not.

I pulled the gun from my waistband, prepared to shoot both Flores and La Araña where they stood if Flores was taking off with Garrett. I prayed my aim was as good as I needed it to be.

"Keep an eye on those two. Don't let them out of your sight!" Flores shouted at La Araña and pointed a finger to indicate the building. "I'll text you once the delivery is made."

"If it goes bad, you want me to shoot them?" La Araña asked.

"Bad, or good. We're gonna shoot them anyway." Flores laughed. "But you gotta wait until I give you the go-ahead in case we need more information. Do it in one of the containers." He leaned out the window and hooked his thumb to show the stack of cargo containers behind him. "Same one as the other guy. Don't go messing up my office."

"Okay, boss," La Araña replied, then he turned and walked back inside the building and Flores pulled out of the lot.

I stepped back into the shadows. A flood of relief washed over me as I dropped the hand holding the gun to my side. I had time. Garrett wasn't being moved. At least not yet. I pinched my lips shut to stop the bubble of panic that threatened to spill out.

All I had to do now was distract the guard so I could get inside to free Garrett and Sid. That's where Tracey came in. It had already been five minutes since I left her, and she was probably panicking. I was about to send her the 'go' text when I heard another vehicle pull into the driveway.

I leaned around the corner and saw an Alfa Romeo Spider. I only knew one person who owned that kind of car. My breath caught in my throat as the driver's door opened and Preston climbed out. He was dressed the same as always—colorful board shorts and a T-shirt—except there was the unmistakable bulge of a firearm in his waistband.

"Holy crap," I murmured as he headed up the stairs and entered the building.

This was what Garrett meant when he said not to trust anyone! Jesus, why hadn't he just told me that Preston was the problem?

I fired off a quick text to the person I'd been wanting to contact all day: Agent Powel. I told her where I was, what was going down and asked that she send help immediately. I hoped she wasn't in the middle of having her scheduled cesarean. I also dialed 9-1-1 and whispered into the phone the address, reporting that there were gunshots at my location. When the emergency operator asked me to stay on the line, I hung up.

Before I could contact Tracey, my phone vibrated with a text from Agent Powel.

I'm close! Don't do anything until I get there!

But there was no way I could afford to wait. With steeled determination, I sent a text to Tracey: Go.

Drawing in a deep breath, I prayed to be brave but only felt a wave of fear and nausea. I was practically deaf from the sound of the blood pounding in my ears. I counted the seconds as I waited for the explosion in the corner of the parking lot that was to be the result of Tracey throwing the Molotov cocktail.

Two minutes went by and there was no fire and no big *KABOOM*.

Something must've gone wrong. Maybe Tracey chickened out. Hopefully, she didn't get caught by some armed guard I didn't account for.

"Oh God, I hope she's okay." My lips trembled.

I looked over my shoulder and briefly considered running back to check but, suddenly, there were loud voices inside the building. Shouts followed by the sounds of a scuffle. I couldn't wait any longer, so I took a step out of hiding and pointed my gun. I mumbled a curse under my breath as I fired a shot into Preston's car. My aim was true, and the driver side window exploded.

Immediately, Preston and La Araña burst out of the building with weapons drawn. I tucked myself into hiding but poked my head around the corner to watch. They spun around wildly with their guns at the ready but I stepped back before they spotted me. After a moment, I peered around the corner. Abruptly, they realized they were targets and started to walk backward toward the door to go inside.

With my lower lip clenched tightly between my teeth, I steadied the handgun in both hands and fired a round that caught La Araña in the thigh. He hit the ground screaming and clutched his leg, while his gun skidded under Preston's car.

Preston figured out where the shot had come from

and began firing in my direction repeatedly but I'd pressed my body behind the container before he could see me. I could hear his footsteps as he tried to make his way back inside the building. His shots ricocheted off the sea can that provided me protection. He couldn't see who had shot at them and I hoped to encourage him to get in his car and take off or come closer, so I could kill him, but he was inching back to escape into the building. There was no way I could let him return to Garrett. Keeping my body pressed against the sea can, I stuck my hand around the corner and fired blindly.

Immediately I heard footsteps crunching on gravel as he came toward me. When the sound of his feet stopped I knew he was close. I felt like a sitting duck. With the expectation that he would shoot me in the head, I crouched down low and flung my ball cap high around the corner. He fired at the cap and, still in a squatted position, I came out from behind the crate and fired two rounds.

I'd aimed for the heart, but my shaky hands landed only one shot into his right shoulder. He dropped his gun at the impact, and as he reached for it I fired again as I made my way toward him. That shot took off a piece of his ear and he dropped to the ground. I reached his weapon before him.

"No more neighborly love," I growled as I snatched up his gun in my other hand. "Move and I'll blow your face off."

"Holy shit, Julie! Get the hell out of here! You don't know what you're doing." Preston writhed in pain, grabbing the right side of his head.

I had no time to chat. I was already running toward the building as he yelled after me, "You'd better be sure you get out of here before Flores returns or your brains will be all over this lot!"

La Araña was passed out and bleeding profusely a few feet away from the front of the building. I reached under Preston's car to grab La Araña's gun, then hurried inside. When I entered the building, I found Garrett and Sid both tied up and bound to chairs with cloth sacks over their faces.

An anguished cry burst from my throat as I reached Garrett. "It's me, baby."

I hugged him tight and clawed at the sack until I got it off. His face was battered, caked with dried blood and his swollen eyes tried to open wide with shock. I removed the gag around his mouth.

"Good God, Julie! What the hell?" he sputtered. He nodded with his chin. "Box cutter's in the desk. Quick! Cut us loose!"

I ran to the desk and opened the drawer. I grabbed the blade and took it over to him and sawed through the plastic straps that bound his hands behind him and his feet to the chair. Then Garrett snatched the tool from my hand and began to work on Sid.

"I've got their guns." I put Preston's and La Araña's weapons next to Garrett as he worked to release Sid.

"Oh my God, is he dead?" I gasped when I saw Sid's face. He was even more bloodied than Garrett, and his head was slumped forward.

Garrett felt for a pulse.

"Unconscious. Took a hard blow to the head." Garrett grunted as he cut the last of Sid's ties, and his brother-in-law slumped onto the floor. "We'll have to drag him out." Garrett slipped both handguns into his waistband as he talked. "You should get out of here."

"I'm staying. I only injured Preston and La Araña but the police are on their way and Agent Karla Powel said that she's close by and—"

"Powel?" Garrett ripped one of the guns out of my hand. "You called Powel? Jesus, she's the problem! I thought it was Preston, but he was just working undercover and he was about to free us when La Araña tackled him from behind and—"

The door burst open and there stood Agent Powel holding a massive automatic weapon against her swollen belly. She expertly lifted the large gun and leveled it in our direction.

"Garrett. Julie." She nodded at us and smiled maniacally. "Drop your guns."

When we didn't immediately comply she added, "Garrett, dear, I will shoot off your legs so you're a stump but still alive enough to watch me blow off her head."

"Just drop it," Garrett told me gently as he tossed the guns he held and then kicked them a few feet away.

"B-but you're an agent… FBI…his partner," I mumbled as I dropped my gun to the ground and nudged it with my foot to be next to Garrett's.

"I was questioning whether Preston was the dirty one." Garrett shook his head slowly. "But then I figured it out. I thought you were mishandling the information on Flash Imports because you were fatigued from your pregnancy, but you were deliberately leaving names out of the investigation and trying to lead us in another direction."

"Preston was too stupid to take the bribe," Powel said.

"But you did," I spat the words out. "How could you do that?"

"Having babies is expensive." Agent Powel shrugged. She looked at her phone. "It won't be long now. Just waiting to hear from Flores that the shipment made it through." She smiled at me. "Your boy here told the other investigators the arrival date of the shipment had been delayed to next week. That way our incoming Mexican Mud will sail into customs without problems. All I had to do was show him pictures of your blown-up Jeep and next thing you know, he's cooperating. Just had to allow him back in your house to get a file he needed to alter in order to convince the other agents working the case that the shipment date had changed."

"So once the heroin makes it through, you'll let us go, right?" I asked hopefully. "Flores will be happy, so just as soon as the drugs are in the clear, you can release us and be on your way."

"That's never going to happen," Garrett told me with a slow shake of his head.

"Your man is right."

Agent Karla Powel tossed back her head in crazy laughter just as a huge explosion rocked the building.

Powel turned toward the source of the sound, and Garrett leaped forward and tackled her to the ground. She instinctively grabbed her belly and dropped her huge weapon. Garrett spun her onto her side, and I kicked the assault rifle away and snatched up the handguns.

"Grab the plastic ties off the desk!" he shouted.

He held Powel down, and I used the ties to bind her hands behind her back. Then I handed Garrett a gun and ran out the door. A massive ball of flames had erupted in the corner of the lot and I could hear a woman's screams.

"Tracey!"

Agent Preston had propped himself up to a sitting position against a cargo container. He'd taken off his shirt and wadded it up to stop the bleeding at his shoulder.

"Sorry!" I called to him as I ran on by in the direction of the flames.

I reached the corner of the lot and scrambled through the cut fence to find Tracey flat on her back and Wookie straddling her.

"Wookie, off!" I shouted, and the dog came running toward me. "Oh my God!" I knelt next to Tracey and took her in my arms. "Are you okay? What happened? Did Wookie attack you?"

"N-no." She shook uncontrollably in my arms. "H-he helped me."

I held her at arm's length and realized there were angry blisters appearing on her arm.

"You're burned! Help is on its way." I hugged her close.

"I'll be fine." Her voice trembled, and tears flowed down her face. "I got your message, but I couldn't get the damn thing lit. I shook the bottle in frustration and, when I did, I guess some splashed on my sweater, so I lit up like a candle. I didn't even notice right away until Wookie jumped on me. He ripped the hoodie off me. He saved me."

I looked over at Wookie, who was lying nearby. He was licking his face and his muzzle was singed.

"Aw-w-w, poor boy." At the sound in my voice he came over and nuzzled close. "You're a good boy. Yes, you are."

"You really are." Tracey reached a tentative hand out to stroke Wookie's fur. "What happened? Did you save him? Are they... Is Garrett okay?"

"I saved him, but you saved us all." I helped her to her feet, being careful of her arm.

Over the roar of the flames licking the sports cars nearby, Garrett called my name.

"Wait here," I told Tracey. "I'll make sure the EMTs get a look at you."

"I'm good." Tracey reached a tentative hand again to pet Wookie. "I've got this big boy to keep me safe."

I squeezed through the fence into the lot and found Garrett running in the direction of the flames. I quickly explained to him that it was Tracey, and the explosion was part of our distraction plan.

"Her arm is burned." I pointed through the fence at Tracey.

"The police and ambulance are here. Agent Powel is in the back of a police car. The EMTs will look her over to make sure she's not going into labor. They're also going to take Preston, Sid and La Araña to hospital. I'm going to go tell them about Tracey too."

"How is Sid?"

"He regained consciousness as the paramedics were taking his vitals. Looks like he has a concussion and possibly a broken arm." His face grew grim.

I wanted to ask more about everything else that happened but there wasn't time for that right now. Garrett hurried back to tell the paramedics about Tracey, and a fire truck arrived to extinguish the cars still blazing in the corner of the lot.

When Garrett squeezed back through the fence, Tracey was sitting on the concrete. Wookie's head rested in her lap and she was gently patting him.

"This is new," Garrett said, taken aback by the sight of the two of them so chummy.

"He's my hero," Tracey said.

"Definitely new." Garrett smiled

Wookie got up to greet his dad with some enthusiastic licks and Garrett's smile faltered when I explained the details of our wonky plan and how Tracey's Molotov cocktail toss went awry.

He bent and looked at her arm. "You are so lucky that it isn't worse."

"I could say the same about you." She giggled and pointed at Garrett's bruised and battered face.

The EMTs came to check Tracey over and when it was time to go in the ambulance, she was obviously afraid.

"I'll take your car and meet you there," I told her. "We're going to have to give our statements first and there's, um, one more thing I have to do."

"Okay." She nodded, the fear slipping from her

face and being replaced with a tentative grin. "Don't be long."

We watched her go off in an ambulance, then I snapped a leash on Wookie's collar and we all made our way back through the fence. The firefighters had quickly doused the flames. All that was left of the sports cars were charred metal carcasses. As we made our way toward the building Garrett reached for my hand and held it tight in his.

In addition to uniformed cops and EMTs, the area was now flooded with guys in jackets that had various abbreviations. Present and accounted for were the FBI, DEA, CBP, and TOC.

"The entire alphabet is here." I shook my head as I led Garrett around the corner to where I'd placed my dowsing rods on the ground.

Garrett frowned but didn't stop me when I picked up the dowsing rods and handed him Wookie's leash. I began to walk, allowing the rods to lead me down the row of shipping containers. I felt all the activity from law enforcement come to a stop as dozens of eyes followed my slow walk. The rods swung dramatically to indicate a particular sea can. This container happened to be close to the police car holding former Agent Powel. There was a large lock on the crate and as I put my rods away, Garrett waved a group of men over.

Eventually they managed to cut the lock. I turned away, tucking my head up against Garrett's shoulder, but then I forced myself to look back as the doors were swung open.

"Jerry Mayer," I said on a large exhale of breath.

Immediately inside the door lay Jerry Mayer with a bullet hole in the middle of his forehead. Sid's co-worker, the arrogant asshole who'd threatened me with a gun outside the bar, was as dead as he could be.

"Yes, but how do you recognize him?" Garrett asked.

"He stuck a gun in my stomach."

Garrett put a protective arm around my shoulder and pulled me to his side. Wookie growled at the sight of the body and we stepped aside so the rest of the team could get a look. As we moved to allow a clear view inside the shipping container, a guttural scream cut the air. It was Karla Powel. She had her face pressed against the police car window and was shrieking uncontrollably as she looked at the body in the container.

"Jerry Mayer is the father of her baby," Garrett explained to me.

And another piece of this puzzle slipped into place.

FOURTEEN

"How DID A thug like Mayer hook up with an FBI agent like Karla Powel?" I asked Garrett, unable to keep the horror and surprise from my voice.

"That's kind of where it all began. I'll explain later."

We walked past the police car where Powel was held, and she screamed a barrage of curse words at us and butted her forehead against the window for effect. Wookie barked at her, and Garrett and I laughed at the dog's attempt to protect us from the crazy person.

Ambulances had separately taken Sid, Preston, La Araña and Tracey to nearby hospitals. It had been determined that former Agent Powel wasn't going to go into premature labor and would, instead, make it to her cesarean appointment. Although she wouldn't be raising her child, that was certain.

I was itching to go and be by Tracey's side, but there were statements to be given to many different agencies.

Even though Garrett kept insisting he was fine, I made sure he got looked at on the scene since he refused to go to the hospital. Although he didn't appear to have a concussion or other serious injury, his nose was most likely broken, and he'd need to see his doctor soon. After an hour more of being part of the investigative process, I insisted that I be able to leave to check on Tracey.

I drove my friend's car and Garrett immediately nodded off. I left him and Wookie in the car together while I went into the hospital.

When I found Tracey, I was happy to see she wasn't alone. Craig was standing next to her bed, holding her small left hand in his meaty one.

"Looks like you're all fixed up." I walked over and smiled down at her bandaged right arm.

"It hurt like crazy when they cleaned it but now they gave me the good stuff." Tracey grinned, and I could see the dopiness of the drugs in her eyes.

"She's going to need her bandages changed daily and more antibiotic ointment on the burn," Craig said. "The nurse showed me how to do it so I'm going to stay with her until she's all healed up."

"That's good." I raised my eyebrows at Tracey, asking the question if she was okay with that. "Right?"

"Yes." Tracey nodded. "It'll be good to have his help. Did you know he was fifty miles away when I texted him and he just dropped everything to race here and be by my side?"

"Well, of course I did!" Craig leaned over and kissed Tracey on the forehead. "You're my boo."

Tracey blushed until her face went pink to match her hair and I began to feel like my presence was unnecessary.

"Have the police and FBI come to get your statement already?"

"Yeah. Some female officer who looked younger than me came in and wrote down everything I said. She took my information and address and said she'll come see me at my apartment once I'm less traumatized." She pointed a finger to a curtained-off bed across from her. "She also went to see that guy. I guess that's Garrett's brother-in-law, Sid."

"Oh wow! Did the officer talk to him too?"

"He was talking but I couldn't really hear what he said."

"Okay. I'm going to pop my head in and see if he's all right, so I can let Garrett know." I gave her hand a squeeze and turned to Craig. "If you're okay taking her home, I can drop her car off to her later."

"I'm sticking around until she's sick of me," Craig said.

Tracey giggled at that and I was wondering if it was the pain meds or the blush of love on her cheeks.

I parted the curtains across the hall to find Sid Klein sitting up holding a cup of water and trying to put a straw between his swollen lips.

He froze at the sight of me.

"I'm Garrett's girlfriend, Julie."

"Thank God." He put a hand to his chest and exhaled. "I thought you were another one of the crazy Flores gang."

"Garrett's resting so I thought I'd check to see how you're doing."

"I've got a killer headache, but the doc says that's normal." He offered me a lopsided grin. "One of the feds came in and said you're the reason we made it out of there alive, so I owe you, man."

"I did it for Garrett," I said coolly.

"Look at you." He wiggled his eyebrows comically. "You're gorgeous and tough as nails." He scraped his eyes over me then, his gaze pausing on my breasts before they returned to my face. "Wow, Garrett went young, huh? You gotta respect a guy who's able to pull that off. What are you, twenty-five or something?"

"Excuse me?"

"I'm just messing with you." He winked. "Garrett's always been cool to me. That's why I reached out to him when I was in over my head with this gang stuff. Handy to have a bro in the FBI, am I right?"

A sizzling burst of hatred exploded in my heart. I wanted to tell him to stay away from Garrett and never involve him in his life again. But that was not my place. This douchebag meant something to Garrett; even if it was just loyalty because of his dead wife.

"Next time reach out to someone else," I said. "No offense, but I have no desire to save your ass again, or have Garrett risk his."

"Hey, I'm done." He put up both hands in surrender. "I'm walking the straight and narrow from now on." He traced an X over his heart with the tip of his finger. "Cross my heart."

"Good." I was still pissed he'd risked the life of the man I loved and nearly had me and Traccy killed. I reminded myself that this was Garrett's brother-in-law and the man obviously meant something to him, so I added, "I'm glad you've learned your lesson. Fancy cars and a big house might be great but they're not worth risking your life, right?"

"Yeah, but the car and house were total babe magnets. You have no idea how often I got laid just because I climbed out of a Lambo!" At the stunned look on my face he rolled his eyes. "Oh c'mon, you girls are all the same, right? You see a guy in a fancy car, maybe a Rolex on his wrist and you want to drop your panties." He erupted in a loud bellow of laughter that went on for far too long.

"I think maybe you're on too many painkillers."

"Not yet. The service in this place sucks."

"Soon you'll be home in your big, beautiful house."

"Nope." He frowned and shook his head. "Not ever going back to that place. No way."

"It was tossed pretty good, but a little cleanup and it'll be good as new."

"Doesn't matter. Never going back there." He visibly shuddered.

Whatever.

"This sucks. I've got a big appointment tomorrow. I can't wait around all day," he huffed. "Tell the nurses I'm hurting, and I need some good drugs."

"Garrett almost died for you," I hissed, and my hands formed fists at my sides as anger boiled in my gut. "And I risked my own life and that of my best friend to save you. None of this is funny."

"I am super grateful. Really." Sid tilted his head as a confused look tripped across his face. "Is that…" He pointed at my chest. "Is that my dead sister's wedding ring you're wearing around your neck?"

I grabbed the pendant and tucked it inside my T-shirt. Even though I had a perfectly legitimate reason for using the ring, the heat of embarrassment colored my face and neck. I wasn't about to explain my talents to this idiot.

"Feel better," I told him. "If you need anything…"

"Yeah, yeah." He smiled. "I'll give you a call."

"No. Don't."

I left him and stormed back to the parking lot. In the car both Wookie and Garrett were still softly snoring, and they only stirred briefly when I climbed into the driver's seat. The fury burning in my stomach dissipated when I looked at Garrett. I kissed the tip of my finger and gently placed that kiss on his bruised cheek. I started up Tracey's car and drove home.

I pulled into the driveway of our place, and Phil burst out of his house and ran over to us as if he'd been watching for our return.

"Oh my God! I'm so glad to see you. I'm on my way to see Preston at the hospital." He hugged me tight as I got out of the car. "I heard you saved everyone. Thank you." He kissed my cheek with a loud smacking sound. "Thank you so-o-o much."

"Um…" I untangled myself from his tight grip. "You do know I was the one who shot Preston, right? I mean, I didn't know he was working undercover—and I sure didn't know he was an agent—so it wasn't intentional, but I was the one who shot him so sorry about that."

"That bitch Karla Powel would've slaughtered them all." He nervously rubbed the back of his neck. "You only fired enough to stop him in case he was working with the cartel. Nicked his ear and one through the shoulder. Powel was preparing to gun them all down." He put his hands on my shoulders. "Thank you."

The fact that I hadn't fatally wounded Preston was only because of my own nervousness but I didn't tell him that. Phil walked over to Garrett and gave him a firm welcome home hug.

"I left you some baking and did some grocery shopping for you," Phil said. "If there's anything you need, anything at all, give me a shout."

"Thanks for that," Garrett said as he made his way toward the house. Then added, "Go be with Preston. We're probably going to sleep for a week."

Waiting for Wookie to happily pee on his own bushes in a glad-to-be-home way, I grabbed Garrett's hand and whispered in his ear. "My hands were shaking too much to shoot Preston dead. I could've frickin' murdered a federal agent!"

Garrett let out a long breath. "You had no way of knowing and you never should've even been there in the first place."

"Good thing I was. And speaking of feds, you could've told me that one of the reasons you were so pumped about having Preston and Phil move in next door was because Preston is a fellow agent." I punched him playfully in the shoulder and I unlocked the front door.

Garrett shrugged. "It wasn't my place to mention it. I'm sure he would've told you himself. Eventually."

"Oh my God!" Garrett stopped short inside and I nearly slammed into the back of him. "I forgot all about the burst pipe. When I was brought back here for the files, I saw the floor was torn up, but Powel literally gave me only a minute to get in and out of the house. Just enough time to grab the file."

"And leave me a note and a gun," I added.

"That gun was for protection, you know. I didn't expect you to go hunt me down."

I chuckled and pointed at the floor. "I sent you pictures. Even asked your choice on the wood but I didn't know then that you didn't have your phone."

"I was captured almost immediately after I left here that day. La Araña ran me off the road and took my phone. They found it in Agent Powel's purse."

"So, she was the one sending me texts? Leading me with the one saying Sweet pea?" I frowned. "She was trying to get me to go to the nursery."

"Of course." His face got dark. "They would've loved to capture you and torture you in front of me. La Araña shot at you that night you followed us from the nursery. Flores told me all about it. He also gave La Araña heck because he was supposed to go back and kidnap you, but by the time he drove back to the ditch, you were gone." His face twisted in pain. "You'll never know how much Flores got off on telling me, in great detail, the things he planned to do to you in front of me."

"It's over now." I tried to change the subject but the look on his face was agony. "The floor is called Nevada Maple. You like it?"

He looked down and frowned. I could tell that he wasn't even registering what I was saying. The look on his face said his mind was still on Flores.

"Look at all this baking Phil did for us!" I waved my hands as I walked toward the kitchen. The counter was covered in plates of home-baked cookies, muffins and a huge basket of fruit. Phil had really outdone himself. "You're probably starved. What can I get you?"

"Nothing." He stood like his feet were frozen to the same spot.

I got out Wookie's bowls and gave him his food and water. Then I grabbed us each a muffin and a glass of water and put them at the kitchen table.

"Come. Have a bite." I pulled out a chair for him.

He walked toward me but ignored the chair and the food.

"We need to get something straight." His voice shook with emotion as he looked at me. "I left you a specific message telling you *not* to come looking for me. I also said not to trust anyone or try to contact me."

I pulled the folded piece of paper out of my pocket and held it up. "I know."

"Right. You know!" He drilled his shaky fingers through his hair. "So you should've also known I would *never* not *ever* in a million years send you words like *Sweet pea* that are really some kind of coded messages forcing you to become a detective to try and save me by putting your own life in danger!" He squeezed his eyes shut. "You could've been killed."

I dropped the paper onto the table and went to him, but Garrett began pacing the floor.

"You could've been tortured! It was pure luck

that didn't happen." He blew out a breath. "Jesus, I almost lost you."

I grabbed his hands in mine. "But we're home and safe now. I went looking for you because I love you and I was concerned about you," I said softly. "And thank God I did because otherwise there's a good chance you'd be dead right now."

"I would've found a way. Preston would've rescued us somehow. I even called the landline to let you know I was okay." He shrugged his hands out of mine and his voice grew louder. "The point is, you put your life at risk and you jeopardized Tracey too!"

Wookie looked up from where he was eating and tilted his head in confusion that Garrett was raising his voice.

"It was a scary situation but you need to calm down. Have something to eat and then get a good night's sleep."

"And you were talking with Powel!"

"Obviously I didn't know that Agent Powel had gone rogue and was using your phone to send me messages. I had to go with my instincts."

"You figured your instincts were better than those of all the trained federal agents working this case?"

He was angry and the very realization I could've been killed was just hitting home to him so I tried to remain calm and not get drawn into an argument. I drew in a deep breath, walked into the living room and slouched onto the sofa.

Garrett followed and looked down at me. His voice had quieted, and I could tell he was trying to work through all of this in his head.

"Right up until recently, I still thought Agent Powel might be in the clear," he explained. "It wasn't until video surveillance caught her banging some guy in a fancy car in the Flash Imports' parking lot."

"Jerry Mayer," I said.

"We couldn't see the guy but, yes, that's who we assumed. Then we followed the money. We didn't know how corrupt she actually was." He sat on the sofa next to me. "When La Araña apprehended me and took my new phone, he called someone to tell them it had been done. I saw him punch the number on his phone and recognized it as Agent Powel's. Even then, I thought she was maybe working the case from a different angle. I'd admitted to the higher-ups my connection to Sid. I was trying to reach out to Sid and get him to turn himself in when I left here but La Araña got to him first and then got me."

"Oh my God, we should tell Meg!"

"Meg? Who's that?"

"Sid's girlfriend, Meg." I pulled out my phone and scrolled through my messages to find her. "I met her when I went to Sid's house looking for you."

"Sid doesn't have a girlfriend."

"Sure he does. About my age, drives a yellow VW bug. Long hair. Dragonfly tattoo on her collarbone. Tough girl. I had to tackle her to the ground because she was making a run for it."

"Wait a second…" Garrett held up a hand. "The person you're describing is Mateo Flores's wife, Josephine." He looked stunned. "Flores probably had his wife hanging at Sid's house, waiting for him to come home because he'd gone into hiding. You tackled a drug cartel's wife! What the hell, Julie?"

"First of all, I hadn't planned on tackling her, but she ran, and I was trying to find information on you. She told me she was Sid's girlfriend. How was I to know that she was Flores's wife?"

"You couldn't know. That's exactly why you should've stayed out of all this!" He put his hand to his forehead and cringed. "How did you manage to go toe to toe with Josephine Flores and live to tell about it? That woman is danger on steroids. Flores is bringing in the drugs, but he groomed her to make the distribution connections out here. She saddles up to all the dealers, whispering sweet nothings in their ears and making all kinds of promises. Meanwhile any dealer who doesn't fall in line and drop their previous heroin connection immediately goes missing." His voice suddenly got louder. "Do you know how many men she's suspected of killing? And she's still in the wind…probably on her way back to Mexico by now."

"I read about all the missing drug dealers when I was trying to come up with information about Flores. A dozen low-level dealers have gone missing in the last two months, and law enforcement says it's connected to the drug turf war in Seattle."

"Flores has been in Mexico for a couple months. His mother was ill. He put Josephine in charge while he was gone but news of all the missing dealers reached him. He came back last week to oversee this mega shipment of heroin. He was unhappy about

Josephine throwing her weight around and drawing too much attention to the cartel."

"Sid's house was tossed. It looked like Meg—I mean Josephine—was staying there, and it also looked like she was a fan of Mexican Mud herself."

"I'd told Sid to run. I was going to bring him in. I'm guessing Josephine figured Sid would go back home eventually and she'd be there when he did. They wanted him bad once they realized he had a brother-in-law with the FBI. Just one word from me would change the date the custom agencies would be looking for that huge shipment of Mexican Mud. Sid admitted he got in over his head."

"I met Sid in the hospital when I went to see Tracey."

"You did? How was he?"

Arrogant. A complete asshole. "Fine. He seemed perfectly fine."

"All Sid's problems started with Jerry Mayer," Garrett said angrily. "He flaunted the cash and fancy car he got from Flores for greasing the import gears. Flash Imports became an easy way to import drugs, but Jerry couldn't handle all the wheeling and dealing on the inside to get a big shipment through the ports. He needed someone new, so he recruited Sid and poor Sid had no idea what he was getting himself into."

"Poor Sid. Right."

Garrett tilted his head at my sarcasm. "Well, obviously he's going to have to answer for his involvement. He told me all about how Jerry Mayer sucked him in and then threatened him. Just a few small loads, at first, and Sid figured what was the harm, right? He was too naive to realize that kind of easy money always came with a price. When he heard about the big shipment coming in, he tried to get out of it but, of course, a visit from some of Flores's thugs set him straight that he wasn't going to be able to just walk away. He sent me a message and went on the run." He exhaled hard. "I owed it to Faith to help him. Unfortunately, once the cartel knew he had a connection to the FBI, that put him in more danger."

I'd spent only five minutes with Sid and felt like I needed to shower the scum off me. Garrett didn't see it because, to him, Sid was family. I was betting that Sid had played the sympathy card to get Garrett's help. Maybe he even set him up to help the cartel.

"You don't think it's possible that Sid reached out to you exactly for that reason? To play big man to Flores by flaunting a connection with the feds?"

"Don't be ridiculous! If all they wanted was a connection to the FBI, they already had Powel."

"Yeah, but she was on maternity leave, right? She didn't have access to know whether the feds had information on the exact date of the big drop. Plus, she's going in for a C-section tomorrow, so I can't imagine Flores wanted to trust her on something this big."

"Stop it." A flash of anger crossed his face. "Just leave the theories to me and the rest of us who are trained to do this job. Please. Just stop."

Garrett got up and walked to the den. I followed, wanting to talk things through and get that angry look off his face. In his office, he reached behind a stack of hardcover books on his shelf to grab a pint of whiskey. He unscrewed the bottle, took a long drink and coughed.

He looked at me and shrugged. "I needed that."

"You don't need to hide booze from me. This is your home too." My voice hitched with sudden emotion. I'd never seen him take a drink around me before. "I'm the one with the problem. You're welcome to drink whenever."

Garrett opened his mouth to speak and then thought better of it. He knew he had to hide that bottle, and the truth of that sat between us like a fat dancing elephant in the room. Neither of us wanted to talk about it. He walked back to the living room with the bottle in his hand.

I followed close on his heels, suddenly fuming. "Look, I know you're pissed that I got involved in your case but try to look at it from my point of view." I added heatedly to his back, "You weren't acting like yourself. You left here and sent me a coded message calling me *Sweet pea* and I thought you really wanted me to try and find you."

Garrett turned to face me in the kitchen. "There are so many things wrong with that statement that I don't even know where to begin."

Wookie came between us and began to whine and paw at me. He'd never seen us fight. I bent forward to offer Wookie a reassuring scratch behind the ears and, as I did, the pendant slipped out from the front of my shirt.

"Is that…" Garrett put down the whiskey bottle on the counter and reached for the ring. His voice held a spark of controlled anger. "That's Faith's wedding ring."

"Yes." I unclasped the necklace and placed the ring on the kitchen counter next to me. "She... Um... it... The necklace helped me find you."

His eyes were softened briefly but his next words were harsh.

"Julie, I am a trained federal agent." His face was contorted in pain and the reek of alcohol left his mouth as he leaned into me. "If I was in danger and needed help do you think for one bloody second I'd waste time sending you coded messages? I called the house landline to tell you I was okay, so your cell phone number wouldn't show up on Karla Powel's phone. I didn't want her to have your cell number since that's the one you always have with you. God, I didn't think for a second you'd reach out to her! If I had access to a phone, don't you think I'd call for reinforcement from other agents? Do you *really* think I'd text my girlfriend and put her in danger?"

The derision he used when he said *girlfriend* caused me to flinch like I'd been struck. I whispered, "I thought you needed me."

A brief pause stretched between us.

Take me in your arms. Tell me you do need me, and we'll be okay.

"I just can't handle thinking about you almost dying for me." He quickly put up his hands, palms out, and I found myself taking a step back from him. My obvious recoil caused his tone to falter.

"Don't you see that I can't do my job and keep you safe too?" His voice broke. "You need to stick to doing your own stuff and leave drug cartels to the FBI."

I felt tears burn in my eyes, but I'd be damned if I'd let him see them. As I turned away, Garrett said to my back, "I'm getting in the shower."

I stood frozen to the spot for a good five minutes. I heard him slam the door to our en suite bath with much more force than was necessary and I listened to him turn on the water.

While he showered I went to our bedroom and repacked my duffel bag with fresh clothes.

I scribbled a brief note—*Gone to Tracey's*—and left it propped up against his small bottle of whiskey, next to Faith's ring on the counter. An evil voice inside my head told me to gulp the remaining whiskey before I left. It took all my willpower to smother that malevolent murmur.

"Be a good boy," I told Wookie, with my hand on the door.

I turned off my phone and put it in my duffel, then tossed it into the back seat of Tracey's car. Tears blurred my eyes as I peeled out of the driveway.

FIFTEEN

When Tracey opened the door to her apartment all I said was, "I need somewhere to stay."

Her eyes searched mine, but she didn't ask for more and I didn't offer. It was late, and I'd obviously woken her and Craig, but they made it feel like it was the most natural thing in the world that I was there. The only annoyed person was Fluffy, who flicked his tail with irritation and clawed at my feet while I tried to walk inside.

The small room smelled faintly of beer and I spied a couple empty bottles on the kitchen counter, then tore my eyes away. Craig fussed over me and went to work bringing me a pillow and blanket for the sofa before he made himself scarce in the bedroom of the small apartment.

"You're going to be okay." Tracey leaned in and hugged me with her one good arm. "Tomorrow we'll ditch Craig before he smothers me to death and we'll go get a really unhealthy breakfast and you can talk all you want or not at all, okay?"

I just nodded because I didn't trust my emotions enough to talk.

Most of the night I stared at the ceiling, replaying everything that happened over the past few days. Then my mind went to work replaying Garrett's hurtful words over and over in my head like they were on my music playlist and the song was set on replay. He was banged up and had lived through terror and that alone allowed me to cut him enough slack that we might get over this hump. But the derision and fury in his voice slammed me back to a place in my childhood I thought I'd put behind me.

I'd been happy to be home; to have rescued my love. Now it was something ugly, and a sea of self-doubt washed over me, leaving me to wonder if I'd really done the right thing. Maybe he would've gotten out of that situation without me. There's a chance I risked Garrett and Tracey being killed for nothing, not to mention my own life. I bit my lower lip as I worked through all the thoughts that piled on one after the other. No matter what, I needed to be away from Garrett right now to clear my head.

"God, I need a drink," I whispered to the ceiling.

The few empty beer bottles on the counter meant possibly more in her fridge. Tracey didn't drink in front of me, and my alcoholism wasn't something we talked about. She kept liquor in her fridge casually for guests the way people without addiction could, and if I drank what was there she'd still be my friend. I got up, walked to the kitchen and opened the refrigerator. Three bottles of beer stared back at me. In the far corner behind the milk was a half bottle of wine. Maybe it would be enough. I stood staring at those bottles. The only light in the entire apartment illuminated me from the fridge. My hand reached for a beer and I jumped when a furry lump wound between my legs.

"He-e-ey."

I smiled down at Fluffy, who began to purr. Closing the fridge door, I went back to the couch followed by the cat. When I lay back down, Fluffy jumped onto my chest and curled up. After a while, I drifted off to sleep, stroking his soft fur; the rumbling of his contented purring was like soothing white noise.

Sometime near dawn I woke and Fluffy was nowhere to be seen. I sat up on the couch and yawned. My head was pounding like I had a hangover, but the headache was pure stress. The sun streamed in through the kitchen blinds, causing me to wince. I combed my fingers through my hair and considered my options as I listened to the sound of Craig's snoring coming from the bedroom. The first thing I needed was to get out of here.

After leaving Tracey a note with her car keys, I left her apartment and got into a taxi with my duffel bag and backpack. I had the driver bring me to a restaurant a few miles away that was located across from a car dealership. I nibbled some toast and looked through a newspaper as I nursed coffee after coffee until the car lot opened for the day. I paid my bill, hoisted my backpack onto one shoulder and hefted my duffel bag onto the other and walked across the street.

In the car lot I immediately spotted a two-year-old Jeep that was nearly identical to the one that had been destroyed, except this one was blue. It took less than a minute for a young salesman to spot and target me. Then I made his day by buying the Jeep on the spot without even a test drive. The insurance, paperwork and small talk in between took a whole lot longer than my decision to purchase the vehicle, but as soon as I had the keys I was gone.

Within minutes I was headed south on I-5 and I didn't even know where I was going until I'd pulled into a parking spot outside the high-rise that housed Dr. Chen's downtown Seattle office. The receptionist let me sit in the waiting room even after she reiterated that I didn't have an appointment and Dr. Chen did not take walk-ins.

Even without a scheduled appointment, when Dr. Chen saw me sitting in the waiting room she invited me into her office since her next appointment hadn't arrived yet.

"What's going on?" She motioned for me to take a seat. "We've only had phone appointments for so long I almost forgot what you looked like, and now here you are in a surprise visit."

Her friendly smile did nothing to break open that happy part of me.

"We had a fight."

"You and Garrett?"

I nodded.

"I take it this was a big fight. I can't see you showing up out of the blue because he didn't like how you squeezed the toothpaste."

I let out a jagged breath but didn't reply.

"People fight. Relationships sometimes end and sometimes they recover." She folded her hands in her lap and gently added, "Do you want things to end?"

"No." I shook my head. "He was so mad." I closed my eyes and remembered his words and the memory was jumbled with the recollection of every hateful, angry word ever thrown my way.

"People get mad." She shrugged. "Did it get violent?"

"No. He would never."

"How did his anger make you feel?"

I looked down at my hands, surprised to see them shaking, and unable to speak.

"Julie, you are not the person you were before," Dr. Chen said gently. "You are strong enough to handle this, no matter which way it goes."

"Am I?" I asked on a whisper. "The quicksand..."

The dark and sticky quicksand thoughts that sucked me into the horrible memories of my abusive childhood.

"There is no more quicksand. You are beyond that." She sat up straighter. "Have you had a drink?"

"No." I licked my lips despite myself.

"But you've thought about having one?"

"One?" I laughed mirthlessly because the idea of only one drink was a ridiculous understatement. I stiffened. "Sure. But I'm not going to cave." I met her gaze for the first time since I entered the room. "I won't."

She nodded. "I believe you." She softly clapped her hands. "And I believe you will get through this hardship and come through stronger. Just like always."

Yes, I'd come through many hardships. My body carried the scars of a childhood fraught with the kind of abuse most people couldn't even imagine, and I was still triggered. They called it PTSD and there were times it felt like a life sentence.

Yes, I was stronger than I was the first time I'd

met Dr. Chen. But there had to be a limit. How much could one person take? I'd broken before. How much more could my mind take before it snapped? Again. Was it fair to Garrett to expect him to stick around through another breakdown?

"You have learned all the skills you need to help you in hard times, and I'm confident you'll use what you've learned to help you now."

She said it with such force that I almost believed it to be true in my head, if not my heart.

We sat for a few more minutes while she brought me through some meditation rituals that I knew as well as I knew the freckle on the back of my right hand. When I left her office, my knees were wobbly with mental fatigue, but my insides felt stronger.

I'd kept my phone turned off since I left my house, but I turned it back on as I walked to my car. One missed call from an unknown number and a few texts from Tracey asking me to check in so she knew I was okay. I called her.

"Sorry for leaving like that," I told her. "Figured it was time to get a new car and also wanted to do a few, um, errands."

"Just glad you're okay." She added, "Ouch!" Then apologized to me, "Sorry, Craig is changing my bandages, and apparently he thinks that the quicker he does it, the less it'll hurt. He's wrong about that."

"I feel so bad about your burn."

"Don't."

That was easier said than done.

"So-o-o…"

I allowed a pause to stretch between us because

the answer to my next question weighed so heavy on my mind.

"Yes, he called here," she said, following up with a string of curses meant for Craig.

"Garrett?"

"Of course, Garrett." She sighed. "You need to call him back. I can give you his new number. Make nice-nice with your man. You'll feel better."

"Maybe…" I chewed the edge of my thumb. "Or maybe we both need some time apart. Things were said and—"

"Words can't be taken back but apologies can't happen unless you communicate." She shouted to the side, "Goddamn, Craig, you're absolutely killing me!" Then to me she added, "I've gotta go. Check in with me later so I know you've not been abducted by aliens or drove off a cliff, okay?"

I told her I would. I unlocked my new Jeep and climbed inside. As I was doing up my seatbelt the same unknown caller from earlier sent me a text. It was Garrett.

My new phone. I'm sorry about last night. I love you.

I closed my eyes and drew air deep into my lungs. My fingers poised over my phone in reply. I wanted desperately for those words to be enough. And they could be. If only I'd let them.

Instead of replying, I turned off my phone, picked up my backpack from the passenger seat and stuffed it inside. I needed to think about whether I was ready to go back home and pretend everything was okay.

Maybe I was one of those people who wasn't meant to be in a relationship. My sketchy upbringing, alcoholism and line of work weren't exactly conducive to the type of person Garrett needed to come home to. I wasn't wife or mother material. I was the weird dowsing girl. I'd always been a loner. I could do it again.

Could you really? A small voice inside me sneered.

"Shaddup," I replied as I slowed my vehicle into an upcoming traffic snarl.

Driving through Seattle traffic might not seem like the ideal way to relax, but it gave me something to concentrate on besides Garrett. I crossed over into Bellevue and thought about my last trip there and my run-in with Meg who'd turned out to be Josephine. My fingers tightened on the steering wheel. If I'd known then that she was the wife of Mateo Flores who was suspected of single-handedly disappearing drug traffickers who challenged her and who was partly responsible for kidnapping and hurting Garrett and Sid, I wondered if I would've killed her on the spot.

Soon, I found myself parked again outside Sid's house. There was no crime scene tape. Nothing to indicate the feds had been by to check out the blood puddle in the bathroom off the den. Because, of course, the only person I'd contacted about that had been Karla Powel. I hit my forehead with the heel of my palm. No doubt the feds would get around to going through Sid's house. I'd told Garrett that I thought Josephine Flores was staying here. He'd definitely report it to his fellow agents, so they could check here for her, even though she was probably long gone to Mexico along with her husband.

"Remember what Agent Garrett Pierce told you." I did a mocking impression of his deep baritone. "You need to stick to doing your own stuff and leave drug cartels to the FBI."

The hurtful words were burned into my head and heart.

He'd been the one to show up at my single-wide trailer years ago asking for help on a case. He'd arrived as an FBI agent needing my help to find bodies. He'd needed my help. But things were more complicated once love was involved.

I sat staring at Sid's house and questioning my reason for the drive besides running away from my life. I decided to call Tracey and ask if she'd mind putting me up for one more night. Reaching for my backpack to get my phone, I felt my divining rods jerk with so much force that I had a difficult time keeping them from flying right out of the bag.

"What the hell?" I murmured.

But suddenly I knew the reason I'd felt like I needed to return here. I called 9-1-1 before I even got out of my vehicle and told the dispatch operator where to send police. I told them I'd found a body and then I disconnected.

Garrett had been wrong about one important thing. Sid hadn't decided to go into hiding at Garrett's insistence. When I'd called Sid's office, his assistant said Sid had been on leave for several weeks due to a death in the family. He'd gone into hiding, and Mateo Flores's wife, Josephine, had taken over here. That's why, when I saw him at the hospital, Sid had told me he'd never return here. He knew Josephine had taken over his house and was using it as her personal home base. I was guessing Sid reached out to Garrett only because he could use him to save his own ass.

I wondered if Garrett had any idea what a low-down scumbag his brother-in-law was, or if he'd always believe poor Sid just got roped in by the money. Shaking my head, I thought about all those notes I'd taken away from Sid's den when I was here. The bag of notes was still crammed into the bottom of my backpack. A brief tickle of remembrance tried to come through, but I had no time to think it through. The dowsing rods were tugging me hard.

As if being pulled by a strong rope tied to my wrist, I followed the rods and found myself crossing the beautiful landscaped yard. Directly in front of the large garden shed built to resemble a gingerbread cottage, the rods crossed.

My throat tightened as I put the rods in my pack. I retrieved my bandana and used it to cover my hand so as not to disturb evidence or leave my own prints behind as I placed my hand on the door. I tried the handle and found it locked, but even through the cedar boards I could smell the stench of death. A quick search around the cutely painted door frame and then under a flower pot led me to the discovery of a key.

Before I opened the door, I steeled myself for what I would find. Even though I thought I was prepared, the sight and stench of the bodies of a dozen young men knocked me backward. They'd each been bound, gagged and shot execution style in the cen-

ter of their foreheads. Flies buzzed noisily in the stifling room and my head swam as I closed the door
and walked away.

When the police arrived, they found me still vom-
iting in nearby bushes.

I told the officers about this being a federal case
because of the connection to the Flores cartel and
gave them Garrett's number. It took him only an
hour to arrive.

When he approached, the concern and love on his
face warred with his need to be a professional FBI
agent. I saw the conflict on his weary face but when
his eyes met mine there was only raw love.

I looked away. I wasn't ready.

Garrett was surrounded by other officers and I
took that opportunity to leave. Everyone concerned
had all my information and would be in touch. This
wasn't my first rodeo. I knew how the business of
finding the dead worked and Garrett would be tied
up for hours.

Sid had said he would never return to his house.
And now I knew why. He'd known this was where
Josephine was stashing the bodies. No doubt he'd
reached out to Garrett only because having an FBI
officer on his side would help the cartel and save
his own ass.

I'd just started the Jeep when a rap on my window made me jump. It was Garrett. I rolled down
the window.

"We need to talk," he said.

"You've got work to do, Agent Pierce. Remember
your own words; I did my job." My words were cool

and calm, hiding all the emotion beneath. "Now it's your turn to do yours."

"I'm sorry about last night." He reached in through the window and put a hand on my shoulder. "I was out of my mind thinking about you risking your life for me. That's not an excuse for my behavior. I was way out of line. I should never have spoken to you that way."

"Yeah, well…" I cleared my throat. "I've gotta go."

"Go home. I'll meet you there once I'm done here." He gave my shoulder a light squeeze. "Please."

"I'm going back to Tracey's." I looked down in my lap. "I think we need some time apart, Garrett."

"No, we don't." His voice was urgent. "We just need to talk things out."

"Maybe it's just me then. I guess I'm the one who needs some time."

He thought about that for a few seconds and removed his hand from my shoulder. "Take as much time as you need. I love you, Julie. I'll be waiting for you."

With that he turned and walked away, and I drew in a deep jagged breath that I expelled on silent prayer as I pulled out of the driveway.

The driveway and street were lined with various undercover and marked law enforcement vehicles. I drove carefully between them to turn onto the main road. I was low on gas and headed in the opposite direction that I'd come, to make my way toward a gas station. Two driveways down from Sid's was another large house tucked behind a hedge of brown, dried cedar trees. I caught a glimpse of color between the thin, frail bushes. There was a yellow car in the driveway near the house. I slowed and squinted as I went by. Definitely a Volkswagen Beetle like the one I'd seen Josephine get into when she left me at Sid's house. I kept driving a little farther down the street and then made a U-turn. I pulled over near the driveway where I'd seen the yellow VW.

I kept my Jeep running as I reached for my phone. I'd taken a picture of Josephine's car and license plate when she'd pulled out of Sid's garage. Before I called all the authorities away from the bodies found at Sid's place, I needed to be sure that the car I'd spotted belonged to Josephine Flores.

As I scrolled through my phone I saw up ahead that a group of federal agents, Garrett's coworkers, were standing on the side of the road in front of Sid's driveway. They were waving in the arriving coroner's vehicle and pointing to where the van could squeeze onto the driveway. As the clutch of agents stepped onto the road, movement in the bushes up ahead on my side caused me to turn my head. A woman stepped out of the trees and onto the road. It was Josephine Flores and she was carrying an assault weapon nearly as large her petite frame.

The agents all had their backs turned and I watched in horror as Josephine took aim at them from the edge of the road only a few yards away. Even if the agents could spot her it would only take one pull of her finger and she could easily take them all out before they could react.

A furious scream exploded from my throat, and

I punched the accelerator of my Jeep and pointed it directly at the woman. The sickening crush of impact tossed Josephine Flores as if she were weightless, and she landed twisted and broken in the ditch a half dozen yards away.

Reactions were swift. A clutch of agents had their weapons drawn and pointed in my direction and a few made their way toward the body. I sat with my hands in the air and waited.

Garrett stepped out onto the road, trying to take in what had happened. He jogged over to my vehicle and opened the driver's side door.

"Josephine Flores." I pointed a shaky finger in the direction where the woman's body lay. "She— She was going to kill all of them so I—" A choked whimper broke my throat. "So, I had to..."

But I couldn't finish, and Garrett leaned into the door and turned the vehicle off.

"Jesus, I thought you'd left!" he exclaimed. "Instead, you decided to stick around and mow down Mateo Flores's wife?" His voice held anger and terror simultaneously. I wanted him to hold and comfort me but, instead, he pointed a finger in my face. "Stay here. Seriously. Don't move."

I couldn't have moved if I wanted. My entire body was shaking.

For an hour I waited around. My vehicle was impounded and, after my statement was taken by other agents and officers, a uniformed policeman was told to take me home. I sat in the back seat, an aching emptiness in my chest. Garrett was going to be tied up until late and I was going to be happy to be home to be comforted by Wookie's licks as I hugged him tight.

When the officer dropped me off in the driveway, Preston came out of his house. His head was wrapped in a bandage with a large bulge over his ear, and his arm was in a sling. He walked toward me with Phil at his side.

"Sweet new ride," Preston joked. He walked around me and had a few words with the officer, after showing his identification.

Phil gave me a hug. "You look like an absolute mess." He nodded toward the police car. "And you have to get a different car."

"I did." I took in a breath and laughed. "Long story but I guess my new Jeep will be returned to me. Hopefully soon."

"At least you got a new one. I guess there's something to be said for getting your old one blown up."

"And having a pipe burst," Preston added. "Blown-up car got you a new Jeep and burst pipes got you a new floor."

"I'd rather make those changes without having the old stuff ruined." I forced a smile, then added to Preston, "I'm sorry about shooting you."

"Under the circumstances you did what you could with what you knew. I'm just glad you weren't a better shot!"

"Me too." I laughed as I picked up my duffel bag and backpack. "You heard about the bodies in Bellevue?"

He nodded, and his face grew serious. "And about you running over Josephine Flores." He let out a low whistle. "I wanted to go with Garrett when he got called but he said I wasn't healed enough to be working. He can be a stubborn dick when it comes to protecting people."

"Tell me about it."

"They found Mateo Flores too," Preston said. "He was hiding in the back seat of some yellow VW."

"Good," I said. "I'm glad this is over."

Wookie was barking at us through the window, obviously happy to see me and probably desperate to go out.

"Go tend to your baby," Phil said with a bright smile.

"He really is like my child," I admitted. When I opened the door, Wookie ran up to greet me. "Hey, sweet baby boy, are you ready to go out?" I asked in a singsong voice.

I laughed and rubbed his head then let him out into the backyard. The new fence looked great and Wookie enjoyed the freedom to run all over. It wasn't the acreage I'd had at my house before this one, or on the farm before that, but Wookie didn't care. And maybe I didn't either. Maybe I didn't mind having neighbors as much as I thought. I left the patio door open, so Wookie could come back inside while I went and brought my bags to the bedroom.

I sat on our bed with a sigh. This was home, but I could only call it that if Garrett and I could work things out. I thought about the anger in his voice when he'd talked to me in the Jeep. I'd needed him to comfort me, but he'd just left me sitting there. If I couldn't work things out with Garrett, then I'd just find another place to live. As I sorted through my bag, I debated refilling it with more clean clothes and going to spend another night at Tracey's.

Garrett had placed Faith's wedding ring on our dresser and I got up and touched a gentle finger to it.

"Thanks again for your help," I told Faith. "I don't know what'll happen between me and Garrett, but I'm still glad you were able to lead me to him. Even if Garrett doesn't think he needs my help."

"I was wrong about that," Garrett said from behind me.

I turned to see him, embarrassed at having been caught talking to his dead wife, and wishing I'd gotten out of the house before he came back home.

"I thought you'd have to stay on scene until things finished up," I said, taking a step back and sitting on our bed.

"Those bodies aren't going anywhere, and it's not like anyone's interrogating Josephine Flores. They know where to find me if they need me." He sat down next to me on the bed and reached for my hand. "I'd told the officers that I was going to take you home but then I found out someone had beaten me to it. Miscommunication there."

"Look, Garrett…" I pulled my hand from his.

"Don't say it." His voice was low and colored with hurt.

"We need time apart to think about us and—"

"No." He shook his head vehemently. "We need to stick together. Forever." He reached again for my hand and this time squeezed it tightly. "Nothing is resolved by us being apart. I was an idiot. I let my fear for you turn into anger and I said some horrible things."

"You did." I wasn't going to let him off the hook. "But I am who I am. I am the dowsing girlfriend. That's not going to change."

"I don't want it to." He brought my hand up to his lips and kissed my wrist.

"You want what you had with her...with Faith." I nodded to the ring. "Who am I to take that from you? I don't know if I'll ever want to be a wife. Or have children. I can't ever promise you any kind of family. Even though, sure, I wouldn't mind wearing your ring on my finger, but—"

"Really?" He grabbed my shoulders and turned me to face him. "I'd love for you to wear a ring from me, and it only has to mean that we are a team. Forever."

"I'd like that too, but only if you realize that I'm not going to change who I am or what I do, even if it makes you uncomfortable. I don't need you to save me. I just want you to support me while I save myself."

He pulled me against him and breathed into my neck. "I'll do that and, because I never said it before..." He kissed my ear. "Thank you for saving my dumb ass."

"There's no other dumb ass I'd rather save." I laughed and then Wookie bounded into the room, happy to have both of us at home with him. "He's our baby, you know?"

Garrett laughed and scratched Wookie behind the

ears. "He must take after your side of the family, because he doesn't look anything like me!"

We chuckled and suddenly I was on my feet frowning.

"Did I say something wrong?" Garrett asked and then cringed. "I didn't mean that about the dog looking like your side—"

"It's not that. It's the baby…"

"What?"

"Sid's notes…" I went to the corner of the room and picked up my backpack. I found the bag of notes and dumped them all onto the bed and began searching. "First time I went to his place, I gathered up all his notes, hoping they'd lead me to you, but most of it was nonsense. But this one…" I held out the piece of paper excitedly.

"All it says is '4-26 Burke.'" Garrett looked at me and shrugged. "Does that mean something?"

"Tomorrow is April 26, so that's what the numbers 4-26 represent." I snatched up my phone and began doing a search. "And Burke is Dr. B."

"Dr. B?" Garrett frowned.

"Karla Powel's obstetrician."

Garrett looked down at the paper in his hand as if still trying to connect the dots.

"You thought Jerry Mayer was the father of Karla Powel's baby but he's not." I tapped the note still in his hand. "Sid's the father."

SIXTEEN

"SID'S NOT THE FATHER. How could he be?" Garrett shook his head as if trying to shake the very notion from his brain. "If Sid is the father of Karla Powel's baby, that would mean that Sid didn't call because he needed help, he…"

"He needed someone on the inside who was preparing to intercept that big shipment of Mexican Mud. With Powel on maternity leave and no longer able to get up-to-date intel on when you feds were going to intercept that large shipment, she suggested he reach out to you. She used and manipulated him into roping you into helping him."

"The original delivery date of all that heroin had been moved up because Josephine's happy trigger finger was making things too dicey around Seattle," Garrett said. "They sped up the date and Powel could no longer guarantee the shipment would get through by messing with the intel she provided the Bureau. She gave us incorrect information before, and that's why we were always a day late on other shipments. She needed me so she could feed accurate information to Mateo Flores. Pretending both you and Sid would be slaughtered unless I turned away and allowed the shipment to get through."

"She left Sid's name off the original list of employees," I said. "Because, in the beginning, she was handling all the inside work. Getting pregnant changed that."

"Sid used me. He knew I'd try to help him. For Faith." Garret looked up at the ceiling as if the answer to that level of exploitation lay written up there. "How could I have been so blind?"

"You were just protecting the people you care about. It's what you do," I said gently.

We spent that night wrapped in each other's arms and making love with a kind of desperation to try to cleanse our minds.

A week later, when Garrett's face only showed a faint yellow tinge where bright bruises once lay, and after I'd had a couple more face-to-face visits with Dr. Chen, we packed up my repaired Jeep and headed north. Tracey and Craig stayed at our house with Fluffy and Wookie while Garrett and I drove across the border and up to Whistler Mountain.

We stayed in a chalet just outside of the ski village. The May air was still crisp from mountain snow, and the chill woke our minds and bodies to long walks and deep talks. One evening after dinner in the village, we walked past an artisan jewelry shop and decided to go inside. There we chose matching platinum bands that were etched with a scene of mountains and sea. The ring felt more right on my finger than any diamond, and the look of love on Garrett's face was every vow I'd ever need.

After a few lazy days, Garrett began returning calls to his office and I began looking through my overflowing email inbox for my next case. There would always be more criminals for him to catch.

And the dead would always be waiting for me to help find their way home.

* * * * *

ACKNOWLEDGMENTS

Many thanks to my agent, Melissa Jeglinski. This book is made better by the tireless efforts of my editor, Deborah Nemeth, and all the wonderful people at Carina.

Also by Carina Press and Wendy Roberts
Latte, espresso, cappuccino & murder!

Read on for an excerpt from
Grounds to Kill,
now available at all participating e-retailers.

THERE'S A SUPERSTITION that says if the palm of your hand is itchy you'll soon be receiving money. If that were true, I'd be a gazillionaire instead of an under-paid barista. Instinctively, I felt my itchy hand might one day bring me luck. So far, nada.

I rubbed my burning palm on the countertop while I concentrated on whipping up a large café mocha, no sugar, no whip, extra-dry, half-skim, half-whole milk, with chocolate syrup.

"Watch your back, Jen." My coworker Mitch squeezed behind me to get to the cooler for more milk.

Mitch was tall and muscular with golden hair and eyes like hot espresso. When Mitch worked, Merlot's Café saw a fifty percent increase in female clientele. The estrogen-enriched customers flocked to flirt with him. They tended to hang around too long and talk too much, but I didn't mind. Mitch's hundred watt smiles had a direct correlation to how the tip jar overflowed, and we shared gratuities. I reaped the benefits without having to sell my own soul with plunging necklines and pushup bras.

My palm was itching even more, so I snagged a wooden stir stick and scraped it roughly against my hand.

"Eczema acting up?" Mitch asked, raising his eyebrows.

I merely shrugged. No sense in complicating our working relationship by telling him I was crazy.

Mitch took a woman's coffee order, then elbowed me good-naturedly.

"Hey, look." He indicated outside the coffee shop with his chin. "It's your pal, Mr. Stinky."

He chuckled, but I didn't. My teeth clenched as I glanced out the coffee shop's window. A disheveled homeless man took up his usual sloppy stance on the sidewalk across the street.

"He's not my friend."

I took an order for a medium, extra-dry café mocha with raspberry syrup.

"You say he's not your friend but I doubt you've bought anyone else on the planet as many coffees as that guy."

Mitch was bent at the waist restocking the pastry case and looked up at me with a smarmy grin. He was trying to be funny so I resisted the temptation to send him flying into the lemon scones.

"Admit it," Mitch chided as he got to his feet. "As far as coffee dates go, you and Mr. Stinky are on a roll."

"Right. You caught me." I tucked a wayward strand of brown hair back into my loose ponytail.

Normally, working with Mitch was a coaster ride of wit made even more fun because he was so easy on the eyes. But it was only halfway through my shift and my feet already hurt in my new espadrilles. Don't mess with a girl with sore feet.

"Oh you li-i-ike him," Mitch teased. He elbowed me in the ribs as he passed.

"You got me. I'm a pushover for skinny fifty-year-olds that smell like a dumpster."

"Fifty? You think he's fifty?" Mitch straightened, tilted his head and stared out the window. "I'd say a hard sixty."

A bouffant-blonde regular stepped up to the counter in thigh-high boots and an impossibly tight blue dress.

"What do you think, Molly?" Mitch asked her. "How old do you think Mr. Stinky is? Jen says fifty and I'm going with early sixties."

"Who?" she asked, looking confused.

"The homeless dude who's been sitting across the street every day the last month or so." When Molly continued to offer him a blank stare, Mitch added, "You walk by him every morning to get your tea."

Molly glanced quickly over her shoulder.

"He's there every day?" She frowned and blinked long false eyelashes. "I never noticed."

I poured Molly her usual peppermint tea, but the steam rising came from between my ears, not from the small vent at the top of the plastic lid. Pushing Mitch aside, I thrust the cup into Molly's hand and took her two dollars. I gave her a quarter in change, and she deposited it into the tip jar. Great, I could plan my trip to Hawaii now.

"Thanks, Mitch." Molly fluttered her eyelashes.

Once Molly was out the door with her tea, I picked up a rag and began energetically wiping down the counter and pastry case.

Merlot's Café was just one of thousands of independent coffee shops in Seattle. I'd been whipping up java there for nearly two years. It was located on the main floor of an old, five-story brown brick office building on James Street halfway between Yesler and Second in Pioneer Square. The place was owned by a seldom-seen owner named Mervin Lo. Here at Merlot's we served fair trade, shade grown, organic coffee usually with a smile. The inside was long and narrow with lots of exposed brick, a wide glass pastry case, half a dozen tables and counters with bar stools at the front windows. The walls were lined with framed black-and-white photos from long-ago Seattle when vegetable stands stood where Pike's Place sprawls today.

"Amazing that she could walk by every day and not even see him," I snarled under my breath. "Obviously her dresses are too tight and have cut off circulation to the gray matter beneath her dyed roots."

"Nothing amazing about it, Jen. Hundreds of people walk down the streets of Seattle every day and I bet most of those don't give the homeless a second thought." He stood next to me and nudged my shoulder. "C'mon, even you must've had times when you crossed the street to avoid a panhandler or pretended not to hear the guy asking you for spare change."

"Whatever. Just drop it."

My gaze cut sideways to the guy across the street. It was starting to rain. My throat constricted. You'd think if you chose to be homeless, you'd at least have the sense to thumb a ride south until you hit the California sun instead of hanging out in Seattle. The burning itch in my palm ramped up a notch and I rubbed my hand against my blue-jean-clad thigh.

Mitch caught me staring across the street and said, "I told you when he started coming round a few weeks ago that if you feed him he'd keep coming back." He paused. They're kind of like cats, and for him…" he nodded across the street "…coffee is like tuna."

"Shut up!" I slammed my palm on the counter, somewhat for emphasis but also to help relieve the itch. The half-dozen customers in Merlot's looked up from their newspapers and laptops to regard me curiously.

We served the last of the customers in a long line and I picked up a pen in my left hand to offer my itchy palm some solace. I doodled on the thick pad left near the register.

"How come you write with your right hand, but you always doodle with your left?" Mitch asked.

"Guess I'm just talented." I winked.

I wiped the already clean counter and Mitch went off to make small talk with a petite brunette. After a minute, I began to feel restless.

"It's slow." I two-pointed my rag into a nearby sink. "I'm going on my break."

Mitch wisely kept any snarky comments to himself when I poured a large black coffee in a to-go cup, snagged a bran muffin from the basket containing the day-olds and headed out the door.

As I crossed the street, I observed Mr. Stinky was still getting organized. He finished a smoke and ground it under his toe as I walked over. Placing a twelve-inch square piece of cardboard on the damp sidewalk, he sat down, crisscrossing his legs clad in dirty blue jeans. He had on a denim jacket and leaned his back against the gray concrete slab of the parking garage behind him. In a death grip in his left hand he held the orange JanSport backpack containing all his worldly possessions.

His eyes looked dead ahead at Merlot's, and he didn't acknowledge me in any way as I dodged traffic and risked becoming the victim to an angry Prius driver. Once I was right in front of him, I crouched down to eye level. The stench of him brought tears to my eyes. At least I told myself it was the smell.

A curl of steam rose from the vented lid of the hot coffee that I placed on the concrete sidewalk. He took the muffin from my outstretched hand and unzipped his backpack using a small yellow compass dangling from the center pocket zipper pull. He placed the muffin gingerly inside next to the oatmeal bar I gave him yesterday and the cinnamon roll from who knows when. Then he reached deeper to the bottom of the pack and pulled out two things—his usual worn paper coffee cup with "change please" scrawled in black Sharpie and a lost dog flyer. He placed the cup in front of him and handed me the sheet.

I sighed, barely glancing at it.

"Right. Lost black lab. Got it. You've given me the same paper every day for a month. You know that you don't have a dog, right?"

I ran an impatient hand through my hair, tugged out the ponytail then scrunched up my hair and pulled the elastic around it tighter than before.

"Look, you gotta find somewhere else to hang out." I dug in my pocket for a folded index card. "I've made a list of all the shelters and soup kitchens in the area. The one up on Third even has a daytime program. You could, you know, be inside all day. No more sitting in the rain. Wouldn't that be nice? Plus, they'd feed you so, um, yeah…wouldn't that be good?"

I held out the card but he continued to look straight ahead. Not *at* me but *through* me. For a minute we

stayed like that. Him staring. Me holding out the list.
I'm sure he could've easily done this all day but I had
a life. The rain ramped up from mist to drizzle and
pasted my hair to my head and made my mascara run
but did nothing to wash away his eau de toilet. Finally,
with a small exasperated sigh, I tucked the card into
his donation cup along with a twenty I couldn't afford.

I was about to get to my feet then changed my
mind and leaned in to snap my fingers in front of his
face to try to get his attention. His gray eyes flicked
to my face then away.

"I don't get it." I threw up my hands in exaspera-
tion. "Why the hell do you come here every day if
you don't even want to talk to me?"

He reached out a grubby hand and tapped the lost
dog flyer I still held in my left hand.

"The dog? There is no dog!" I crumpled the sheet
and tossed it at him angrily. It bounced off his stained
jacket and landed in his lap.

"You can't keep coming here." My voice hitched.
I placed a hand on his shoulder. "Sorry, Dad, but
you just can't."

* * * * *

Don't miss
Grounds to Kill *by Wendy Roberts,*
Available wherever
Carina Press ebooks are sold.

www.CarinaPress.com

ABOUT THE AUTHOR

Wendy Roberts is an armchair sleuth, fan of all things mysterious but a huge chicken at heart. Her mind is often in a secretive cloak-and-dagger world of intrigue while her physical presence is usually at home feeding feral cats and demanding guinea pigs. Wendy resides in Vancouver, Canada, where she happily writes about murder and is always at work on her next novel.

You can find Wendy on the web here:

Website: www.WendyRoberts.com
Twitter: www.Twitter.com/Author-Wendy
Instagram: @WendyRoberts_Author
Facebook: www.Facebook.com/WendyRoberts-Author